ten little
words

ALSO BY LEAH MERCER

Who We Were Before
The Man I Thought You Were
The Puzzle of You

ten little words

words

LEAH MERCER

LAKE UNION
PUBLISHING

Text copyright © 2020 by Leah Mercer
All rights reserved.

No part of this book may be reproduced, or stored in a retrieval system, or transmitted in any form or by any means, electronic, mechanical, photocopying, recording, or otherwise, without express written permission of the publisher.

Published by Lake Union Publishing, Seattle

www.apub.com

Amazon, the Amazon logo, and Lake Union Publishing are trademarks of Amazon.com, Inc., or its affiliates.

ISBN-13: 9781542007634
ISBN-10: 1542007631

Cover design by Heike Schüssler

Printed in the United States of America

For my son.

CHAPTER ONE

JUDE

April 1988

Jude yanked open the door and squinted into the grey sky, the filtered light stinging her eyes. She hadn't been outside for days – weeks, even – and each breath of the damp, salty air burned her throat like whisky. She'd kill for just one more shot of alcohol, but her stash was gone now. Sunk into her, bottle after bottle, absorbed into her blood.

Into her body.

Into her soul.

But it wasn't enough. Not enough to blot out the images of him – of his fingers gripping her arm, of the stink of tobacco when his hands covered her mouth, of the coiled tightness of his body as she struggled against him.

Not enough to erase the memory of a soft mouth on hers, either . . . of how his fingers stroked her hair, of the tenderness in his voice when he said her name.

Of the ten little words he echoed before sinking into her, like a promise, like a vow.

I am always with you. I will always be here.

Jude had echoed those words, fiercely pulling herself against his body even as, inside, part of her pushed him away. And later, when he was gone, she'd repeated the words to her daughter – whether as a desperate pledge to remember or to delete the past, she didn't know.

But nothing would be enough to erase what had happened. God knows, she'd tried everything: from antidepressants to counselling (a wasted hour, where she'd sat in silence), to giving her daughter every last piece of herself in the hope she'd magically morph into a mother, to drinking as much as she could. And she couldn't bear it any longer. Couldn't bear what she'd become in her quest to bury it all; couldn't bear her daughter shaking her awake each morning, jerking her back to the torturous present. She couldn't struggle any more through stale-bread breakfasts, forgotten lunches and hasty suppers of baked beans because that was all the pantry contained.

Maybe if it had just been her, she'd have let the days unroll until her body couldn't take it any longer. But it wasn't just her, and she wasn't just damaging herself. 'If you can't live for yourself, live for your daughter,' one clueless GP had told her, back in the early days when her sister, Carolyn, had managed to drag her out of bed. Jude had wanted to laugh so hard the whole rickety clinic would collapse. Didn't the doctor know that Ella *was* the problem?

Jude loved her daughter, of course she did. But she didn't want to stare into a face that was a constant reminder of all that was bad . . . of all that was good. Didn't want that twisted torment of hate and love, of anger and loss, to claw at her heart. Didn't want *her*.

That sounded horrible. That *was* horrible. How could you love your daughter but not want to be her mother? How could you wish she had never existed and at the same time want to protect her from everything? Want to keep her safe from life . . . from you?

It didn't matter. Nothing mattered now. Nothing, but leaving all this behind. Jude gazed out to the sea, the waves rolling towards her, one after another. She could feel them calling; feel her body respond. The urge to be oblivious, weightless in the briny water, was overwhelming.

Behind her, the flat was silent. Ella was still sound asleep, tangled in her duvet with one bare foot flung out like it was trying to run off on its own. She wouldn't be alone when she finally woke; Carolyn should be here soon, on her daily mission to haul Jude back into life. She was more of a mother lately to Ella than Jude had been, and when Jude was gone . . . well, Ella would belong to Carolyn, be the child her sister had never been able to have. Carolyn would throw herself into mothering Ella, the same way she had mothered Jude after their parents died.

Pain twisted Jude's insides, and she let out a strangled cry. She didn't want to go, but she couldn't stay. It was the story of her life.

The story of her death, too.

She closed the door behind her and stepped forward.

CHAPTER TWO

ELLA

July 2018

'Have some cake, Ella!' Jane waved a huge piece of cream-laden Victoria sponge under my nose. I glanced up from computer screen, trying to keep the annoyance off my face. Stuffing myself with cake didn't appeal to me any more than chit-chatting with my colleagues, and most of the time my headphones were firmly in place. Thankfully, my job as an audio archivist at the Musical Museum – built in an attempt to elevate Hastings above other fading seaside destinations – made that seem more conscientious than rude.

I forced a smile. 'I'm okay, thanks.'

I winced as my co-workers started a rousing rendition of 'Happy Birthday' that even my blaring sound file couldn't block out. For my first few months here, my boss, Jane, had tried everything to involve me in work social life, inviting me to nights out and stopping by my cubicle to chat each morning. I hadn't been unfriendly – I hoped – but I wasn't interested. Jane and my colleagues were lovely, but I didn't need the unnecessary clutter in my life. I wanted to go from my studio flat to work and back again, rolling along nicely in my cosy little cocoon. Minimal interaction, minimal distraction.

Cheering and clapping erupted as Siobhan blew out her candles. Then someone turned up a godawful song on the loud-speakers. The one thing my self-imposed bubble couldn't do was block out rubbish pop music, so with lunchtime celebrations for Siobhan's thirtieth (I'd pegged her at forty, at least!) well underway, I yanked off my headphones and admitted defeat.

I pushed back my chair and grabbed my lunch bag, thinking today might be a day to escape to the museum cafeteria. Filled with throngs of screaming kids and sunburned holidaymakers in the summer and earnest OAPs trying to wring the most from their waning years in the winter, I usually shunned it at all costs. But right now, I'd take anything over some bloke crooning about the shape of his girlfriend's body.

I eased past my colleagues, who were clustered around Siobhan's desk, and made my way up in the lift to the cavernous lobby. Already I could smell the coffee from the café, positioned just off the entrance to catch any visitor, big or small, in its net of exorbitantly priced stale cakes and weak lattes.

I fixed my eyes firmly on its door to avoid the staff members dotted about in their annoyingly bright red 'Can I Help You?' shirts and made a beeline for an empty table in the corner, well away from the raucous mum-and-babies group blocking off half the space with their oversized prams (they must be planning to take their infants off-roading, by the size of those things; I wouldn't be surprised if they were fully motorised). The mums were staring down at their newborns with a mixture of awe and fear, and I tore my gaze away. Not that *I* longed to have a baby – God, far from it. My cat, Dolby, was more than enough responsibility. But just seeing mothers and children was dangerous territory for me, and I never strayed too far from the boundaries I'd set years ago.

School holidays had yet to begin, so, thankfully, the café was quiet, apart from the mums and babes. I sank into a seat and stared out of the window at the sea in front of me, watching the waves whip the water white and gulls fighting the wind. No matter where you went in Hastings, the sea would draw your gaze, as if the whole town was built for nothing but to offer up awe and admiration for its vast expanse. As a child, I'd stared for hours, willing the water to part and my mother to emerge like some mythical mermaid. I believed she'd meant those ten little words she always said to me each night.

I am always with you. I will always be here.

Through the days and months – through *years* – after my mother left, I'd held those words close to my heart. Police had long since closed the investigation, ruling her disappearance a suicide after finding her clothing and jewellery on the beach, with witnesses claiming they'd seen a dark-haired woman enter the sea the morning she went missing. Still, I believed.

I knew she'd return, even as my aunt Carolyn closed up the dingy council flat Mum and I had lived in, moving me into her huge, empty house. Despite the nightly nightmares that my mum had drowned – despite the memory of her face and arms around me growing fuzzy – I trusted she'd come back. Every night I fell asleep without her was like a kick to the gut, but hope is a funny thing. It has a way of springing up anew after withering away, like daffodils each spring.

Slowly, though, the soil inside of me grew drier, until the very part that hope fed off was dead: unfertile ground, barren and wasted. The tender shoots stopped growing, leaving behind thistles of longing, anger and pain. I still stared out at the sea, but now each breaking wave was like a tombstone marking my mother's grave, reminding me over and over that she'd left. That she'd *chosen* to leave, despite the words she'd said to me each night. Wherever my mother's final resting place was – for her body had never been found – she wasn't here.

I'd been wrong to believe in her. I'd been wrong to trust. She didn't keep me safe – just the opposite. She'd hurt me, so much that some days I hadn't been able to catch my breath.

Now, thirty years later, I felt neither anger nor pain. My mother was gone, and life carried on. I couldn't say I was *happy*, but then, I didn't want to be happy. Being happy meant you had something to lose, and I wasn't about to risk that. I might have moved past hope, but those brutal years of longing had made their mark, the sole of their boot permanently imprinted on my heart. I was moving through life in a comfortable bubble of my own making and the only person who had the power to hurt me was *me* . . . and maybe Dolby, when she rejected my lap in favour of her fuzzy blanket. I'd take the vicissitudes of a cat over those of other people any day, though.

I tore my gaze from the café window and unpacked the little lunch I put together each morning, running my eyes over the familiar items: ham (honey-roasted, two slices) and cheese (Emmental) sandwich (granary bread), raspberry yoghurt (sugar free), ten celery sticks and my refillable water bottle. I'd eaten this lunch for years and when I laid it all out on the table it was like being with an old friend – a friend who demanded nothing in return, with whom I could eat in comfortable silence.

Halfway through crunching my celery, I spotted the colourful front page of *The Post* on the next table, complete with a lurid headline about a footballer's affair. A man handed out the paper on the promenade each morning, always smiling at me as I passed (I don't know why because I always rejected his outstretched hand – reading free newspapers full of gossip never appealed). Now, though, I drew it closer, always eager to place another barrier between me and the outside world.

I aimlessly flipped through the pages, running my eyes over articles on the latest summer trends and celeb weddings. Reading this newspaper made me feel like an alien from another planet. Who *were* these people, and why would I care? I was just about to fold it up and push it away from me when a tiny boxed advert in the classifieds caught my eye. The text leaped out at me, each word hammering my eyes.

I am always with you. I will always be here.

My heart pounded and everything inside me went cold. The words echoed in my mind, growing larger and larger until they pressed on my skull. Images of my mother holding me close each night as she whispered those same ten words clawed and scratched at my soul, demanding entry, and I shoved the paper away from me.

I sat frozen for a minute, forcing air in and out of my lungs as I batted away those memories. Then, I let out a little laugh. God, how silly was I? It was just ten words. Ten insipid words, uttered a million times by a million people all over the world. Maybe whoever had placed the advert – for there wasn't any contact information – meant them, but my mother hadn't. My heart may have sizzled and smoked painfully for years after her death, but hard scar tissue had finally formed. Any memories were just that: memories, echoes of events long past that couldn't breach my defences.

I gathered up my lunch things and slung my cooler bag over my shoulder, looking out to the sea again. My mother had chosen to die. She wasn't coming back.

And I was perfectly fine with that.

CHAPTER THREE

JUDE

July 1980

Jude fizzed with excitement as she pulled on her tank top, struggled into her favourite pair of skin-tight jeans, and shoved her feet into the high-heeled sandals she'd been dying to wear all summer but would have frozen her toes off if she'd tried. It was her twentieth birthday today and after weeks of rain and fog, it felt like summer was actually here. She was itching to take advantage of the fine weather. Sun brought out way more punters than the endless drizzle and cold she'd been struggling through. More punters meant more money . . . and more money meant an even greater chance of moving to London at the end of the summer.

She made a face, thinking of the meagre two pounds she'd earned yesterday after singing for hours in the freezing wind on the promenade, trying not to shiver, even though she was already wearing four layers. God, she couldn't wait to get out of this godforsaken town, where people's dreams of seaside holidays went to die. London, baby . . . that was where it was at. That was where she would start her career as a singer. She could feel it in her bones, though Carolyn always rolled her eyes when Jude said that, asking if 'her bones' knew for certain that she'd be able to earn a proper wage and make a living once she was there.

But Carolyn was always like that: the practical older sister, doing everything in her power to keep Jude out of trouble ever since their parents had died in a car crash when Jude was fourteen. Carolyn had just turned twenty-two, but she'd taken on the role of both mum and dad with a sense of responsibility that Jude both admired and hated, often at the same time.

Even her parents hadn't been as strict as her elder sister, and Jude was certain that had played a major role in her acting up and getting excluded from school at seventeen – although she had to shoulder the biggest chunk of blame; no one had forced her to smoke dope on school grounds. Carolyn had begged and pleaded the headteacher to take her back, but Jude hadn't bothered to turn up to the meeting her sister had arranged. She wanted to be a singer – she was *going* to be a singer – and that was that. Why did she need to learn anything else but music?

She'd spent the next few years working part-time at the supermarket (Carolyn had insisted she either get a job or go to school) and taking music lessons in piano, guitar and voice. Music was her life – the place where she could go to be herself and to escape from the dull, cloistered world – and even Carolyn couldn't stop smiling when Jude sang. Singing and writing songs made her free, and she couldn't wait to do it for the rest of her life.

First, though, she had to get to London. She had almost enough saved up for rent in a bedsit – she'd looked through the London newspapers at the library to see how much it might cost – and all she needed was a little bit more. If the weather would just cooperate, come September she would be on her way.

Twenty years old and a Londoner. Jude couldn't wait to say those words.

She closed the door behind her and stepped out into the blinding light. Hastings on a sunny day was dazzling: the sea reflected the sun and lit up the whole place, whitewashing the town. It was the polar opposite of a rainy day, when the ocean swallowed whatever light filtered through the clouds and the whole place was deserted and grey. Despite the new sandals pinching her toes, Jude strode down the promenade as if it was a catwalk, smiling at passers-by as they turned and stared. With her curly brown hair, dark eyes and curvy body, she never failed to make an impression, something she hoped would help her stand out in London, even before she opened her mouth to sing.

It was only ten o'clock, but the warm air caressed her bare skin and she could feel the promise of heat in the sun. The promenade was packed already, and she quickened her pace to reach her favourite spot, far enough from the funfair so it wasn't too noisy but close to the main sandy beach and restaurants. If she started singing now and carried on as long as her voice could hold out, she could make a considerable haul.

She took off the straw sunhat she'd bought as a birthday present and placed it in front of her, then backed up a few paces and let loose with one of her favourites, 'Summertime'. She worshipped Ella Fitzgerald. There was something about the singing which just gripped her heart, kneading it with warm hands, until it felt like the emotion was being pushed up from her very soul, through her throat, and out of her mouth. If Jude could even begin to be as good as her idol, then she'd be happy.

It only took a phrase or two until punters began to gather, their eyes focused on her. She loved this moment: when people were transfixed, falling under the spell of the song and her voice as

11

everything else faded away. Music had a way of immersing you in it and holding you there until it ended.

As she sang, her gaze lingered on a man towards the back of the crowd. He held himself away from the rest of the people watching, like he was marking out an invisible boundary. He was fair and slight, wearing trousers and a long-sleeved shirt, as if he was afraid to expose his skin. The way he was standing apart, with his gaze fixed on her, made Jude think he was really *listening* – that every note was important. He wasn't there for the sun or to soak up the ambience of the promenade. He was there for her music, and that alone.

'Summertime' ended, and Jude plunged straight into another song before anyone had a chance to move. She tried not to look, but her eyes kept darting to where the man was standing, her heart jumping each time she spotted him. She wasn't normally attracted to fair men, but it wasn't his looks that drew her to him – it was something else. A charge of electricity went through her when their eyes connected, and her cheeks went warm. The crowd grew larger the more songs she sang. People peeled away from the front to put coins in her hat, only to be replaced by the next row of audience, and on and on. The sun grew high and sweat streamed down her back, but she couldn't stop. She didn't want to stop. She didn't want the man to move, and it felt like her music was the only thing anchoring him in place.

Finally, though, her throat began to feel scratchy and dry, the sun stung her skin, and Jude let the last notes of her final song fade away. She closed her eyes and bowed, the applause rushing over her and into her soul, filling up an empty space she never knew was there until she stopped. She straightened up and looked towards where the man was standing, but he was gone.

Gone, without even a coin in her hat.

Oh, well, she thought, sitting down on the bench as disappointment swirled inside. Served her right for thinking there was some sort of mystical connection between them. That kind of thing didn't happen in real life – not in hers, anyway. Usually, the most connection she had with a bloke was a drunken conversation in a bar before sleeping with them, then sneaking back to Carolyn's afterwards. Anyway, come September, she'd be out of here, on her way to making it in London.

The fewer complications in her life, the better.

CHAPTER FOUR

ELLA

I stayed late at work that night, waving off the rest of the staff on their way to the pub to continue Siobhan's birthday celebrations. Jane had asked if I wanted to come along, but she was almost out the door by the time I'd said no. Not that it mattered – she knew my answer, anyway. It was nice of her to keep asking, after years of rejection.

When my co-workers were safely gone and the archives sank into darkness, I stood and stretched. I hadn't moved since returning from lunch, burying myself in cataloguing a new batch of sound files. The local radio had sent over live studio recordings from the 1940s and despite the huge pile of work on my desk, I couldn't have been happier. I loved the thrill of listening to the husk and rasp of voices from the past, of immersing myself in other people's soundscapes and imagining their lives. They were suspended in that one moment; their present became my present, where neither the past nor the future could touch us. It was how I wanted to live my own life.

I glanced into the darkened café as I passed by, the advert in the newspaper flashing into my mind. I rolled my eyes at how it had shaken me, even if just for a moment. By tomorrow, the paper would be in the bin, those ten words buried under layers and layers of rubbish – just like they'd been buried within me. They meant nothing now. They'd caught me off guard, and that was all.

I hurried home along the promenade, glancing up at my aunt Carolyn's house on the hill. I could just imagine her and my uncle Rob eating supper at the cosy kitchen table with Classic FM playing in the background. Carolyn would be buzzing around the kitchen, glancing out the window to provide a running commentary on the promenade's action. Rob would be rolling his eyes and telling her to sit *down*.

I always walked home as quickly as I could. I could feel her eyes on me, watching me, imploring me to drop by for a quick bite, a quick drink, a quick chat . . . as if using the word 'quick' would convince me our encounter didn't have to mean anything.

And while for me it wouldn't, I knew it would for her. Ever since she'd taken me in, I'd felt the weight of her longing . . . longing for me to love her as a mother; longing to unleash on me the love she had been waiting to lavish on her own child, which she'd never been able to have. Carolyn would have built her whole world around me if I'd let her, but how could I? How could I let someone step into my heart when I'd believed my mother would return?

That first night after my mum left – after she *died*, although I couldn't think that then – Carolyn had tucked me into the guest bedroom, smoothing back my hair as she said the same ten words Mum had repeated to me each night. I'd leaped from the bed as if my aunt had slapped me, screaming 'No!' so loudly that Rob burst into the room to see what had happened.

'Only Mum can say that,' I remember crying, my slender body shaking in the thin pyjamas Carolyn had packed for me. They still smelled of home, and I burrowed my nose into them and tried to

15

block out the scratchy, starched sheets, so different from the soft, worn duvet I was used to.

Everything about Carolyn's life was different from what I was used to, as if she and Mum lived in two separate worlds instead of just streets apart. Their contrasting worlds reflected their personalities: Carolyn was an ordered, conservative woman with a job as headteacher at a local primary school, while Mum was a bohemian who had shunned uni to busk at the seafront, singing in pubs around the town and hoping to catch a break – before she fell pregnant with me. Carolyn had a respectable husband, while Mum was a single mother with no man in her life. It had been just me and her ever since I'd been born . . . until she'd left me alone.

By the time I'd stopped hoping Mum would come back, anger made me force my aunt away. And when I'd finally reached an equilibrium – achieved my perfect cocoon – the barriers between me and Carolyn were already too well erected to pull down. I'd spent years building them up, and I wasn't about to dismantle them. I knew my aunt loved me, but it didn't filter through my defences. It *couldn't*.

I unlocked the front door of my block and, shunning the lift as usual, trundled up the three flights of stairs. I told myself it was good for my legs, but really, I was avoiding the possibility of any small talk with other residents. I could feel myself relaxing more and more the closer I got to my studio. This was my space – well, mine and Dolby's – and it was the one place I could let myself unwind. If I wanted to dance, I could dance (not that I ever did; I loved classical music, and it was hard to groove to Bach). If I wanted to turn up the music (not too loud, of course, the walls were about as thick as wallpaper), I would, and if I wanted to just sit and gaze out at the sea while Dolby dozed on my lap, I'd do that, too.

In fact, that was what I did most often. When I'd first bought this flat right on the promenade, I was a little unnerved by the fact that my huge front window stared straight out at the sea, with nothing between it and me. I'd shied away from staring at it, closing the blinds and turning on music for some background noise. But after a week or so, I realised I was being ridiculous. It was the sea for God's sake – an inanimate object; not something that could hurt me . . . not something that *had* hurt me. Only people could do that . . . if you let them.

I'd opened the blinds and faced the water, forcing myself to stare at it without turning away. The moon was full that night and light danced on the waves – the scene was like something from a postcard. I stood there for what felt like hours until Dolby started meowing. Then, I turned away, and I've rarely closed the blinds since.

The vast, wide expanse of the sea echoed the clean, uncluttered lines of my flat. Despite living here for almost seven years, I had only a pull-out sofa, a lamp and a laptop which I also used as a TV. The walls were bare, the breakfast bar and counter-top free from knick-knacks, and the whole place was painted white. The room's uncluttered lines made me feel safe, as if there were no hidden secrets to fear.

Dolby curled around my legs when I let myself inside, and I leaned down to scratch the spot beside her ear. I'd found her as a kitten under the promenade one day when I was walking home. She'd been in a horrendous state: her fur was patchy, she was only skin and bones, and there were so many fleas it was a wonder she wasn't driven mad. I still don't know what possessed me to take her home, but several exorbitant vet bills later, she was definitely mine. In fact, I don't know if I adopted her or she adopted me. She's my alarm clock, companion and hot-water bottle all rolled into one – the only flatmate I'd ever want.

I was just about to plop down in my favourite spot on the sofa when the mobile rang. Dolby performed her usual leap of surprise in the air before shooting me an evil look. I cringed when I saw Carolyn's name pop up on the screen. Had she been watching me from her window, like I always suspected? Was she calling to give me a bollocking over not speaking to her and Rob for so long? Guilt needled me as I tried to recall the last time we'd spoken. It *had* been a while.

Sighing, I hit 'answer', then scooped up Dolby again and plonked her on my lap. I'd learned it was best to answer Carolyn's calls, or she'd keep ringing until I picked up.

'Hi, Carolyn.' I didn't know when, but somewhere along the way, I'd dropped the 'Aunt'. She didn't feel like an aunt – she did everything a mother should, but she didn't feel like that, either.

'Just calling to check in and see how you're doing,' Carolyn said, in that soft, caring voice that was a particular speciality of hers . . . a voice that seemed to work on everyone but me. As the headteacher at my primary school, I'd seen first-hand how all the kids loved her. When I was younger, they used to tell me how lucky I was to be living with her. I'd wanted to scream at them if they thought I was lucky to have my mum disappear, too, but all I did was nod and smile, telling myself over and over that my mum would be back.

'I'm fine,' I said, in the same carefully neutral voice I'd been using as long as I could remember. 'And you?' I grimaced, thinking how formal my words were. Carolyn deserved more, but I couldn't give it.

To my surprise, instead of her usual cheery answer, Carolyn sighed. 'I'm all right. As well as can be expected today, I guess.'

My brow furrowed. *As well as can be expected today?* What was she talking about?

'I miss her, you know,' Carolyn said, and I squeezed my eyes closed as the realisation filtered in: today was my mother's birthday. Every year I managed to forget, and every year Carolyn remembered, ringing in the hope that this would be the one year I'd finally open up and tell her how I really felt, not knowing I had nothing to say now. Any words about my mum had long since faded away.

'She would have been very proud of you,' my aunt continued. 'A great job in a museum, your own place . . . She would have been so happy to see what you've accomplished.'

I nodded, but I couldn't help wondering if that was true. What would Mum make of my quiet, controlled life? What would she make of *me*? I pictured the photo of my mother that used to hang in Carolyn's lounge – until I'd angrily turned it face down so many times Carolyn had moved it to her room. Mum's dark, curly hair had been blowing in the wind, she was wearing a yellow T-shirt and skin-tight jeans, and her smile was so bright it seemed life was bursting from her. I was almost her exact opposite: skinny, my dark hair cropped short so it couldn't get messed up, wearing mostly grey and black.

What would I have been like if Mum had lived? What would my world have been like?

I shoved the thought from my mind before any answers could filter in. Mum *hadn't* lived. There was no point even contemplating otherwise. I'd managed to make a good life without her.

'Right, well, I'll let you go,' Carolyn said, when it became obvious I had nothing to add. 'We'll be around all weekend if you feel like coming over. I'm cooking lasagne.'

I raised an eyebrow at her mention of lasagne. When I first went to live with her and Rob, I couldn't eat. My stomach was constantly twisted – the pains left me gasping for breath. Multiple visits to GPs uncovered no problems; the doctor told my aunt it was simply the trauma of what had happened. Night after night, Carolyn would serve up perfectly prepared meals she thought I'd like, from fried chicken with ice cream for dessert to spaghetti Bolognese finished off with sticky toffee pudding. And night after night, I'd sit at the table with the feast in front of me, only able to think of my old place with Mum and longing for the baked beans we used to have – not because I loved them, but because that would mean we were together again.

One night a few weeks after I'd come to stay, Carolyn spent hours assembling a lasagne after my teacher told her I'd eaten some of the lasagne at school. She was sliding it from the oven when it slipped from her hands. I'd heard the glass dish shatter on the floor and come running, only to see Carolyn standing in the middle of a tomato-splattered kitchen, tears streaming from her eyes. I'd backed away slowly, worry and fear surging through me at seeing my capable aunt so sad. I forced down the grilled cheese we had that night for supper in a desperate bid to make her happy again.

'Maybe I'll swing by,' I said, both of us knowing I wouldn't. I said goodbye and put down the phone, then stroked Dolby again as I stared out the window. The blue of the sea stretched out to meet the azure sky, forming an endless space. I let it blur before me, ordering my brain to echo its emptiness.

The advert flashed into my mind again, and I shook my head. Seeing those words had reminded me how much my mum had hurt me; of how she'd betrayed my absolute trust. She wasn't with me. She was dead – we weren't celebrating her life, blowing out candles like my colleagues had with Siobhan. I didn't want to commemorate my mother, either. She'd forfeited any right to that by choosing to die.

I padded to the bathroom and hopped into the shower. I turned up the hot water, concentrating on the stinging sensation of my skin as it turned an angry red. I waited for the warmth to filter into me and my body to relax, but somewhere deep inside – a place I tried to identify but couldn't – something was twisting and turning, its sharp edges niggling like a tiny splinter I could feel yet couldn't see.

A good night's sleep, I thought. That's all I needed. Come tomorrow, everything would be fine once again.

CHAPTER FIVE

JUDE

August 1980

'I'll be back right after the break.' Jude did a low bow and forced a bright smile at the ten or so people not watching her perform in the pub. Hell, she could probably do a striptease and they'd still stick their noses in their drinks, preferring swilling beer to watching a real, live performer – even one who was taking off their clothes, not that she'd ever resort to that.

She sighed as she ordered her usual water from the bar and sat down in the corner, telling herself once again that every chance she got to perform was practice for London, where there'd be a million and one girls like her clamouring to perform. Still, singing jazz on a Monday night to punters who looked like they wouldn't know good music if it hit them upside the head was a tough go.

One more set, she told herself, and then she'd be out of here. Carolyn would be waiting up for her, like she did every night, even though Jude was twenty now. Sometimes, although her sister was only eight years older, she acted like she was closer to fifty than to thirty. Jude had hoped Carolyn would loosen up once she'd met her now-husband Rob, but he was just as bad as her. The two of them never went out, saving every single penny for the old dump they planned to move into and do up. Jude planned to be in London before that ever happened.

She was about to put down her drink and head back to the 'stage' (the area furthest from the telly, so people could also watch the match – thankfully, there was no competing game on today) when two men came into the bar. Her eyes widened and a thrill went through her. One was the man who'd watched her on the promenade for ages last week, the one where she'd felt that strange little spark of electricity whenever her eyes met his. He was with a younger bloke who looked more like her usual kind: floppy long hair, dark jeans, and a T-shirt showing off his muscles. She couldn't help smiling when she noticed that the man from the promenade hadn't exactly dressed for the pub – it was like he hadn't brought the right wardrobe for a holiday. Despite his stiff white-collared shirt and trousers, she felt that same zing of attraction when she looked at him. Had he felt that, too, or had it all been in her mind?

The manager of the pub gestured her to the stage, and she sighed. Hopefully, the man would stay long enough for her to find out this time. She went to her little corner and picked up the mic, straining to make out where he was with the blinding lights the manager had so helpfully switched on for her. She launched straight into 'Summertime', the song from the promenade when she'd first noticed him. He'd seemed to like that then, so maybe he'd stick around now, too.

She couldn't see anything but she sang every song – every note – for him, hoping he was just as entranced as he'd been a few days ago . . . hoping her music had managed to capture him once more. After thirty minutes, she smiled, said thank you, and ducked out of the spotlight, sweeping her eyes around the bar as her heart pounded. *Please may he still be here.*

She let out a little snort to quell the butterflies inside. He was just another man, she told herself, and for all she knew, he could have the world's worst BO or breath that would kill you. There was no need to get so worked up.

'Hey.' A male voice at her side made her turn, and she was smiling before she made out who it was. It had to be him. But her heart dropped when she saw it was his friend, the bloke in the tight T-shirt. Up close, he wasn't quite as good-looking as she'd thought: his swarthy skin was pitted with acne scars and his eyes were a little close together. But even if he'd been an Italian film star, she didn't care. He wasn't the one she wanted to talk to. Where had the other bloke gone?

'Hi.' She craned her neck, trying to spot him.

'You're a really good singer,' he said, leaning even closer. 'And I should know. I've worked in the industry.'

Jude's pulse picked up pace, and she felt her cheeks redden as happiness swirled inside. He worked in the industry and he thought she was good? She thought she was okay, but no one who knew anything had ever complimented her on her singing.

She opened her mouth to say thank you, but before any words could emerge, he put a hand on her arm. 'Can I buy you a drink? Let me buy you a drink.' Without even waiting for her to answer, he'd signalled to the bartender and ordered her a beer.

She raised her eyebrows, grudgingly admiring his confidence. It took a lot of guts not only to assume she'd say yes, but to make an executive decision on what she'd drink. She didn't really like beer, but she didn't want to offend him. He thought she was good! She held the thought in her mind, repeating it over and over as a little

24

thrill ran through her. An industry professional thought she was good. What exactly did he do in the industry? she wondered. Did he know anyone in London?

The man lifted his arm, interrupting her thoughts. 'Hubert! Over here!' He smiled down at Jude. 'I'm Frank. And this is my brother, Hubert.'

Jude's heart lifted as she took in the man from the pier. Finally, here he was. Thank God she hadn't lost him.

'Hi.' Hubert smiled, and she loved how his whole face changed from sombre to sunny. 'I saw you on the promenade the other day. I love how you sing, and that song . . . the one about summer . . . it was brilliant.'

'Clever choice, too. Ella Fitzgerald is always a crowd pleaser,' Frank said, and Jude felt a pang of delight that he'd complimented her not only on her singing, but also on her savvy selections. 'Most people recognise her songs, even if they don't know her name, and once the music starts, you can't help but sing along.' He hummed a few bars of 'Summertime', and Jude nodded enthusiastically.

'Exactly!' she said, thrilled to have someone who understood how hard it was choosing the right music to keep people engaged. 'And she's such a musical icon. I can only hope that, one day, I'll be half as good as she was.'

'Keep singing like you did tonight and I'd say you're on the way.' Frank raised his beer and excitement leaped inside her. If an industry insider thought that, maybe she did have a solid chance of making it, after all.

Hubert shifted beside them and Jude turned in surprise. She'd almost forgotten he was there for a second. 'I'm sorry I couldn't leave you anything that day on the promenade,' he said. His cheeks flushed, and he looked down at the counter. 'I didn't have any change, or I would have stayed even longer. But let me get you a drink now, to make up for it?' His cheeks flushed even more, but he managed to raise his head to meet her eyes, and Jude felt that same zing go through her. It felt like he was really looking at *her*, as if he really saw her . . . not like countless other men, who only saw her chest.

'I've already got her one,' Frank said, gesturing to the beer in front of Jude. Hubert's face dropped and Jude squeezed his arm, thinking that, for brothers, they couldn't seem more different. And while, normally, she'd be more drawn to Frank's brash confidence and their musical connection, Hubert's quiet, calm demeanour was so soothing. Already, after only one minute in his presence, she could feel herself relaxing, her insides unwinding.

'You know, I am quite thirsty after all that singing,' she said. 'I'd love a gin and tonic, too.' Actually, she'd never had a gin and tonic, but she liked the way it sounded.

Hubert met her eyes, his smile returning. 'Coming right up.'

Hubert ordered her drink and Frank pushed back from the bar, telling her he needed the loo. Jude watched him go, both glad and anxious that he'd left them alone – she was itching to find out more about his ties with the music industry, but she was also desperate to talk to Hubert. Frank would be back again, she told herself, and she'd have plenty of time to chat to him about the music industry. Right now, she wanted to get to know this man in front of her.

She sipped her gin, enjoying the cool, woodsy taste in her mouth and wondering what to say. Usually, she could talk for hours about anything, not caring what she came out with. Men only listened to her with half their brain, anyway. But there was something about Hubert which made her want to weigh up her words, to not throw them at him like he wasn't important.

'Do you ever go by Hugh?' She cringed. She'd been thinking for a minute about what to say, and that was what she came out with? But Hubert just shook his head.

'No. But Frank calls me Bertie sometimes,' he said. 'Says Hubert sounds like an eighty-year-old at a church picnic.' He laughed. 'You can always trust my younger brother to tell it like it is.'

Excitement leaped up in Jude again. If that was true, then Frank really *must* think she was good.

'Can I call you Bertie, too? Hubert just seems so . . . formal.' She bit her lip, hoping he wouldn't take offence, but Frank was right. Hubert *was* better suited to an eighty-year-old at a church picnic.

He smiled, an endearing lopsided grin. 'I'd like that.' He stuck out a hand. 'Bertie McAllister. Nice to meet you.'

Jude placed her hand in his, loving how his fingers closed firmly around hers. 'Jude. Jude Morgan. Lovely to meet you, too.'

The bell rang for last orders, and Frank grabbed Bertie by the arm. Jude bit her lip, hoping they weren't about to leave. 'I don't know about you two, but I'm famished. Let's grab something from the chippie and eat it down on the beach. Come on.' He charged off towards the door, and Bertie shook his head.

'Sorry about him,' he said, smiling and rolling his eyes in the same exasperated way Jude was sure Carolyn did about her sometimes. 'He comes across a little strong at times. I'm the typical older brother, always trying to rein him in.' Bertie paused, uncertainty flashing across his face. 'Do you want to come and get a bite to eat with us?'

Jude nodded. She could never eat before a show – if you could call this a 'show' – as singing on a full stomach was torturous. She was ravenous now, and even though she usually spurned the greasy chippies at all costs, she could murder some hot, steaming, crunchy battered fish.

But that wasn't the real reason, she knew. The real reason was that she wanted to spend more time with Bertie. And, afterwards, have a chat with Frank and pump him for information. It wasn't often – okay, it wasn't ever – that she ran into someone who knew anything more about music beyond the dire pop songs the local radio station played.

'Let's go, then.' Bertie held out his hand, and she followed him into the dark night. Usually, she hurried home as fast as she could along the promenade to Carolyn's, rejecting Carolyn's plea to call a taxi but never feeling one hundred per cent safe, either. Now, with Bertie clutching her arm, she let herself relax and breathe in the summer air. The city was quiet on a Monday night, except for the laughs of punters leaving the pub behind them. She stood on the promenade and stared out at the sea, marvelling at the vastness in front of her. She shivered, leaning back against Bertie.

'Here we are.' Frank appeared, clutching huge paper bags already soaked through with grease. 'Come on, let's sit down by the water.'

They picked their way through the rocks and over to the sandy stretch, plunking down on the soft sand. The tang of the salty air made the fish and chips taste miles better than she ever remembered, and she devoured her meal.

'So, is this your first time in Hastings?' she asked Bertie, who was trying to eat his fish and chips without making a mess. She couldn't help smiling at his futile attempts.

Bertie nodded. 'Yes. I came to visit Frank.' He gestured to his brother, who was now paddling in the sea. 'He moved down here to help build . . . something or other.'

Jude's heart sank. Frank was a *builder*? Had he been lying to soften her up?

'He mentioned to me that he worked in the music industry?' She couldn't keep the hope from her voice. Perhaps she'd been an idiot, but she'd wanted to believe that someone who knew something thought she was good.

'He's done some work setting up for bands on tour and in pubs, that kind of thing,' Bertie responded. 'It's a hard industry to get regular work in so he does other odd jobs when he needs to, but his heart is really in the music scene. He says it's where he wants to be, so he takes whatever comes his way.'

Jude nodded. She could certainly understand that. And while Frank may not be an industry bigwig with loads of contacts, it sounded like he did have a little experience. He'd been around professional musicians; he knew what it took. If he thought she was good, it carried *some* weight.

Enough about Frank. Jude forced her thoughts from the future and smiled at Bertie. 'What about you? What do you do?'

'I live in Edinburgh,' Bertie said, and Jude's heart dropped. Edinburgh? That was miles away! But it didn't matter, she told herself. It wasn't like she was about to dive into a relationship with this man. She barely knew him. Anyway, she had other things she wanted to do.

Things like moving to London and getting started on her dream.

'And I work as an accountant,' he said, making a face. 'Not the most exciting job, I know, but I like it. There's something about working with numbers that just makes me feel . . . like everything is okay. Like the world is a sane, solid place, instead of all this craziness.' He laughed and shook his head. 'I know that sounds strange.'

Jude squeezed his hand. 'It doesn't, actually. Not at all. It's exactly how I feel when I sing.'

He reached out an arm and placed it gently around her, and she told herself to stop thinking about the future and let herself enjoy the night – and Bertie. Even if it was just for a few hours, she'd found someone she could have a real conversation with; a connection that was more than just physical.

The waves crashed in her ears, and she leaned back against Bertie's chest and closed her eyes.

CHAPTER SIX

ELLA

After my shower, I crawled into bed with Dolby and grabbed my book. As a child, books had always been my shield against the images waiting to ambush me at night. Now they were a comfortable companion, gently lulling me off to sleep. This time, though, the book I was reading lacked its usual anaesthetising power. When I did manage to fall asleep, I jerked awake after what felt like just seconds, my heart beating fast as I struggled to take in air. Dread seeped through me, and I sat up in bed.

I'd had the dream again – the dream that had played in my mind for years, starting the night after my mum had left me.

It began with her walking into the sea in the black of the night. I was on the beach, trying to call out to her, but the howling wind swallowed my voice. Mum kept walking, waves crashing into her, higher and higher, until one went right over her head, enveloping her in dark water. I tried to run, but I couldn't move. I could do nothing but watch the waves, praying to see her head re-emerge, unable to do anything to save her.

When I was younger, I always awoke screaming and crying. Carolyn and Rob would run to me, Carolyn cradling me in her arms even as I pushed her away, with Rob biting his lip and his face creased with worry. Carolyn always asked me to tell her what the dream was about, saying talking about it would make it less scary. But I couldn't. I couldn't begin to explain I was dreaming that my mother was dead. That would make it true.

The dream stopped when I'd finally accepted that my mother *was* dead . . . when I'd finally stopped hoping. The scenario that had played out in my subconscious was no longer a nightmare but a reality.

I crawled from the warm covers and padded to the window. The sea was dark except for white foam capping the waves, and I shivered as I stared at it, feeling exposed and vulnerable. Before I could stop myself, I yanked the blinds closed and burrowed back under the covers, pulling Dolby's warm body up against me.

This was ridiculous. My mother had been gone for thirty years. My mother had been *dead* for thirty years, and any hope – any longing to see her once more and have a mother again – had vanished ages ago. I was over the swamp of fear, the panic and the desperation I'd lived in for so many years as a child. Life was moving forward, carrying me with it, and it would take more than a random advert to burrow through my barriers and plunge me backwards.

But in the days that followed, I felt just that: plunged into the past again. My mum's voice lingered in my brain, those ten words looming larger each time I closed my eyes. The comforting, soothing concoction of safety, trust and love I'd felt in my mother's arms slid over me – a feeling I hadn't had since she'd disappeared – followed swiftly by the brutal see-saw of hope and loss that had engulfed me when she'd gone.

And instead of providing an escape, the nights made it worse: every time I sank into sleep, I was pulled into that same old dream of waves breaking over the top of my mother's head as I screamed in vain. I'd awaken with Dolby crouched under the bed in fear and my pillowcase soaked in sweat.

I told myself over and over that I was past it all, but my subconscious wouldn't listen. I went into work early and left late, but even the huge list of sound files to digitise didn't distract me. In fact, I'd made my first ever mistake at work after cataloguing the files in a completely different era, then accidentally deleting the whole folder when I'd tried to move them. Luckily, we'd been able to restore them.

'Are you all right?' Jane had asked, tilting her head to look closely at my face.

'I'm fine,' I'd said, although I knew I looked anything but. Nights of little sleep had left dark circles under my eyes, and I'd run a hand through my hair so much I resembled a hedgehog. I'd neglected to do my weekly shop, which meant my familiar packed lunch was now down to three Babybel cheeses I'd found in the back of the fridge. I'd been so off-kilter lately that I'd forgotten to do my usual Wednesday night load of laundry, so I was sporting a T-shirt that a diplomatic person might say was 'a little snug'. I looked a mess, and that was exactly how I felt inside, too. For God's sake, I'd almost forgotten to feed Dolby this morning.

'Just . . . er, well, just be careful next time you add a file, okay? Siobhan almost lost a few months' work.' Jane had looked uncomfortable giving me a warning, since I'd never made a mistake before. I prided myself on my concentration and my accuracy.

'Okay.'

Jane had given me another look and then backed off, and I knew she didn't believe I was fine any more than I did.

Because for the first time in years, I *wasn't* fine. I could decry it as much as I liked, but seeing that advert had punctured the neat, ordered bubble I'd been living in. A chink somewhere in my subconscious had allowed those ten words to penetrate, igniting the charred remains of memories I'd thought had long since burned out but were obviously still smouldering. And those memories of my mother's death and the painful aftermath were burning now, trying to consume the defences I'd worked so hard to build; the *life* I'd worked so hard to build.

I couldn't sleep. I couldn't eat and I couldn't work. All my attempts to ignore the flames and carry on as usual were failing, and I couldn't keep going like this. I needed to find a way to put out that fire for once and for all . . . to patch up my armour and get my life – get *me* – back again.

But what could I do?

I drew my knees to my chest as my brain whirled. Perhaps instead of trying to run from the memory of my mother's death, I should invite it in full force. It might sound implausible, but I'd never allowed myself to wonder why my mother had killed herself, and I'd never permitted myself to remember that day. I *couldn't*, if I ever wanted to move forward. And while my efforts might have worked as a stopgap to let me live the life I wanted, clearly it wasn't a permanent solution.

Clearly, some part inside of me still needed rooting out.

But . . . I wrapped my arms around my legs as hesitation filtered in. Was I prepared to fully abandon my defensive stance? To ask the questions I'd buried and bring back that day – the day my mother had died; the day the waves had broken over her head and the sea had swallowed her under?

I had to. I had to, if I ever wanted to return to normal. By knowing what had happened, my subconscious would finally be at peace and the dream would disappear for ever. I'd have my life back again.

I crossed to the window and opened the curtains. I wasn't a hurt, confused little girl any longer. I knew my mother was gone, and years had passed since she'd died. That advert with those ten little words may have stirred up something inside me, but I was stronger.

I'd douse the flames with the truth of the past. It was time, and I was ready.

CHAPTER SEVEN

ELLA

I was desperate now to tear into the past, as if the faster I ripped off the makeshift plaster inside of me, the faster the wound would heal. I sighed, realising the logical person to talk to was Carolyn. She was the only one I could remember in our lives back then, and she'd known my mum better than anyone. She'd be more than happy to talk to me now about my mother; she'd been trying in vain for ages, often inserting little titbits about her in our daily conversation. I'd tune her out or interrupt, willing her to stop talking. Not that she ever got the message. You couldn't will Carolyn to do anything.

Would she ask why I wanted to know about my mother now? I wondered. After all, I'd put her off for years, always slamming the door closed with every attempt. I swallowed. No way would I tell her about the advert I'd seen or how much it had unsettled me. I didn't want her to know that, somewhere deep inside, some part of my subconscious still smarted from what my mother had done.

I could barely believe it myself.

I made it through the day at work, hurried home to feed Dolby, then threw on my jacket. Dolby looked up at me with an enquiring gaze. It wasn't often I went out in the evening . . . actually, it wasn't ever. I spent the whole day avoiding people at work, so why would I voluntarily meet up with them after hours?

'Just going out for a minute or two,' I said, scratching her behind her ears. 'Won't be long.'

The soft summer sun had given way to fog, and I hurried along the promenade with my chin tucked down against the wind. A few minutes later, I was standing outside Carolyn and Rob's, staring up at the brilliant white facade that was dazzling, even in the dim light. At huge expense, they had it painted every three years or so; Rob hated any bit of potential peel. The house was their baby – they had rescued it from demolition after it had fallen into a state with squatters, who'd almost burned it down at one point. With Carolyn a newly qualified teacher and Rob only just starting out as an engineer, they'd bought it for hardly anything and spent the next ten years making it into the home it was today.

Not that I'd ever considered it my home. After almost fifteen years here, right up until I got my job at the museum and had saved enough money for a deposit on my studio, it still didn't feel like that. This house would only ever be the place where my life had changed. It was here that, after years and years, I'd finally accepted Mum wasn't coming back.

It was here that I lost a mother, and here where I was no longer a daughter.

But that first morning . . . oh, how sure I was that my mother would never leave me. It never crossed my mind that she didn't mean the words she uttered every night. Memories tugged at my brain now, and for the first time, I didn't stop them. I urged them forward, welcoming them into me.

I'd known my mother was gone the second I opened my eyes. Everything was unfamiliar, from the scent of frying bacon (made Mum ill) to the radio blaring BBC4 (gave Mum headaches). I could hear the clanking of plates and Carolyn's cheerful yet tuneless humming, and for a second – a second I'm so ashamed of now, yet at the time I had no idea of its true significance – I wished this could be my reality: that Carolyn was my mother and every morning started this way, instead of the heavy silence pierced only by my mum's snores.

But that morning there were no snores, and I was happy. That meant my mother was up and about, and I wouldn't have to creep into her room and try to wake her up . . . though for what, I didn't know, since her piano students had long since stopped coming for lessons. That morning, there'd be a hot breakfast on the table and I could fill my tummy until bursting, and Carolyn would still urge me to eat. I'd slid from the covers, grinning.

What had happened next? I strained to remember, but for a morning that had blown my world to bits, everything seemed fuzzy. I recall Carolyn asking where my mother was, and me saying I didn't know before tucking into the breakfast – funnily enough, I remember the toast was black on one side; Carolyn didn't know our toaster liked to 'keep us on our toes', as Mum always said.

And then the hours are a blur of Carolyn ringing round – although I couldn't imagine who she was calling, because it's not like we knew anyone. I remember night falling and Carolyn taking me to their house in the car, me only too happy to sit in front of the telly we didn't have at our place. It was only at bedtime when it really started to hit me: Mum wasn't here. She'd promised she'd always be with me! Where was she?

I remembered asking Carolyn that question over and over. In all of my five years, my mother had never *not* been there. Carolyn responded that she wasn't sure, but my mum must have had something important to do and would probably be back in the morning. At last, my eyes grew heavy and I slept.

I woke up on the soft, downy mattress at Carolyn and Rob's house. Voices drifted up from the kitchen, and I raced down the stairs in my pyjamas, which Carolyn had brought over from home. I couldn't wait to see my mum and hear her stories of where she'd been. When she was in a good mood, Mum had a way of making even the most mundane event sound like the funniest and most exciting thing in the world.

I'd rounded the corner into the kitchen, my bare feet skidding on the unfamiliar polished tiles. I froze at the sight of two policemen sitting at the table with Carolyn and Rob. What were they doing here? But before my five-year-old brain could begin to even conjure up answers, my gaze fell on the clear plastic bag on the table in front of them. In that bag were things I recognised: the cardigan full of holes that Mum always wore, her gold hoop earrings, the butterfly bracelet I'd broken once and Mum had managed to fix . . .

What were all those things – those pieces of my mother – doing there, in that bag?

Where was she?

Carolyn took me by the hand and led me the lounge – one of them, anyway, the one they called the sun-room. She sat me in a wicker chair and told me I'd be staying with them for the next little while. I'd shaken my head, saying I had to get home. Mum would be wondering where I was. If she wasn't here, she'd be waiting there – waiting for me to crawl into her bed, to hear those ten words and say them back again.

I slid from the chair and opened the door. Carolyn tried to grasp me, but I was too quick for her to catch hold. Forgetting I was only wearing my nightclothes with nothing on my feet, I slipped out the door and into the fresh morning air. The sky was a heavy grey, and as I streaked across the manicured lawn dew coated my bare feet. On the beach in front of me, I could see police officers sifting through the rocks and chatting to people with dogs, usually the only ones out so early. A boat was moving back and forth, back and forth, people on board prodding at the water as if looking for something they'd lost.

'Ella.' Carolyn had touched my arm, and I'd jumped. For a second, I'd forgotten where I was. 'Come back inside.'

'What are they doing?' I remember asking. 'What are they looking for?'

'Come inside.' Her voice had sounded unfamiliar then, miles from the usual cheery tones I'd been used to. Even though I'd been intent on going home, a little voice in my head had urged me to follow her. Her feet had been bare, too, and they couldn't have been more different from my mum's slender, delicate ones. The door closed behind us, and although questions bubbled up in my brain, I couldn't get them out to ask. Somehow, I knew those policemen on the beach were connected to my mother, but I didn't know why. I couldn't put it together.

I *wouldn't* put it together. Mum would be back for me, and that was that. Even when Carolyn sat me down a few days (a few weeks? I don't know; time had lost all meaning for me) later and said that although police hadn't found my mother, they didn't think she was coming home, I still wouldn't believe it. Even when Caroline and Rob held a private memorial service on the beach one wind-swept morning in autumn, I clung on. The marker on my mother's empty grave on the hill became weathered, but I held out. The rose-bush my aunt had planted in memory of my mum grew and grew, sprouting more heady-smelling blossoms each summer. And still I thought my mother would come back for me. I was certain of it.

Mum wouldn't break those ten words. And more than that, if she *really* was going to leave me for ever, she would have left one thing behind: the necklace with the heart pendant that she always wore. It hadn't been in the plastic bag I'd seen that morning. She'd promised it to me when I grew up . . . when I was old enough to have a love – a life – of my own. Her eyes always looked sad when

39

she said that, and I'd throw my arms around her and say that I'd never leave her.

My eyes widened at the memory. I'd forgotten about that necklace. I strained to recall when I'd first seen it around my mother's neck, but of course I couldn't remember. It was just always there, a flash of gold against my mother's creamy skin. I'd loved the heavy heart, always begging my mum to take it off and let me prance in front of the mirror, playing princess. I'd hung on to the fact that she hadn't left me the necklace as proof she was going to return.

But gradually, like those ten little words, I'd realised it was just another promise my mother wasn't going to keep. I'd shoved the memory and her empty words to the back of my mind; to the back of my soul . . . until now. Why *hadn't* she left the necklace? I wondered. Why hadn't she left a note, something – anything – or me, her only child? Anger darted through me, but I managed to block it quickly, a quiet confidence seeping through me as the rogue emotion faded away. I could do this. I could face the past and walk away unscathed.

I took a deep breath and headed to Carolyn's door.

CHAPTER EIGHT

ELLA

I pressed the doorbell, shifting back and forth as I waited for my aunt (it was always Carolyn who answered, pushing past Rob if he ever tried). It was like she was living in a permanent state of expectation, waiting for me to come home again.

'Ella!' Her eyebrows flew up. 'Come in, come in!'

I paused for second, wondering if she was going to try to hug me, but thankfully, she'd stopped trying. She opened the door wide and I stepped inside, struggling to remember the last time I'd been here – in December, probably, for Christmas lunch. I'd dragged myself out of bed as late as possible then thrown on my clothes and headed over. It was the one day I didn't have to tuck my chin down to avoid passers-by; the city was quiet and still, like I was the only person in the world.

'I'm so sorry, but we've finished all the fish pie,' Carolyn was saying. 'I can knock you up a nice grilled cheese, if you like?'

I shook my head. 'No, thanks.'

Carolyn didn't look surprised by my rejection. 'Come in, then. Rob's in the lounge, struggling with sudoku.' She rolled her eyes and I couldn't help smiling. Every night, Carolyn and Rob competed to complete the day's puzzle. And every night, Carolyn won. They used to ask me to join in, and I'd pretend I wasn't playing, even though I was trying to figure it out, too. I loved puzzles: a simple problem contained within a nice, neat box that could always be solved.

'Look who's here!' Carolyn ushered me into the stuffy room. Even though it was summer, a fire blazed in the hearth. Carolyn always kept the place on jungle-setting, as if heat could banish the house's emptiness. Warmth seeped into me and I could feel my cheeks flush.

'Well, well.' Rob glanced up with a grin. 'It's good to see you. Come and sit down and let me know what you've been up to. Thank God you came – I was about to lose it with this puzzle!'

I sat down beside him. I never felt the same discomfort around Rob that I did with Carolyn. Maybe it was because I'd never had a father in my life; someone whose place he'd tried to fill. My dad had died shortly before I was born, but even if he'd lived, I sensed he wouldn't have been on the scene. Mum had always said I was hers and hers alone. She hadn't even named my father on my birth certificate, showing just how superfluous he was.

I blinked, remembering the time Carolyn applied for my passport. I must have been around ten, and even though my mum had been gone for five years, I still believed she'd be back. I'd picked up a document on the table, noticing it was my birth certificate, my eyes tearing as I ran my fingers over my mother's name. The box for my father's name was blank, but that didn't faze me. He'd always been just that: a blank, and I'd never felt the urge to fill it in. Seeing the document had made my mother's words even clearer: I was hers. She *would* come back.

When she didn't, I realised I was no one's but my own. Only I could protect myself, keep myself safe.

That's exactly why I was here.

I bit my lip. Now that I was ready to face the past, I wasn't sure how to start. I shifted in the chair, drawing a cushion into my arms. Much to Rob's dismay, Carolyn had a habit of cluttering every sofa and chair with cushions. She claimed to love the contrast of colours and I'm sure she thought she was making everyone as comfortable as possible, but to me it felt like she was smothering every surface. Now, though, I was happy for their presence. I held it against me like a shield.

'So' – Carolyn cocked her head and smiled – 'how are things at the museum? I've been meaning to see their new exhibition . . . songs of seabirds, isn't it? Did you help put it together?'

I nodded, my mind flying through the hours upon hours I'd spent combing through the sound archives, pulling the right files for the exhibition. Others might see it as a tedious task but, for me, there was something hypnotic about listening to the sharp cry of birds above the rolling sea. If that was the last thing my mother had heard before the water took her under, then she was lucky. In a way, I almost longed to duck under the salty, cold water myself.

I cleared my throat, shaking myself from my reverie. I wasn't here to talk about the exhibition. The sooner I got this over with, the better.

'Look . . .' I clutched the cushion tighter. 'I just, well . . . I've been thinking of my mother a lot lately.' That much was true. Ever since seeing that advert, I'd barely thought of anything else. Carolyn shot Rob a questioning glance before her face returned to a careful neutral expression I knew very well. 'I guess I just . . . well, I was wondering *why* she took her life. Was she really that unhappy with me?' The last question slipped out before I could stop it, and I wanted to kick myself. I sounded like the five-year-old I once was. It was more than obvious she hadn't been happy with me – with being my mother – wasn't it?

'Oh, Ella.' Firelight flickered on my aunt's face, the glow highlighting her sympathetic features. Annoyance and irritation darted through me. I didn't need sympathy. For a second, I regretted opening up this Pandora's box. But I had to. I couldn't turn around now. Not if I ever wanted to be at peace again.

'Jude loved you very, very much.' Carolyn reached out to touch my hand, but I saw her stop herself. 'Her death had nothing to do with you.'

Anger flared inside, and I tried to keep my features from twisting. My aunt meant well, but my mother's death had *everything* to do with me. We'd been connected in a way only a mother and child could be, and even though I'd got over it, her leaving had torn me apart for years. I drew in air, forcing away the emotion. Now wasn't the time to succumb to feelings.

'But Jude had . . . well, she had some issues,' Carolyn continued. 'Depression, you know.' She gazed into the fire. 'At first, we thought it was just the baby blues, after having you. Hers seemed a bit more serious than usual, so I took her to the GP. She took some medication for a while and seemed better, but then . . . then I'd find out she'd cancelled all her lessons, and that neither of you had left the house in days.'

I tilted my head, trying to cast my mind back. Had my mum been depressed? I remembered her sleeping a lot, but I'd thought that's just what adults did. I'd very often get up and make my own breakfast (a piece of bread and some milk, if we had any), then play with my toys until she stirred. There were days she'd sit and stare at the sea for hours as I played around her, trying to poke and jab her and get a reaction. Eventually, she'd drag herself upstairs into bed and I'd crawl in next to her, listening to her heartbeat and telling myself it was okay; she would always be here.

But I hadn't known any different. I'd thought that was what everyone did; what every mother was like.

'I tried to get her on to her medication again, but she refused to see the doctor. Before she died, I think she was drinking quite a bit,' Carolyn said. 'It was her way of dealing with her depression, I guess. She tried to hide it from me, but I could smell it on her breath.'

I nodded, remembering the sweet, cloying smell of my mum's breath sometimes when I crawled into the bed – and those thick glass bottles filled with clear liquid I'd sometimes find under the sink. I hadn't known what it was then, other than it seemed to make Mum better. In my head, I'd called it her medicine.

'So she was depressed and she drank,' I said. 'Was there anything else?' My tone was matter-of-fact, but that's how I needed to be: business-like and removed, as if this had happened to a stranger, not my mother – as if it hadn't happened to me. I couldn't let emotions touch me again.

Carolyn slowly shook her head. 'No.'

The room was silent for a minute as I thought about what else to ask. 'And the police . . . did they do much investigation? When was she officially declared dead?' It hit me once more how little I knew. I'd been so young, and of course Carolyn and Rob had kept the finer details away from me. I'd never wanted to know until now.

'After I told the police about her depression, combined with the reports of people who'd seen her walking into the sea and her belongings on the beach, well . . . it didn't take long for the police to decide she must have taken her own life. The currents that day were strong and although the police made every effort, they said the chances of finding her body after a few days were very slim. I almost didn't want them to. I wanted to keep Jude in my head exactly as I remembered her: beautiful and full of life.'

Carolyn paused, her shoulders lifting in a sigh. 'All that evidence, along with the fact that she hadn't taken any money from her bank accounts or used any cards for weeks after her disappearance . . . It was enough for all of us to know she wasn't coming back.'

Enough for everyone but me. My heart panged at my five-year-old self's steadfast belief and trust in my mother, and I shook my head to clear the emotion.

'We had to wait a few years before we could get her death certificate but, by then, the whole thing was really just a formality. We only got it in case—' Carolyn cleared her throat. 'Well, for logistical reasons, really.'

I raked my mind for more questions to ask, but nothing came to mind. I wasn't sure what I'd expected, but my mother's death seemed so black and white. She'd been depressed and, without treatment, it had all been too much. She'd left me and walked into the sea, and that was that.

Maybe because I'd refused to think about it for years, I'd thought there would be more – more of a reason; more of a story behind her death; maybe an explosive memory long since buried. Relief filtered through me as I realised everything was out in the open now. Despite what my subconscious may have conjured up, there wasn't anything else there to fear.

'I have some of your mother's things packed away upstairs,' Carolyn said. 'I've been saving them for you, whenever you were ready.'

I drew in a breath, remembering Carolyn asking me throughout the years if I wanted to take a look. I'd always shaken my head – after giving up hope that my mother would return, I hadn't wanted anything to do with her. Why would I want to comb through her precious things? Nothing had been enough to keep her from the sea. Not even her very own daughter.

I still didn't want to. I'd come here to learn about my mother's death, not her life. I didn't need to know her as a person. She'd been a mother who'd left me, and that was all. I wasn't scared – I simply wasn't interested.

'There's some jewellery there I'm sure she'd like you to have,' Carolyn said, and I jerked towards her. Jewellery? Did she mean the pieces they'd found on the beach that day, or had the heart pendant been found? Maybe it had been uncovered in the sand at some point. Carolyn wouldn't think to tell me. She didn't know my mother's promise that the pendant would one day be mine.

Before I could stop it, hope flared inside me . . . hope that maybe my mother had left something, after all. Something she'd known I would cherish; a piece of her I could hold close to me, knowing it had been precious to her, too.

Maybe she'd kept one promise, after all.

Stop it! I shook my head so hard that my neck hurt, swearing at myself under my breath. I was done here. I'd faced the past. Nothing had touched me, and nothing would. But before I could gather myself to say anything, Rob was already halfway up the stairs.

'I'll get the box for you,' he said, his voice floating down. 'And don't worry, there's no rush – you don't need to go through it here. I'll drive you home and you can take your time.'

Relief filtered through me that I wouldn't be forced to open the box under Carolyn's watchful eye. I'd shove it in the back of my wardrobe, and it could stay there until I had a chance to return it to my aunt.

Carolyn and I watched Rob head up the stairs and, this time, Carolyn did reach out to touch my hand. I tried not to shy away. 'I'm so pleased you're ready to talk about all of this,' she said. 'If you have any other questions, you know where to find us. Call any time.'

I tore myself away from her intense gaze and looked at the fire. 'Great. Thank you.' I didn't want my words to sound so forced, but I couldn't help it.

Rob came down the stairs with a cardboard box tucked under his arm. 'Ready to go?'

I said a quick goodbye to Carolyn and followed Rob out to the car.

Rob unlocked the car door and put the box in the back. 'Hang on a sec, Ella. I found another box of your mum's things in the shed – I think Carolyn must have forgotten about it. Just one minute and I'll get it for you.'

I nodded as he scurried off, returning with a small shoebox.

'Right,' he said, sliding into the driver's seat. 'Let's get you home.' He started the engine and I clenched my jaw. In the back seat, the boxes felt like my mother's crouching presence, watching us. I couldn't wait to pack them away.

'You know, it was really nice to see you,' Rob said. 'Carolyn, well . . . she worries a lot about you.'

'I'm fine,' I said tightly. 'Just tell her not to worry.'

Rob laughed. 'Telling her that is like telling the sea to stay still,' he said. 'But talking to you a bit more, well, it'd do her good.'

I swung my gaze towards him. 'Is she okay?' Something in his voice made me wonder.

'Oh, yes, she's all right,' he said. 'Just a few minor issues with her blood pressure – the doctor thinks it's to do with her heart. They're going to do a few more investigations.'

'Right.' I swallowed. 'But she'll be okay, right?'

'Oh, yes, as long as she doesn't get herself too worked up. Right, here we are.' Rob pulled up in front of my block of flats. 'Do you want me to help you carry the boxes up?'

'No, that's okay. I can manage.' Rob hadn't been in my flat since he'd helped me move in – there was hardly any room for me and Dolby, let alone entertaining other people. 'Thanks for the lift.'

'My pleasure.' He touched my arm. 'See you soon?'

I nodded, although I didn't know what he meant by 'soon'. I reached over to the back seat and hauled out the two boxes, then set them down and closed the car door. Rob lifted a hand and the car pulled away, leaving me alone with the remains of my mother's life.

CHAPTER NINE

JUDE

August 1980

Jude hadn't realised time could pass so quickly – well, not in Hastings, anyway, where one hour could sometimes feel like a century. But over the next few days, the minutes flew by. Despite her declaration that she didn't need any complications right now, she and Bertie were spending almost every second together . . . from the moment she woke up and rushed to his hotel (Frank's place wasn't fit for a rat, he'd said) to the late-night walk back to Carolyn's. Sweetly, Bertie hadn't tried to convince her to stay over – not yet, anyway, although she couldn't wait. If their kissing was anything to go by, making love was going to be amazing.

She smiled now as she hurried along the promenade to his hotel, recalling the moment they'd locked lips on the night they'd first met. They'd spent that whole night on the beach (she'd had a lot of explaining to do about that one with Carolyn). Bertie had walked her along the promenade in the dawn, asking if he could see her again. She'd grabbed his hand and nodded, saying how about right now, for breakfast? She'd been so happy she hadn't even been tired, and she could see he felt the same. They'd got breakfast in the one place that was open, then sat down on a bench in the glowing sun and fallen asleep in each other's arms. It sounded like something from a romance novel – and it had felt like it, too. When Bertie had lowered his lips to hers, light had filled her, banishing any lingering darkness.

Bertie was so far from her usual type that she couldn't even begin to describe what made him attractive. It wasn't just his impeccable manners, how he always turned up on time without a million excuses, like the other blokes she'd dated, or how he really listened when she spoke. It was just . . . *him*. There was something about his soul, about the very essence of what made him Bertie that clicked so well with her. They were two very different pieces of a puzzle that slotted together perfectly. He made her feel anchored and safe, like she wasn't about to float off untethered, the way she'd been feeling since her parents had died.

Her smile grew wider as thoughts of yesterday filled her head. Like every day she and Bertie had been together, they'd had breakfast then gone down to the promenade, where Bertie watched her sing. He'd stood quietly at the back of the crowd as always, his gaze fixed firmly on her face as if nothing in the world was as important as her. The blue sky had clouded over and a sharp wind whipped the water, and Jude could feel cold seeping into her more and more with each gust. The punters started melting away and she'd been about to grudgingly pack it in when Bertie had appeared at her side, wrapping her in his thick coat and rubbing her arms.

'Keep going,' he'd said, urging her on. He'd understood that, for her, this wasn't just busking – this was working towards a dream; towards starting the life she'd always wanted. She'd taken a deep breath and started to sing again, warm now from her very core.

When she'd first told Bertie about her plan to go to London, she'd been worried that he'd think she was crazy, just like Carolyn had. Jude knew it wasn't the most practical idea, and anyone could see the odds were stacked against her. Even if she did manage to get a job at one of pubs Frank had mentioned when she'd pumped him for information, that was only a very slim foothold on the long ladder she'd need to climb. Jude had braced herself, unsure if she could bear hearing anything negative from this man who'd made her feel that, finally, someone actually *saw* her.

But Bertie had surprised her. He'd hugged her tightly, saying how brave she was to follow her dreams and how much he admired her passion for singing – that he could hear it in every word. And as he'd stood there yesterday, watching her sing, his arms bare as the freezing wind whipped in from the sea, she realised that not only did he understand, but he wouldn't try to change her. She could be *her*.

When she really couldn't sing any longer, she and Bertie would abandon her pitch and head down to the beach for a break before her pub gigs started. Sometimes Frank would join them, sitting still for just one second before trying to drag Bertie into the frothy water, often succeeding. Jude would lounge on the sand as the laughter from the two men floated towards her, smiling as she watched the two of them cavort in the waves like overgrown puppies. Then, despite the fact that Jude would need to do her hair all over again, she'd plunge into the sea savouring the cold water on her sweaty, sunburned skin. Frank was like crashing waves to Bertie's still water, but despite the differences between the two brothers, she'd never seen them clash – not like she and Carolyn did. Bertie could take it all in his stride, and that made her feel even more comfortable with him. Happiness bubbled up inside, filling her whole world with light.

Even Carolyn noticed what a good mood Jude was in, commenting that she hoped it would last. She'd meant Jude's good mood, of course, and not her fling with Bertie (Carolyn didn't even know about Bertie), but it made Jude think. This *was* just a fling, a wonderful holiday romance that couldn't last. Soon, Bertie would go back to Edinburgh. Hastings would revert from being a wonderland to a wasteland once again and, come September, she'd go to London.

Somehow, though, the thought didn't hold the same appeal.

CHAPTER TEN

ELLA

I carried the boxes into my flat and shoved them to the back of the wardrobe, the only place in my studio where I could put things out of sight. They were just boxes, I told myself, trying to shake the unnerving feeling that my mother had invaded my sanctuary. They were only objects – inanimate things, nothing more, nothing less.

Moving methodically and deliberately, I went through my usual bedtime routine: shower, pyjamas, then curling up under the duvet with Dolby and my book. Ten-thirty came and I switched off the light and lay in the darkness, counting my breaths in and out and waiting for sleep to come. Tonight, I'd nothing to fear. I'd faced down my memories and put my terrible nightmares to rest. I couldn't wait for a full night's sleep in peace.

Each time I closed my eyes, though, the boxes in the wardrobe loomed larger and larger, questions needling my mind like poisonous darts. Was the heart pendant in there? Had my mother thought of me in her last moments? *Had* she left something of herself for her daughter?

I pushed the questions away. I told myself over and over how ridiculous I was being. I twisted the duvet around my limbs, as if I was physically preventing myself from getting up to rip open the boxes. But no matter how hard I clenched the covers or pressed myself into the mattress, I couldn't stop the urge building inside.

Sighing in frustration, I threw aside the duvet and got out of bed, switching on the light. I was done with all of this, but if the only way I was going to sleep tonight was to open those boxes and prove to myself the necklace wasn't there, then I'd do it. Why not? Jewellery or not, my mother was gone. She'd still left me, and I'd long since accepted it. After tonight, I knew there was nothing more to fear; no reason my subconscious would linger on painful memories.

I opened the wardrobe doors and slid the boxes on to the sofa. Then I grabbed a knife from the kitchen cupboard and ran it down the centre of the bigger box, lifting the flaps. It was full of clothing I didn't recognise, bright colours spilling out into the gloom of the dim light. A soft red silk shirt, a jade-green jumper, an orange pair of trousers, a purple velvet dress . . . so unlike Mum's typical outfit of faded jeans or jogging bottoms along with whatever T-shirt she'd pulled from the laundry pile on the sofa that day. I pawed through the items, determined not to pause. I didn't want to think about her. I was only doing this to put my mind to rest and get some sleep.

I spotted a clear plastic bag with the glint of metal inside. Despite myself, my stomach flipped: this must be the jewellery that was found on the beach. I tore open the bag and drew out the tangle of necklaces and bracelets. The butterfly bracelet, the earrings . . . No, no heart pendant. Not in this box, anyway.

Right, one more box, and then I could sleep. I grabbed the shoebox and slid my fingers under the yellowed Sellotape that attached the lid. It snapped easily, and I lifted the top.

I sat back, taking in the contents. Envelope after envelope was neatly stacked inside, some thick and some thin. I sifted through them, noticing none had been opened. There were dozens of them, and they were all addressed to my mother at Carolyn's house. There was no return address, but the handwriting looked the same on each.

Why hadn't my mother opened any of these? I wondered. And why had Carolyn kept them all this time, even those that had arrived after my mother's death? Why hadn't my aunt written to this person and told them my mother had died?

I shut down the questions in my mind as I scanned the inside of the box, looking for a glint of gold, but it was empty. I took a deep breath, steeling myself against any hint of disappointment. My mother hadn't thought of me, but that was hardly news. How could she have killed herself otherwise? She might have been depressed, but she could have let Carolyn help her. She could have taken medication, but she'd decided not to.

She could have stayed, but she'd chosen to leave.

Case closed.

I replaced the letters in the box without giving them a second glance. I'd only opened it to see if the pendant was there. Whatever else – *whoever* else – my mother had left behind, well . . . I didn't care.

It was time to get my life on back on track.

CHAPTER ELEVEN

JUDE

August 1980

Before Jude could even blink, Bertie's holiday in Hastings was over and it was time for him to head back to Edinburgh. He'd wanted to pick her up at Carolyn's and take her out to a posh restaurant: a 'last supper', as she'd jokingly called it. And while she'd have jumped at the suggestion with previous dates, now she'd shaken her head. She didn't need to dress up and go out; she didn't need fancy food and expensive wine. She just needed Bertie.

Besides, she didn't want anything special to mark that this was over. Sure, she'd known that Bertie was visiting for only a short time and that he had a life in Scotland (though she struggled to picture him anywhere but here, by her side). And, sure, they both knew that in a few weeks, she'd be leaving here anyway. But despite realising they'd soon go their separate ways, Jude had plunged headlong into their remaining days together, giving him her everything. He made it easy, and she couldn't – she didn't *want* to – hold back. Just knowing Bertie was waiting for her at their spot on the promenade brought a smile to her face.

'What is *up* with you lately?' her sister had asked a few days earlier, when Jude had finished washing up one night with a smile. Usually, she suffered through it as if someone was flicking her skin with the damp towel. Truly, could there be a more boring task in the world?

Jude had jerked, catching herself dreaming of Bertie's arms wrapped around her. 'Nothing.' She didn't want to share Bertie with anyone but herself, least of all her sister. Bertie was like a pleasant dream, and the last thing she needed was Carolyn shaking her rudely awake with her dose of reality. Bertie had wanted to meet her sister, but Jude had steadfastly refused. They had little time together as it was, and she didn't want to waste it over an excruciating dinner where poor Bertie would be subjected to Carolyn's grilling. Although, actually, she suspected Bertie might meet with Carolyn's approval, unlike some of the other blokes she'd been with in the past. He was polite, had a steady job, dressed neatly, and spoke nicely. He and Carolyn were almost the same age, too. Bertie was nearly a whole decade older than Jude!

She shook her head now, a smile creeping across her face as she struggled into her favourite pair of jeans and a gingham top. Bertie might be miles away from her usual type, but she couldn't be happier.

For now, anyway. She swallowed against the sadness that filled her when she remembered that this time tomorrow he would be gone, and life would fade to black and white again.

But there was always London, she reminded herself, sighing as she ran a brush through her hair. Just a few more weeks, and she would be escaping to a city where things were sure to be in Technicolor. Okay, so she still hadn't figured out where she would live and how she'd survive until she made it as a singer. She didn't know a soul and, even with Frank's tips, it was bound to be difficult until she got going. Something like fear shot through her, and she took a deep breath.

But she didn't have to worry about that now. She didn't have to think about that now. Tonight, she was Bertie's, safe and loved in his arms. And she was going to hang on to that with everything she had, even if it would only last for a few more hours.

She sprayed on her favourite perfume, grabbed her cardigan and ran down the hill to the promenade. The sun was shining and the air was warm, but further out to sea she spotted dark clouds and the hazy slant of falling rain. Although she may not be a huge fan of this town, she loved living by the sea. It reminded her that she wasn't trapped; that across the water were other places to see and new things to explore. Hastings might sometimes feel like the end of the world, but it was only a starting point.

In the distance, she could see Bertie leaning against the rail and gazing out at the sea the same way she had just done. She hurried her legs faster and faster, warmth growing inside, the closer she got. Not only was she attracted to him physically – although they still hadn't slept together; Bertie hadn't wanted to push it, but if they didn't do it tonight, when would they ever? – she was attracted to the person inside, too. She'd never felt this combination before, and she revelled in its headiness.

Jude lifted a hand as Bertie turned towards her, and she could see his smile growing bigger in a reflection of hers.

'Hiya,' she said when she reached him, tipping her head up to meet his lips. He folded her in his arms, and she tried not to think yet again that this would be the last night he'd hold her.

They chatted their way down the promenade and over to the fish and chip shop, the same one they'd got their first meal from after meeting at the pub. With every second that passed, no matter how frothy and flirty Jude tried to keep her tone, the heaviness in her heart increased until she felt like she could no longer breathe without a struggle. She could almost see a clock counting down their last seconds together.

As they crossed the beach to their favourite spot, the skies opened and rain poured down. Bertie grabbed her hand and together they ran underneath the concrete of the promenade, into a space strewn with litter that smelled of spilled beer and urine. Jude wrinkled her nose, rubbing her wet arms as goosebumps poked up. This was most definitely not what she'd had in mind for their last night together.

She swallowed. It was now or never, and if Bertie was too shy . . .

'Shall we go back to yours?' she asked. She wanted to keep her tone light and fun, but to her own ears it sounded shaky and uncertain. Bertie wasn't someone she'd shag one night then simply move on. Whatever happened now would mean something to her . . . something she'd clutch close to her heart in the days to come without him. It might hurt – it would hurt – when he left, but she wanted that. She wanted a reminder of him, even if it was painful.

And as he nodded slowly, she could see that he felt the same way, too.

They clutched each other's hands and dashed though the rain to Bertie's hotel. Inside the tiny room, they sloughed off their wet clothes and stood facing each other. Normally, Jude would be worrying whether her boobs were too saggy (the perils of big breasts) or if the fish supper she'd wolfed down was making her tummy poke out, but in front of Bertie, she found she didn't care.

His body was surprisingly sturdy and solid, and when she took a step forward to close the distance between them and his arms came around her, she could feel his heart beating steadily against her ear, a rhythm that grounded and stilled her. Rain lashed the window and the panes shook as they fell on to the bed. The world around them was dark and brooding, and they formed the one spot of light – light that was bursting from Jude as they kissed. Making love with Bertie wasn't just about her body. For the first time, she felt it was about them, not as two separate people but making something new, something wonderful, together.

And when it was over, she lay in Bertie's arms, both of them trying to catch their breath. He rolled over and raised himself up on one elbow, tracing the curve of her hip with his fingertips.

'I've been thinking,' he said, his voice soft.

Jude raised an eyebrow. 'Uh-oh.' She was joking, but her pulse picked up pace at his serious expression.

'I realise we've only known each other for a couple of weeks,' he said. 'Well, even less than a couple. And I know it sounds horribly clichéd, but I feel like we belong together.' He drew in a breath, and Jude could feel his heart beating quickly now. 'You're planning on going to London, and the last thing I want to do is stand in your way. But I have to ask, because if I don't do it now . . .' He swallowed. 'Would you like to come to Edinburgh with me?' The words tumbled out, and Jude jerked in surprise. She hadn't been expecting that!

'I mean, I'd move to London with you, but I have my house there and a job,' Bertie continued. 'And Edinburgh has a great music scene, too. Maybe it'll be easier to get a start there? It's not London, but . . .'

His words washed over Jude as her mind spun. Go to Edinburgh? Be with Bertie, with someone who understood her, who appreciated her – who barely knew her. Carolyn's voice sneaked into her head on those last few words, but Jude pushed it away. It wasn't true, anyway. Bertie *did* know her, in a way her sister never could . . . never would. He knew her better than anyone ever had, even if they had only met just weeks before.

In an instant, she knew what her answer would be. London would always be there – it wasn't going anywhere. Bertie was, and she was going with him.

'Yes,' she said, beaming. 'Yes, I'd love to. I'd love to come to Edinburgh with you.'

And as his arms tightened around her, she felt safer than she had since her parents had died all those years before. She wasn't alone, not any more.

She had Bertie.

CHAPTER TWELVE

ELLA

I sat up the next morning, rubbing my eyes triumphantly. For the first night in weeks, I'd managed to sleep for hours without waking up – or having that horrific nightmare. If my subconscious was a dog, I'd give it a good pat on the head. Finally, it had submitted. I was proud of myself and confident I'd taken the right steps to return to normal.

I was just getting ready to go to work when my mobile rang. My heart dropped as I read the name. *Carolyn.* I sighed and picked up, hoping she wasn't expecting another tête-à-tête, like last night. I knew talking about my mother would make her think I'd let down my guard.

'Sorry to ring so early, but I wanted to catch you before you left for work,' she said.

'That's okay.' I grabbed my jacket and my backpack, ready to head out the door.

'I just wanted to see how you are this morning,' she said, her tone strangely pinched. 'Have you had a chance to go through your mother's things?'

I sighed. I didn't want to reminisce with her over my mother's belongings – not now, and not ever. It was all packed up, both in my mind and in my space. 'Not yet,' I said, thinking it was the easiest answer to cut this conversation short.

'Oh, okay.' Far from the disappointment I was expecting, Carolyn sounded relieved. 'Well, don't worry about the shoebox – it's just a bunch of old letters; nothing to do with your mother. I don't know why Rob gave it to you. I think he was trying to make space in his shed for more gardening tools . . . or at least that's what he told me this morning.' She laughed, but it sounded high and tense, far from her usual affectionate tone when she spoke of her husband.

'I'll send him over tonight to pick it up,' Carolyn was saying. 'There's no reason for you to hang on to it.'

'Sure, that's fine,' I said as my mind whirled. Nothing to do with my mother? They might be old letters, sure, but they had everything to do with my mother. They'd been addressed to her, after all.

'Right, well, have a good day at work,' Carolyn said, in that same strange, stilted tone. 'Talk soon.'

'Bye.' I hung up the phone, an odd feeling sliding over me. Had my aunt actually *lied*? Carolyn had said 'honesty is the best policy' so many times, it was practically tattooed on her forehead. I'd never known her to even fib, that's how truthful she was. Why would she be dishonest about a bunch of old letters?

I gazed at the wardrobe where the shoebox was, picturing the thick stack of envelopes. What did these letters say? Who were they from? Was there something in them Carolyn didn't want me to see?

How could she know, if she hadn't even opened them?

I'll just have a quick look through them, I decided. I *was* over all of this – my subconscious had proved that last night, and reading a few letters wouldn't change anything. Anyway, this wasn't really about my mother. This was about Carolyn. I was curious to see why she'd broken her own advice.

I crossed to the wardrobe then picked up the shoebox and carried it back to the bed. I leafed through the envelopes and picked up the one at the bottom of the pile, which looked to be oldest. I slid my fingers under the flap and unfolded the letter inside, squinting at the neat cursive writing. It was dated 20th July 1983 – my mother's birthday. I paused, doing a quick calculation. She would have just turned twenty-three, and I'd have been just a few months old. An address at the top showed the letter had come from someone called Bertie in 10 Belford Mews, Edinburgh.

Happy birthday, my love. It seems fitting that my first letter to you is on your special day. In a way, it feels like I was born that day, too – the day we first met, when I heard you sing on the promenade. It was the day I fell in love, before I even knew you. It was the day that changed everything for me, whether we both knew it then or not.

I hope you're not angry that I've written to you through your sister. I know you told me not to contact you again, but I had to. Whatever the reason that made you leave me – whatever the reason you felt you couldn't tell me – it's behind us. It's in the past, and only one thing is clear. You are my future. I meant what I said – I meant those words we repeated every night.

I am always with you. I will always be here.

I stared at the page in my hands, unable to believe my eyes. For the second time in as many weeks, those words leaped out at me from the past. Unlike the newspaper advert, though, this time I knew they *were* connected to my mother . . . but it wasn't her saying them. It was a stranger, someone outside the world we'd made together. My gut churned and a bitter taste filled my mouth. I'd thought those words had belonged to just us, but they hadn't been our special mantra, after all.

I forced a laugh, shaking my head. What was I, five years old? Those words meant nothing. So what if she'd said them to someone else? I focused on the page once again.

I can only hope that you meant them, too, the letter continued. *And that's enough for me right now. Hope, and my love for you.*

Hope. The word cut through me, and the letter slipped from my fingers and fell to my lap. Hope was never enough – not after years and years. It hadn't been for me, anyway. I looked at the pile of letters. Had it been for him?

Who was this Bertie? When had he been with my mother? I picked up the letter again, scanning his words. If he'd met her on the promenade, then she must have been in her late teens or very early twenties – Carolyn always told me my mother had shunned uni to busk. If they'd had a serious relationship, they couldn't have been together for more than a year or two before Mum had met my father and had me.

Was that why she'd asked him not to contact her, because she'd been with someone else? Did Bertie know my mother had had a baby? I tilted my head, looking at the pile of letters. He clearly didn't know she had died.

Was he still hoping, even now? God, I hoped not. I hoped he'd given up, like I had. Not that I cared, of course, I reminded myself. Not that it had anything to do with me. I was only reading these to see why Carolyn might have lied.

Right, next letter. There had to be something here that Carolyn didn't want me to see. I picked up another envelope, postmarked a month or so after the first, and scanned the neat writing. My mother hadn't written back to Bertie, but he was still hoping – still loving. I opened the next and the next and the next, brittle pages falling around me like dead leaves as I devoured the words. Years passed, and she still hadn't got in touch. Years passed, and yet he was still writing.

They didn't say much, the letters – just snapshots of their world together: how my mother would hog the pillow, how proud Bertie was of her singing, how she looked beautiful from the second she woke up, how he loved her so much it hurt. Despite the short time they'd been together, they'd clearly had a committed relationship. They'd even lived together, judging by the everyday titbits these lines held.

Was *that* why Carolyn had tried to hide the letters? Because my mother had lived with someone before getting married? I dismissed the thought. My aunt was a traditionalist who believed in 'good old-fashioned values', but I couldn't picture her wanting to hide this from me so much that she'd lie about it. No, there had to be something more.

Reading these letters, I could almost hear Bertie's voice in my head. The more I read, the more their life and his love leaped from the page and swirled around me, transporting me to their past. I could hear their voices mingling, see the patch of sun fall on the white sheets like Bertie described, smell the strong coffee he brewed up each morning, just the way my mother liked it. And—

I blinked as the words on the page jumped out at me. Bertie had given my mother the necklace? The necklace with the heart pendant, the one she'd always said was so precious to her, and the one she'd promised to me? I closed my eyes now as images flashed through my brain: how she'd always touch it when she said those ten words to me; how she'd never take it off, not even when she showered. How it had nestled next to her heart, as if it was keeping her soul safe.

My mother must have really loved Bertie. She'd been so young, and they may not have been together for long, but she must have cared for him deeply to keep wearing that pendant even after she'd left – even after she'd met my father and had me – and to promise it to me, when I found someone to love.

Had she realised she'd made a mistake in leaving Bertie? She hadn't seemed to have much of a relationship with my father. She'd never spoken of him, and she hadn't even put him on my birth certificate.

Why hadn't she answered Bertie's letters, then?

And how could he bear to hope for so long?

I knew I should stop reading, but I tore through the final few envelopes in the box, praying Bertie had accepted my mother wouldn't write back. The letters were shorter with every year, but I could still feel his pain, his longing, his desire for her to return, almost as keenly as if it was my own. Like me, my mother had been his world. Like me, she'd left without an explanation.

Please God, like me, may he have finally given up.

My fingers shook as I lifted the last envelope from the box and ripped it open. It was dated just a couple of years ago, and I unfolded it slowly. Would this be his goodbye? Had he stopped hoping, all these years later?

I scanned the page, my heart dropping.

There were only ten words.

I am always with you. I will always be here.

He hadn't given up. As recently as a few years ago, he was still writing, still longing. I sucked in my breath as a thought hit. Could *Bertie* have placed the advert in the paper on my mother's birthday? He knew those ten words, he didn't know she was dead, and he'd definitely known her birth date. Hell, he'd considered it his, too. God, the poor man. To want to see her so much he'd placed an advert in a national newspaper . . .

I put the envelopes back in the box. I'd read them all, yet I still couldn't understand why Carolyn had tried to hide them from me. Perhaps she'd figured, if my mum hadn't wanted to read the letters, then I shouldn't, either? I was glad I had, though. I could see in those letters what I would have become if I hadn't accepted my mother's death; if I hadn't taken these final steps to douse the flames. My hope would have lingered, taunting me for years – for decades, even, because it *had* taunted me for years.

Thank God there'd been an end. Thank God I'd been able to stop the fire from burning out of control. But Bertie . . . I swallowed. Bertie was still hanging, swinging in the wind with the noose of hope around his neck. He was stuck in the torturous state I'd existed in, with no end in sight.

Unless someone told him my mother had died.

I'll tell him. The thought popped into my mind and I held it there for a second, unable to shove it away for some reason. It was a ridiculous notion, I told myself. I shouldn't care – this person was a stranger. But somehow, Bertie wasn't a stranger. It was odd, but I felt like I knew him. I could see how he'd loved my mother and how she'd been his world. I could understand his devastation and confusion when she'd disappeared, and how he longed for her to return.

We were connected by more than those ten words. We were connected by more than our love for my mother. We were connected by *losing* her, and he deserved to know that she wouldn't come back. He deserved a chance to accept her death and move on, to be able to make a life without my mother in the margins.

Just like me.

CHAPTER THIRTEEN

ELLA

I rifled through the box and drew out the most recent letter, staring down at the return address: *10 Belford Mews, Edinburgh.* There was no phone number and – I flipped over the envelope – no surname. Should I write to him and tell him the news? What if the letter didn't reach him? What if he wrote back, wanting more information? I didn't want to start a dialogue. I just wanted to set him free.

I walked to the window, watching the waves churn as my mind spun. I'd go to him. I'd go up to Edinburgh, tell him what I needed to, then come back to my life. I didn't want to prolong this. The sooner I saw Bertie, the sooner normal service could resume.

The instant I made the decision, I propelled myself into action. I called work to say I wouldn't be in, then booked the train, groaning at the long journey ahead. Even if I managed to make it to the station in the next hour, it looked like I wouldn't get to Edinburgh until eight-thirty tonight . . . if everything ran on time. I didn't fancy trundling around an unknown city in the dark, so I booked a hotel near the station. I'd head to Bertie's tomorrow morning, praying he still lived there.

I let out a low laugh. This was crazy, wasn't it? Asking for unscheduled time off work, taking a train across the country to a city I'd never been in, tracking down my mum's former lover to an address that might not even exist any more . . . all to tell someone my mother had died years ago, and that he didn't need to – he *shouldn't* – hang on to hope any longer?

I shook my head. Maybe it was crazy, but I couldn't let this man continue to suffer. I'd read his words; I knew his pain. Now that I was finally free, I had to help him, too. I had to end the awful legacy of my mother's actions.

I stood in my flat for a second, wondering what to bring – wondering what to pack my things in. It sounded stunningly boring, I knew, but I couldn't remember the last time I'd left England . . . Maybe back in Year 6, when Carolyn and Rob had arranged a trip around Europe for us all? I cringed, remembering how I hadn't spent time drinking in the sights around me. Instead, I'd examined every woman who bore even the slightest resemblance to my mother, asking Carolyn over and over if that could be her.

We never went to Europe again, and the next summer Carolyn said we'd take it easy at home instead.

I dug out the rucksack I used for work and threw in some knickers, a clean pair of jeans, and a few jumpers. I was as low maintenance as you could get, even wearing mascara only for special occasions and my trusty Chapstick to protect my lips from the salty wind when I made my way to work. My keys, my wallet, my mobile phone . . . Oh God, Dolby! I'd only be away one night, but I didn't want to leave her alone even that long. She wasn't used to being on her own. Who could I get to look in on her?

Carolyn would ask endless questions about where I was going, and no way was I about to tell her the truth. For whatever reason – perhaps Bertie could tell me, for there was nothing shocking – she hadn't wanted me to see those letters, and I wasn't about to tell her I'd read them all now. As much as I loved Rob, he had the memory of a parakeet and I didn't trust him to keep a plant alive, let alone remember to visit my cat.

I tapped my foot, for the first time realising how limited my circle was. I hadn't had a best friend since Lizzie, back in primary school. I'd started school a few months after my mum had left, and all the kids were the best of friends from nursery. But it wasn't only the kids that were foreign: it was everything. From the structure of the day, sitting on a hard floor in an uncomfortable cross-legged position while sharing during circle time, the hustle and bustle of playtime, and the smells that made me sick at lunchtime, school might as well have been Mars. And although Carolyn was deputy head when I'd started there, she'd expected me to slot in and had not given me any special considerations, thinking it was best I made my own way. I don't know now if she could have made it any easier for me even if she had tried. I was locked in my own cycle of hope and despair – although I wouldn't have labelled it like that, of course – and school was just one more thing in this new life to drag me down.

I might have sunk if it hadn't had been for Lizzie.

Even now, I can remember the damp, earthy smell of the furthest corner of asphalt in the playground where I used to stand every morning and afternoon playtime. The area was fenced off but I'd latch my fingers on to the chain-links, as if they could anchor me down. If I craned my neck and stood on my toes, I could see the sea. I'd stare and stare, telling myself over and over that my mother couldn't be in there. She wasn't in there. She was coming back for me.

The other kids didn't see me – or if they did, they didn't care. Only Lizzie would venture out to where I stood, chattering in her bright little voice about whatever was happening in her world: her hamster, her annoying brother, how her mum wouldn't get her whatever toy was popular at the moment. I ignored her at first, but she kept coming back, and eventually I couldn't help joining in with her chatter. We'd stayed firm friends through Year 1 and Year 2, but then her mum had remarried and she'd moved to Liverpool, only bothering to return my letters once. I'd missed her chatter – it had distracted me when I'd needed it most. The silence swirled around me, closing me in. I'd soon learned it was easier to bury myself in it.

There was no way I'd invite someone from work to help me; I didn't want them knowing where I lived. It was like crossing an invisible line. Maybe . . . Maybe my next-door neighbour? I hadn't been overly friendly, but I hadn't been *unfriendly*, either. She'd always offered to keep an eye on my place if I ever needed her to, probably hoping I'd offer to do the same for her (I hadn't). I'd no idea what she did, but she seemed to be around an awful lot. I could hear from the terrible music thumping through the walls that she was home now.

I hated to ask anyone to do something for me – even when I'd first got my period, I'd made an excuse to leave the house and gone to Boots to buy sanitary towels myself, rather than risk telling Carolyn and kicking off a cringey 'you're a woman now' talk – but I didn't really have a choice. I scrounged around for the extra key I should have left at work or at Carolyn's, then stepped outside. Steeling myself, I knocked on my neighbour's door, desperately trying to remember her name.

'Coming!' The music was turned down, and I could hear footsteps approaching.

'Oh! Hi, Ella.' Her eyebrows flew up as she faced me. She was taller than I'd remembered and her blonde hair was screwed up on top of her head, the bun secured with a pencil poking out of it. 'Sorry, is the music too loud?' She scrunched up her nose. 'It's terrible, I know, but the worse the music, the better my concentration. If it's too good, I just have to stop and listen.'

I bit my tongue to stop from suggesting that maybe she should try not listening to music at all.

'No, no, it's not that.' I took a breath. 'It's just, I need to go away rather unexpectedly.' You could say that again. I could hardly believe I was going myself. 'I wondered if you could look in on my cat? Make sure she has enough food? I'll be back tomorrow night.'

'Oh, of course!' She nodded so enthusiastically I worried she might hurt her neck. 'I love cats, and I'd love to take care of her. What's her name?'

'Dolby,' I said, and she smiled.

'Dolby. Great name.'

I nodded back, wondering what to say next. Small talk wasn't exactly my forte. I cleared my throat. 'Here are the keys. Dolby's not really used to strangers, so she might be a bit skittish . . . just leave some food in her bowl, if you can't find her.'

'Oh, don't worry.' She waved a hand. 'We'll be fine.'

'Great.' I stood for a second. 'Well, thanks again.' I turned to go.

'Wait! Don't you want to swap numbers? I mean, I'm sure all will be okay, but just in case.'

I felt my cheeks colour. 'Oh yes, of course.'

'Just call me, and then I'll have your number,' she said. 'Oh, you don't have your phone?' she asked, when it was clear I had nothing in my hands. 'I'm never without mine, but I suppose you have only come from next door.' She grinned, and I thought of how I was the exact opposite: I rarely had mine close to me, and if I did, half the time it was either uncharged or on silent. I never would have got a mobile if it hadn't been for Carolyn buying me one for Christmas a while back.

She grabbed the pencil from her hair and scribbled down her name and number on a Post-it note. 'Here you go.'

'Thanks, Lou,' I said, relieved that I finally knew what to call her. I was sure she'd told me at some point, but I was terrible with names. It was like my mind just knew I wouldn't need that information again.

'Give me a call when you leave and then I'll have your number, too,' she said.

'Okay. Well, thanks again.' I smiled awkwardly. God, I was out of practice with this. 'I'd better get going.'

'Have a good trip,' she chirped.

I nodded, then turned and went back to my flat, trying to shake off the uncomfortable feeling that I'd invited a stranger into my protected space. It was only for a day, I told myself. One day, and then my comfortable, closed life would resume.

I couldn't get to Edinburgh and back quickly enough.

CHAPTER FOURTEEN

ELLA

I leaned my head against the train window as the landscape flashed past, feeling like I was in another time, another place. I was miles outside the boundaries of my comfort zone, but I was being driven to do this . . . by the connection I'd felt with Bertie and the feeling that I had the power now to stop the terrible torture of hope.

The train pulled into Charing Cross, and I grabbed the underground to King's Cross station, where I'd begin the five-hour journey to Edinburgh. I joined the crowds of passengers streaming down the crowded platform towards the exit, the quiet of Hastings firmly behind me. I hadn't been in London since a secondary-school trip. After being dragged around the tourist-clogged attractions of the Natural History Museum and the Tower of London, our teachers had taken us for a quick visit to the British Library before heading home – I reckon their main motivation was grabbing a pint at one of the pubs outside while we were doing something 'educational'.

Most of my class had quickly diverted themselves away from the hulking library and dispersed in the cafés, too, but for me, the library was a chance to pull the silence around myself again; to walk the corridors and breathe in the air, uncluttered by anything other the delicious scent of books and years of knowledge.

I suspected now that our teachers hadn't ever visited the library themselves, because if they had, they would have realised that this wasn't a normal place where the public could roam free. To access many of the areas, you needed a special pass, which none of us had. I'd spent my time wandering through the free exhibitions that allowed anyone to enter. One of them featured Sounds of Britain, an exhibition celebrating our nation's soundscape. From the moment I stepped into my own sound booth to have a listen, I was completely absorbed. I heard voices from the past stretch out towards me, as if they were right beside me. I heard animals come alive, music curl inside of me . . . I was transported, in a way I'd never been – away from *me* and my small life. When I closed my eyes and listened, nothing existed apart from that noise. If I could, I'd have shut myself up in that booth for ever.

I knew from that moment on that I wanted to work with sound. To do what, exactly, I didn't know. All I knew was that it had the ability to take me out of myself, unlike anything I'd ever experienced. I'd finished secondary school, enrolled in a sound-technician course at the local college (much to the disappointment of Carolyn and Rob, who were desperate to get me into university), and in a stroke of luck, the Musical Museum opened just when I'd graduated. I had no experience working in any archives, but I'd been keen and enthusiastic – and willing to work for hardly any money.

I'd dreamed of one day returning to the British Museum, with an eye on working there as an ultimate goal. How wonderful it would be to have such a huge digital bank at my fingertips that I could disappear into at the flick of a switch. Striding across the courtyard and through the entrance of the building, then into a room only staff could enter . . . *incredible*. But the past few years had flown by and I'd carved out my niche back home, treading a comforting path. Things were fine now. I enjoyed working at the

Musical Museum, and people – apart from Jane and her unusual persistence – knew to leave me alone and let me get on with things. I didn't have the energy to go through all of that again.

It was dark when the train arrived at Edinburgh Waverley station. I breathed in, bracing myself for the unknown city. Even listening to my favourite classical music playlist on my headphones couldn't calm the knot of tension inside at being so far out of my familiar surroundings. Thank goodness I'd booked a hotel so close to the station.

I forced myself from the safety of the train carriage, through the busy station and out into the night. Had my mother followed this same route all those years ago, when she'd come to live with Bertie? Had she hoped to make a life here? What had made her leave? I shook my head. I didn't need to know, actually. Whatever had happened, I was here to tell Bertie about her death, and that was all.

The air was much colder than it had been in London and the street was buzzing, full of noise as people hurried to their destinations. The sound of bagpipes filtered through the air, and I spotted a man in a kilt belting out Stevie Wonder's barely recognisable music. Light spilled out of restaurants and bars, and a longing to be back at home, tucked under my duvet petting Dolby, washed over me.

I managed to find my hotel without too much trouble, shrugging off my backpack on to the small twin bed barely long enough for me to stretch out. Every bit of me throbbed with exhaustion, and even though the room was noisy and my stomach was rumbling, I turned off the light and crawled under the covers.

Tomorrow, I'd meet a man my mother had loved . . . a man who still hoped for her return. And tomorrow, I'd set him free, then head home and back to my life – stronger and more resilient than ever.

CHAPTER FIFTEEN

JUDE

August 1980

Jude didn't know how long it took to get to Edinburgh. She didn't care, really. All she cared about was being with Bertie – that he didn't have to leave her now, and that they would be together. She was getting out of Hastings with a man she . . . dare she say, *loved?* They hadn't used that word yet, but she felt it.

She couldn't really use anything else to explain her emotions, other than buoyed up and anchored at the same time; like she was flying but wrapped in a million soft blankets so she needn't be afraid. Bertie would catch her. Bertie would be there. And even though she'd never been to Edinburgh – even though she rarely left Hastings – she knew she'd be happy. She knew *they'd* be happy.

Shame Carolyn wasn't so easily convinced, but then . . . that was Carolyn. She and Rob had been together for ages before they'd agreed to marry each other. Jude had expected her sister to kick up a fuss, and that was part of the reason she kept Bertie at a safe distance when she'd gone to pack her bags this morning. The other part, well . . . she'd wanted to keep Bertie to herself. She didn't want her sister to sully anything with her cautions and warnings, not like she usually did.

She'd given Carolyn her address (well, Bertie's address) in Edinburgh, and that had gone some way to mollify her, but it hadn't stopped her sister standing over her as she packed her bags, asking what Mum and Dad would think right now.

Anger had surged up inside of her, and before she could stop herself, she'd turned to face Carolyn.

'Mum and Dad aren't here,' she'd said, her voice loud in the sweltering room. Her face flushed even hotter. 'They haven't been for years. They're dead.' She spat out the word, guilt squeezing her heart as Carolyn winced. But seriously, Carolyn needed to stop acting as if they were still around, watching over them – as if she was their appointed representative in this place. Carolyn was her sister, and that was all. She wasn't and she never would be her parent, and enough was enough.

'Look,' Jude said in a softer voice, reaching out to touch Carolyn's arm. 'I know this seems crazy.' She shook her head. 'Okay, so this *is* a little crazy.' Carolyn met her gaze with a little smile, and Jude could see she was forgiven for her earlier outburst. 'But I need to do this. I need to go.' She couldn't let the one person she'd really connected with since her parents' death fade from her life. She couldn't.

Carolyn sighed. 'Well, you know what I think. But I know I can't stop you, so . . .' She took Jude's hand and looked into her eyes and, for a second, Jude could see a flash of her mother there. 'Just remember one thing. I—'

Jude stepped back before her sister could finish the sentence. She didn't want to hear more. She *couldn't* hear more.

And now, the train was pulling into Edinburgh Waverley station. It was dark and, even though it was summer, the air had a chill to it. She shivered, and Bertie wrapped his arms around her.

'You'll get used to it,' he said, smiling down at her. 'Did you want to get a bite to eat or head straight home?'

'Home,' she said, without even thinking. Her stomach was rumbling and the streets around her were filled with music and people. Normally, she'd be dying to join the throng and explore but, right now, she was desperate to see where she'd be living with Bertie. She shook her head, wonder flooding through her. She'd be living with Bertie!

She waited once more for the trepidation she'd been sure would rear its head once she'd boarded the train. She'd been ready to slap it down but, to her surprise, it had never come. She squeezed Bertie's arm as he led her to a taxi. She was here, in a strange city, about to start a new life, and she'd never felt more certain of anything.

Certain, and oddly relieved.

'Ten Belford Mews,' Bertie said, and she leaned her head against his shoulder as the taxi pulled away.

'Tired?' he asked, stroking her hair.

She lifted her head. 'No. Just excited.'

'Me, too.' He pulled her close, his face obscured by darkness. This was a big move for him, too – inviting someone he'd only just met to live with him. She bit her lip, wondering if he was sure of his decision; if *he* regretted it. She'd been so focused on how she'd vanquish her own emotions that she hadn't actually thought how he might be feeling. What if she had made the move up here, only for him to tell her it wasn't working out?

But then he tightened his grip around her, she leaned her head on his chest and, through the thin shirt he was wearing, she could make out the solid, even beat of his heart. And she knew she was safe here.

Her mouth dropped open as the taxi left the winding main road and bumped down a little mews lined with squat, narrow houses that looked better suited to fairies than to humans. One side of the road gave way to thick foliage and she wound down the window, breathing in the heady scent of damp earth and flowers, so different from the smell of the sea around Hastings. The taxi stopped and Bertie heaved the suitcase from the boot, then came around to open her door. She loved how he took care of her.

She walked out into the night, hearing leaves rustle in the wind, and she couldn't help smiling. Even though she was more of a city-centre, hustle-and-bustle kind of girl, this place was like something from a dream. And when Bertie opened the door and ushered her into his house, that feeling only increased. Everything about the place was narrow and crooked, as if it had been uprooted from its moorings and plunked down here, yet it had survived. From the wood panelling to the fireplace to the steepest spiral staircase she'd ever seen, every inch of it was bursting with character . . . and with comfort. A well-loved puffy sofa stood against one wall, with a colourful blanket thrown over the side. A wooden rocking chair and a mismatched armchair completed the room, and books dotted every surface. Towards the front of the cottage was a tiny kitchen with a little table and two chairs.

'This is an amazing house,' she breathed, taking it all in.

Bertie was watching her with a look of pride. 'Isn't it? My grandfather left me some money a few years ago, after he passed away. Together with my savings, I had just about enough to buy this place. After living in horrific flats for years, sometimes I still can't believe how lucky I am. I love it here.'

Jude nodded. She knew she would, too.

'Come on,' Bertie said, taking her hand. 'Let me show you where you can unpack. I'll make some room for you in the wardrobe – I wasn't expecting to bring someone home with me.' He shook his head with an incredulous expression, and it struck Jude how quickly life could change; how all it took was just one random turn of direction, and everything would be different.

She thought of her parents and her heart squeezed. This wasn't the first time she'd experienced life's vicissitudes, and it probably wouldn't be the last.

She followed Bertie up the stairs and into the bedroom. A queen-sized bed was tucked under the eaves, and Bertie swung open a window. She could hear the river from here, and her lips curved in a smile once again. Like everything else in the house, this was perfect.

'Come here.' She sat down on the bed and grabbed Bertie's hand, tugging him from where he was rearranging his things. He sat down beside her, taking her hand in his. She looked up into his grey eyes and her heart tightened.

'I am always with you. I will always be here.'

The words flew from her mouth and filled the small room, and tears sprung to her eyes. She hadn't said those ten words since she was a child in her mother's arms. But then, she hadn't felt so safe – so secure – since then, either. She meant them now as she'd meant them then, with every fibre of her being. No matter where life might try to take her, she would always be here.

Bertie touched her face, then repeated the words back. She let them curl around her, holding them close to her heart. And as she and Bertie fell on to the bed together, Jude knew that coming here was the best thing she'd ever done.

CHAPTER SIXTEEN

Ella

I jerked awake the next morning, blinking at the sun streaming through the window on to my legs. I'd thought the warmth was Dolby for a second, unsure exactly where I was. Then I remembered: I was in a hotel in Edinburgh, and if things went to plan, I'd speak to Bertie, get on the train as soon as I could, and be home by tonight. God, I couldn't wait.

I yawned and sat up, my mind slowly clicking into gear. First things first: I needed to see how to get to his address – please, God, may it still be his address. I dug out my mobile from my rucksack, grateful for the first time that I had a smartphone. Despite paying for data on my plan (was it even possible to buy a mobile plan without it?), I'd never actually used it. If I ever needed to look up something, I used the computer at work.

But right now, I was only too happy to open up Google and enter the address: 10 Belford Mews. I watched as the little arrow popped up on the map, marking the location. It looked to be a fairly easy thirty-minute walk from here – or, at my usual speedy pace, even less. The few times Carolyn attempted to walk with me, she always laughed and ended up puffing, asking me to please slow down before she collapsed. For me, walking was about getting from A to B as quickly as possible. Luckily, this route didn't seem too difficult: straight down Princes Street, then turning north. With my phone to guide me, I was sure I'd make it there without trouble.

My heart picked up pace and nerves skittered through me. In just a short time, I was – hopefully – going to come face to face with someone from my mother's past; someone who'd loved her and wanted her back just as much as I had.

Someone who was still hoping, even now.

Someone whose hopes I would have to break, just like mine had been.

I swallowed, wondering how Bertie would react when I told him my mother had died. He would accept it with time, like I had, but after so many years of hoping it was bound to be a difficult thing to hear. He needed to know, though. Of that I was sure.

I jumped in the shower, turning it up as hot as it could go (not very hot, actually), sluiced shampoo through my hair, then stepped out. I pulled on my jeans and a fresh jumper, ran a brush through my hair, and I was ready to go. Out on the street, the bagpiper had been replaced by an accordion player who seemed to have an affinity for the same three notes, played over and over. The music, if you could call it that, followed me down Princes Street. The sun was so strong it practically blinded me as I hurried down the busy street lined with shopfronts on one side and what looked like a garden on the other. Part of me longed to meander through the trees, away from buses and punters, but I forced my legs faster.

I left the wide pavement and continued down a smaller road, winding past stone houses on one side and a high wall on the other. After stopping many times to consult the map on my phone, eventually I made my way into a lovely little mews, a maze of cobbled streets with colourful garage doors and tiny houses with hanging flowers and trellises. I kept walking until one side of the houses stopped, giving way to trees and bushes. Finally, when I'd almost reached a dead end, I came to number ten.

I paused to wipe my sweaty face. The air was fresh, but the sun was hot, and the backpack had got heavier and heavier as I'd marched on. And now here I was, standing in front of number ten, about to meet the man who'd loved my mother so much he'd written for years.

I closed my eyes and, for a second, an image filled my mind: my mother humming happily as she moseyed up these cobblestones. She loved bright colours, and she'd have adored the greens and blossoms. I may not have known my mother well, but I could imagine she'd have been very happy here. In fact . . . My eyes flew open. This place looked exactly like the house she used to describe in the stories she'd tell me sometimes, where the princess always found love in the end.

Was she talking about this place when she'd told me those tales?

And if she really had found love, then why had she left?

I pushed the questions aside. I wasn't here to find answers, only to give one. I was here to talk to Bertie, then head home again. I straightened my spine, lifted a hand and knocked.

My heart pounded as I heard footsteps on the other side of the door.

'Hello. Can I help you?' A man about my age, with curly dark hair and a stubbly beard, swung open the door. My heart dropped. Whoever this was, it obviously wasn't Bertie. He was way too young.

'Hello.' My voice sounded hoarse after all my exertions. 'Um, I'm looking for someone called Bertie? Does he live here?' *Please, God, may I not have come all this way for nothing.*

The man's brow crinkled. 'Bertie? No, there's no Bertie here. Sorry.'

My heart dropped. *Shit.*

'Do you know who used to live here, maybe? He would have moved within the past couple of years.' Just my luck that Bertie had lived in the same place for thirty-odd years and then moved on. I bit my lip, thinking about what that might mean. Was he no longer waiting for my mum? *Had* he given up? My mother wouldn't have been able to find him if she hadn't known where he lived now.

The man shook his head. 'The man who lives here has been at this address for ages.'

My heart plummeted, and my brow furrowed as I tried to puzzle it out. Perhaps Bertie had used this address simply to write from? After all, he hadn't written to my mother at her address, either. Maybe he lived somewhere else?

'Okay, thanks.' The strength of my disappointment surprised me, and I realised just how much I'd been looking forward to meeting this man . . . someone who would understand what I'd been through; someone I could free.

But I'll find him, I told myself. There had to be a way to track him down. A fierce determination gripped me, surprising me with its force.

'Can I talk to the man who lives here now?' If Bertie was using his address, then he might know where I could find him.

The man tilted his head, as if he was debating something with himself. Then he nodded. 'All right. He's having a good day, so maybe he can help.'

'A good day?' I met the man's eyes, noticing for the first time how the deep blue of them looked like the sea on a summer's night.

'Hugh suffers from Alzheimer's,' he said, and my heart fell. 'Some days he's okay and others he's a little muddled up. I'm Angus,

by the way. I live next door and I come round to help when I can.'
He stuck out his hand, and I took it in mine. His fingers closed
warmly around my cold ones and, for some annoying reason, I felt
my cheeks flush.

I pulled my hand away, hoping Angus hadn't noticed. It
had been a long time since I'd touched a man, as pathetic as that
sounded. I'd had a few flings with guys in college, but I'd never had
a proper relationship – as soon as anyone wanted more, I'd balked.
And then, as I'd got older, my circle had shrunk, and I hadn't made
the effort to meet anyone new. My lack of relationships had never
bothered me, though.

'Come on through.'

I followed him inside, loving what I saw. The house couldn't
have been more different than my barren flat, but it was so full
of character that you couldn't help but be drawn in. The back
garden was tiny but absolutely bursting with colour. Vines and
flowers spilled over stone walls and, like the house inside, almost
every inch was covered with potted plants. A tall, thin man with
an angular face turned to greet us as we entered the garden. He
looked in perfect shape, and he couldn't have been more than
sixty-five. It was hard to believe someone so young suffered from
Alzheimer's, but I'd heard that sometimes it could happen fairly
early on.

His eyebrows rose as he spotted us. His gaze locked on me,
burning into me as if he could see right into my heart. I blinked
under his scrutiny, feeling my cheeks heat up again.

'Hugh, I've got someone here who'd like to talk to you,' Angus
said. 'She came here looking for a man called Bertie?'

'Haven't heard that name for a while.' The man smiled and
shook his head. 'I'm Bertie.' My heart sank as he came forward.
This was Bertie – this man with Alzheimer's? How could I tell him

my mother was gone if he was clutching those few memories – that hope – close to him?

But then, how could I let him live his last few years in futility?

'And there's no need to tell me who you are,' Bertie said, his gaze unwavering. 'I know who you must be. I can see her in you, clear as day. You're Jude's daughter.'

CHAPTER SEVENTEEN

ELLA

I nodded, barely able to breathe. I'd never thought I resembled my mother, yet this stranger had seen her in me straightaway. But he wasn't a stranger, I realised yet again. He was someone who'd known my mother intimately . . . and someone whose thoughts I knew intimately; someone with whom I'd connected.

Angus put a hand on Bertie's shoulder. 'Why don't we go inside?' he said. 'I'll make you both some tea.'

'Yes, of course,' Bertie said. 'Please forgive my lack of manners. After you—' He paused. 'I just realised I don't know your name.'

'It's Ella,' I said.

'Ah, Ella. Of course.' He smiled, but his eyes looked sad. 'Your mother loved Ella Fitzgerald. "Summertime" was the first song I ever heard her sing.' He beckoned me forward, and I followed Angus back into the house. Bertie settled into a well-worn chair, motioning me towards the sofa. 'Have a seat.'

I shrugged off my rucksack and sat down, almost wishing now that I hadn't come – that I didn't have to tell this kind man news that would sadden him. But it would help him, too, I reminded myself. If he did only have a little time left before his condition claimed him, then he deserved to live in absolute clarity.

'Seeing you now, sitting there. . . well, I almost feel like I'm seeing her again.' Bertie swallowed, and my mind flashed back to one of his letters, where he described how my mum used to throw herself on to the sofa with abandon, then lie there with a smile and sing.

'But I'm nothing like her.' I winced. I hadn't meant to say that. 'I mean, I don't look anything like her.'

'You do,' Bertie said, his eyes filming over like he was looking at something far away. 'It's the shape of your eyes and the set of your mouth; in the way you carry yourself when you move.'

Something shot through me that I couldn't identify – a mixture of surprise and dismay, perhaps, that she *was* there in me, after all? Each time I'd gazed in the mirror as I'd grown, I'd reassured myself that I couldn't look more different. I didn't want to see her there. It was a reminder that I'd been a part of her and she'd chosen to leave me. And as I got older, the differences seemed greater. I'd wanted her as absent from my body and soul as she was from my life.

Angus set two steaming mugs of tea in front of us, complete with a mismatched saucer of milk and a tiny pot of sugar. The clashing china was charming, and I snuck a look at Angus.

'Very domesticated, our Angus,' Bertie said, catching my gaze. 'As well as being a huge help with all the jobs around this old place and keeping me ticking over. Sometimes I feel like it's starting to fall down around me as much as my mind is, but I couldn't leave now. Not yet, anyway.' He sipped his tea.

'I'm sorry I almost sent you away,' Angus said to me now. 'I've known this man for a few years now, but I'd no idea he'd ever gone by the name Bertie!' He raised an eyebrow at Bertie, and Bertie laughed.

'Well, I haven't used that name in a while – over thirty years, in fact.' He shifted in his chair, his eyes taking on that faraway look again. 'My full name is Hubert, but your mother wasn't a fan. She said she'd call me Bertie, and that was that.' He paused, a small smile lifting his lips. 'It's funny how today it's all so clear and sometimes it's hardly there.'

I nodded, sipping my own tea.

'I've lived in this place for years – I'd never move,' Bertie continued. 'I loved it from the moment I bought it, and the memories I have here are so precious – even more so now. It'd take wild horses to drag me away.

'So, Ella . . .' Bertie tilted his head, his dark grey eyes fixed on me. 'Is there a reason you came to see me? Did she . . . Did she ask you to come?'

I could see the hope in his eyes, and I stared down at the well-worn rug, my heart squeezing. I had to tell him the truth. I couldn't let him slide into the fog of Alzheimer's without solidifying the present. He deserved to spend the last few years of his life free from the clutch of hope.

'No, she didn't send me to find you.' I took a deep breath and looked up. 'I'm really sorry, but my mother's dead.' The words sounded so heavy and weighted in the midst of this place where my mother had lived; in the presence of this man she had loved. I could almost see the light in the room fade into grey.

Bertie's face didn't change, but his eyes did. They went flat and the corners tightened.

'I'm very sorry,' he said gently. 'I'm sorry that you lost her. She was such an incredible person and so full of life. She made everything brighter for me. Having her here was like turning on the sun.' He made a face. 'Which, living in Scotland, sometimes you absolutely need. Not every day is like today.' He paused. 'When did she . . . When did she pass away?'

I met his eyes, wondering how much I should say. I'd set him free by telling him that she was gone. I didn't need to inflict more pain or stir up questions by telling him she'd killed herself. 'It's been about thirty years now. I was only five.'

'Thirty years?' Bertie's eyebrows rose, and his head started shaking back and forth, back and forth. 'No, no. That can't be right.'

'What do you mean?' I shot a worried glance at Angus, wondering if Bertie was sinking into confusion. Perhaps a shock could do that to him.

'I saw her. I saw your mother, in London, about two years ago now. I'm sure of it.'

It was my turn to shake my head. 'I'm sorry, Bertie,' I said, 'but she's dead.' I sighed, thinking I'd better tell him everything, after all. Maybe that would make it more real. 'She took her own life.' I tried to make it as palatable as I could. 'She walked into the sea We never recovered her body, but people saw her in the water that day, and the police found her belongings on the beach. I was raised by my aunt and uncle – my father died before I was born.'

'No.' Bertie was still shaking his head. 'She couldn't have done that. I saw her – I'm sure of it. She was down by the river, listening to music. She was older, yes, but I'm sure it was her. I shouted her name, but she didn't hear me, and when I tried to get closer, I lost her in the crowd.'

'Is that why you placed the advert instead of just writing?' I asked. 'You thought you saw her?' But why would he wait two years? If Bertie believed my mother was alive, surely he would have put an advert in the paper right away.

Maybe he had, I thought, and I just hadn't seen it.

'The advert? What advert?' Bertie's brow creased. Did he not remember, or had it not been him, after all?

'In the classified section of *The Post*,' I explained. 'The one that appeared on the twentieth of July.'

'Your mother's birthday,' Bertie said, and I nodded. He remembered that, anyway. Maybe he hadn't put the advert in. 'What did it say?'

I took a deep breath. 'I am always with you. I—'

'Will always be here,' Bertie finished. 'Nothing else?'

'No.'

Bertie breathed in. 'Ella, I may not always remember things perfectly these days, but I can tell you beyond a shadow of a doubt that I did not place that advert. And there's only one person I can think of who would reach out with those ten words . . . on her birthday.'

I stepped back, as if I could stop him from speaking – as if I could stop him from plucking the answer that was hanging in the air around us. But I couldn't stop him. Couldn't stop the words from falling towards me.

'Your mother,' he said, his voice full of hope and wonder. 'It must have been your mother.'

CHAPTER EIGHTEEN

ELLA

I glanced around the room for Angus, hoping he could help me rid Bertie of such a ridiculous notion, but he'd slipped away without me even noticing.

'Bertie . . .' I paused, wondering what to say. I knew it was hard to accept that my mother had gone – and maybe even harder to grasp the information with Bertie's illness – but I couldn't leave here letting him think my mother was reaching out to us. It may not have been him who had placed the advert, but it couldn't have been her. She was dead. She had been gone for thirty years, disappeared into the sea without a trace of her left living.

Not even what she'd promised me.

Bertie may have thought he'd spotted her, but of course he was wrong. It'd been years since he'd seen my mother, he'd only glimpsed her from a distance, and – as much as I hated to think this – I wasn't sure I could trust his memories. My mother, lounging by the river, in London? It was impossible to get my head around. This wasn't some fairy tale, like my mum used to tell me. This was real life. And in real life, people didn't suddenly turn up again after thirty years.

'It's just not possible,' I said quietly. 'She was declared dead long ago. No one has seen or heard from her.' I sighed. 'Mum always said those words to me, too, but we didn't have a monopoly on them, and the fact that the advert appeared on my mother's birthday is purely a coincidence.'

But Bertie wasn't having any of it. 'It must be her, don't you see? I might be old and slightly doddery at times, but my eyesight is as sharp as it ever was. I'd know your mother anywhere, despite the years. She *is* alive.'

'Let's say it is her,' I said slowly, even though I was in no way prepared to submit to his so-called logic. 'You're living in the same place. My aunt Carolyn is living in the same place. Why would my mother put an advert in the paper? Why not just get in touch?'

Bertie met my eyes. 'I don't know, Ella. But I imagine just turning up after such a long time would be . . . difficult. Leaving her family behind, leaving you . . . Maybe it was a way of reaching out to the ones she loved; of letting them know she was all right.' He swallowed. 'You said your father passed away?'

'Yes,' I said. 'He died before I was born.'

'And was there . . . Was there anyone else?'

'No. There was just me and her until she died.'

'So she never married.' He shook his head. 'I always wondered. I thought she must have, and that was why she never wrote back. Still, I couldn't help hoping.' He smiled sadly. 'I wrote for years, you know. Letter after letter. I know it was kind of pathetic – my brother certainly told me so on a regular basis, back when we were still talking. After all, she'd left me with barely a word. But I knew that she loved me. I felt it. And whatever her reason for leaving, I couldn't help thinking that if we could just *talk*, then we could get through it. I sent the letters to Carolyn's place – the only address I had, hoping she'd pass them on. It was a long shot, since she wasn't keen on me, to say the least, but it was the only thing I could do.'

My eyes widened. Maybe my mother hadn't discarded those letters without even opening them. Maybe Carolyn had failed to pass them on to my mum, the same way she'd tried to keep them from me. That would explain why they'd been tucked away in the shed, at least. But why would she do that? I still didn't understand why she'd tried to stop me from reading them.

'Did you and Carolyn ever meet?' I asked.

Bertie nodded. 'Well, sort of. Jude never introduced me properly – I think she and your mother had a bit of a rocky relationship, and Carolyn wasn't thrilled that we were living together so soon after we'd met. I got the feeling she thought I was some kind of Lothario who was dragging her sister back to my lair when, in truth, I couldn't have been further from. I was a shy accountant desperately in love.'

I nodded. I could certainly see Carolyn believing that, but hiding letters . . .

'After your mother left me, I went down to Hastings over and over to try to find her. I scoured the promenade, the pubs and all the places she used to sing, but she wasn't there.' He sighed, and I could see the frustration and loss in his face, even now.

'It was summertime when I ran into your aunt, about a year after your mother had left,' he continued. 'I saw Carolyn one day in the supermarket. She looked so much like Jude that I knew she had to be her sister. Anyway, I tried to talk to her. I told her who I was and asked about Jude, but she hurried back to her house without even speaking. I followed her and knocked for ages, but she never came out. I went back to Edinburgh, happy that at least I had somewhere to write to; somewhere where I might reach your mother. And, believe me, I tried.'

He shook his head. 'Those words I said to her . . . I meant them, as much as I could ever mean a wedding vow. I'd never met a woman like your mother before, and I'd no interest in trying to again. I don't think I could, even if I had tried.' He sighed. 'A few months after I sent my last letter, I was diagnosed with early onset Alzheimer's. Seeing Jude in London that one time, well . . . that was like a gift. Like a bookend to my life. A way of saying goodbye, before I faded.'

He turned to face me, and I was taken aback by the intensity in his eyes. 'But, Ella, maybe that's not the end. If Jude is reaching out now, then I have to respond – before it's too late for me. What's the good of trying to find her all these years, only to turn away now?'

'But, Bertie . . .' Where the *hell* was Angus? I needed his help to convince Bertie not to go on a wild-goose chase in the past. We had to pull Bertie back into the real world, where people did not come back to life.

Bertie smiled at me. 'I know you probably think this is foolish,' he said, and I felt my cheeks colour. 'And maybe you're right. Maybe it is foolish, but I'd rather try than hide away here. If I can see her one last time . . .' He met my eyes. 'Will you help me, Ella? Will you do this with me? Will you help me find your mother?'

I sighed inwardly, wishing I'd never come. Why the hell couldn't I have just stayed home? I'd journeyed here expecting to end all of this, but I'd only stirred things up more.

Guilt flashed through me. Bertie wasn't a foolish old man – in fact, he wasn't even that old. He was someone who had loved my mother and who had hoped, like me, that she'd come back. She had been the only one for him, in the same way I could only have one mother. In very different ways with very different outcomes, we had both waited for her. And instead of setting him free, I'd only succeeded in flaring up his hope once again.

If I could, shouldn't I do something – anything – to help him rest easier, to make his inevitable slide into dementia that much less tormented? The last thing I'd wanted was to make things worse for him.

'All right,' I said, and Bertie's smile made me feel even guiltier. Because I didn't believe my mother was alive, and I wasn't striving for that happy ending. I wasn't helping him so he could find her.

I was helping him so he could bury her, once and for all.

CHAPTER NINETEEN

JUDE

April 1981

Jude groaned as the bed shifted beneath her. She still hadn't got used to Bertie getting up at 6 a.m. every day, even after almost eight months. And this morning – she glanced at the clock and groaned again – he was even earlier than usual.

For their first few months together, she'd tried to get up with him when he left for work, puttering around the kitchen, the two of them knocking hips as they made their breakfast. The sky brightened, the birds sang and gentle rain floated down, making everything outside misty and otherworldly. She'd had grand visions of how much song-writing she'd get done if she arose that early, when the world was quiet. But she'd yawn her way through breakfast, then haul herself back to the bedroom and fall asleep again until around mid-morning. Then she'd settle on the sofa to try to write some music for a while before the deathly silence got to her. She'd throw on a coat and march to the city centre for some noise and buzz. Sometimes, she'd even busk for an hour or two before getting shoved off her pitch by yet another annoying bagpiper.

Life here was great, but . . . if Jude was honest, some days she was even more bored than she'd been in Hastings. Edinburgh was a much bigger city, obviously, but her life had shrunk. She'd never pictured Bertie as the life and soul of the party, but she'd thought he must have *some* friends she could hang around with. Instead, he went to work and came home again, preferring quiet nights in. And as much as she loved snuggling up with him, part of her was beginning to miss the nights she used to dread, singing in pubs to dozy punters.

She'd been trying for months to break into the local music scene, popping into pubs and dropping off her tapes, but with no luck. She'd hoped Frank might have a few contacts he could pass on, but in the past few months the only time they'd heard from him was a drunken late-night answerphone message asking Bertie to send him money in Spain. Bertie had simply rolled his eyes and smiled affectionately, as if he hadn't expected anything different. Jude had thought it'd be easier to get a start here than in London, but Edinburgh seemed a beacon for musicians looking to get a leg-up, too.

Bertie was nothing but encouraging, telling her over and over again that Jude was so talented she could never be anything but a success. She'd smile, despite knowing it didn't work that way: talent wasn't enough. A mind-boggling amount of hard work, sacrifice and dedication went into getting to the top, and even putting in the hours was no guarantee. A million girls with voices like hers were out there trying to make it, and only one or two of them did – probably down to who they knew, or being in the right place at the right time. Jude was working hard, but she wasn't even *in* the right place – not in London – and as for contacts? The one person who might be able to help was miles away in another country. In a way, it felt like she'd taken a step backwards.

Except for Bertie, of course. He was one giant leap forward into a world where she didn't feel like she was hanging on by her fingernails; a place where she could let go. It was hard to believe they'd been together for almost a year now; before him, the longest relationship she'd had was a night. Even with their different personalities – maybe because of it – they rarely argued, and every day rolled away smoothly, as if the path had been neatly paved before them. Okay, so maybe Jude wished that Bertie wanted to go out a bit more to see some bands around the city, or that he would stay up a bit a later and have the occasional lie-in. But that was nothing in the grand scheme of things. That was nothing compared to knowing that she was finally safe.

This morning, though, she would have given anything for an uninterrupted lie-in. She'd been up until three last night, working on new songs for her demo tape, and her head was fuzzy. To make matters worse, Bertie was gently pushing at her shoulder.

'Jude. Jude!' His voice was soft in her ear, but it sounded like a foghorn. Carolyn had always said she'd needed a foghorn to get her out of bed in the morning.

'Hunh?' Jude sleepily lifted an eye, feeling like that was a major concession. Bertie knew better than to try to wake her in the mornings now. What the hell was the problem?

'Come. Come with me.' His tone was wide awake and alert, and she knew that he wasn't going to let her get away with falling back asleep. For all his gentleness, when Bertie got something in his head, he didn't let it go. She admired that about him.

Sighing, she let herself be pulled from the warm covers and into the still-chilly morning. Bertie wrapped her robe around her and tugged her down the stairs.

'Come on, Bertie,' she said, her voice still hoarse from sleep. 'What on earth is this all about? Is something wrong?'

'Just follow me.' Bertie smiled, but his voice wasn't its usual relaxed tone. He pulled her towards the door and she slipped her feet into the sparkly flip-flops she'd been hoping to wear if it ever warmed up enough.

'Where are we going? Bertie, I'm not even dressed!' She gestured to the bright pink fuzzy robe that barely covered her bottom.

'Not far,' Bertie said, an enigmatic smile on his face. 'Don't worry, the only one who will see you is me, and I already think you're beautiful.'

Jude rolled her eyes because, as far as she was concerned, with her curly hair like a bird's nest and dark circles under her eyes, she couldn't look further from beautiful in the morning. She squinted against the sun streaming through the trees, the morning chill taking her breath away. Bertie led her across the narrow street and down a steep path between the bushes and brambles to the river.

'It's a little early for a riverside walk,' she complained as she tripped on a root and a dew-laden branch slapped her in the face. But Bertie didn't stop, and a minute or so later they were at the river's edge. The sun was nearly blinding as it glinted off the river, but even she had to admit it was beautiful down here in the morning light. Birds flitted in and out of the water, and the sound of the river flowing over rocks was like music. She'd never been here so early, and the peace of the spring morning was so calming.

Jude gasped as she spotted cushions, blankets, a huge flask of what she hoped was very strong coffee, and what looked like her favourite extra-greasy bacon baps from the café down the street.

'This looks amazing!' she said, smiling up at Bertie. She threw her arms around him, breathing in his soapy scent as his heart beat that steady, solid rhythm. 'But what's the occasion?'

Bertie sank on to one knee, and Jude's mouth dropped open.

'It's only been eight months since I've known you, but it feels like forever,' he said.

'Hopefully, you mean that in a good way,' she joked, then wanted to kick herself. Why couldn't she just go with the moment? The intensity on Bertie's face made her want to make light of the situation, almost as if she didn't deserve such love.

Thankfully, Bertie didn't respond. 'And it's been better than I ever thought it could be. You've brought me to life,' he continued, his cheeks colouring, and Jude felt something inside her give. 'I can't imagine being with someone else . . . not now, and not ever.' He swallowed, and the only sound was the tinkling of the water. 'So I guess what I'm saying is . . . will you marry me?'

Jude stared down at him, her brain spinning as she tried to digest his words. She hadn't ever thought about marriage – she was only twenty, after all. Sure, it had crossed her mind that Bertie was old – well, eight years older than her, anyway – and since she and Bertie were living together, they might have that conversation eventually. It had seemed miles in the future, though. There was still so much she wanted to do, first and foremost making it as a singer and a songwriter. There was a long, hard road ahead, despite Bertie's confidence that she couldn't help but make it.

But there was no reason that she couldn't be a wife *and* a singer, right? Being married didn't mean the end to hopes and dreams: it just meant there was someone by your side, along for the journey. Her mind flashed back to that day on the promenade when Bertie had given her his coat, encouraging her to not stop singing. He may not understand how difficult it would be, but she knew he'd support her. He knew how important this was to her and he'd never try to change that.

She rolled the word 'wife' around in her mind, partly repelled and partly fascinated by the concept of applying it to herself. She didn't doubt her love for Bertie, nor his for her. She meant those ten little words they exchanged each night with every cell of her body. No matter what the future held for them, Bertie had become a part of her, and vice versa.

So why not make it official? Carolyn would be thrilled to officially release Jude from her responsibility now, and Jude couldn't ask for a better person than Bertie to be by her side. She may be young, but she already knew that a man as good and supportive as Bertie didn't come around often.

And she wasn't going to let him go. She couldn't let him go. They'd been connected since that moment on the promenade. Singing and performing; going to London . . . She'd figure it out. *They'd* figure it out, together.

'Yes,' she said, and Bertie got to his feet. A huge grin shone from his face and he gathered her in his arms, hugging her so tightly her feet left the ground.

'I'm afraid I don't have a ring,' he said when he set her down again. 'I've been saving up and I'll get you one eventually, but right now I wanted to give you this.' He withdrew a box from his pocket and Jude snapped it open, her eyes raking over the gold heart pendant inside. She lifted it up, loving the heavy weight of the heart and the way the chain glinted gold in the sun.

'It's gorgeous. Thank you so much.' Her fingers touched a small latch on the side of the heart and she popped it open, glancing up to meet Bertie's eyes as she spotted a slip of paper folded inside. She carefully unfolded it, her heart swelling as she took in the words written in Bertie's neat script.

'I am always with you,' she read. 'I will always be here.' The words spun around them in the air, and she thought how, for the first time since her parents had died, they seemed more of a promise of potential than a desperate plea.

Bertie fastened the necklace around her neck, and Jude reached up to touch it. It felt like she was wearing his heart next to hers, and she never wanted to take it off. She'd do everything she could to keep it safe – to keep *them* safe. That much she could promise.

Bertie's lips met hers and, as the river flowed and the sun rose in the sky, she wished they could stay here, in this place where nothing else could touch them, for ever.

CHAPTER TWENTY

Ella

'Where should we start?' I asked Bertie, praying I'd somehow be able to quickly snuff out his notion that my mother was alive. I bit my lip. How could you convince someone that the love of their life was dead if they simply didn't want to believe it? God, I wished I'd never come here. 'The advert doesn't have any contact details, but maybe I can call the newspaper office and see if they can tell me something.' If they could say who had placed that advert – and clearly it wouldn't be my mother – it might go some way towards placating Bertie.

'But then, I'm not sure they'll be able to release any details,' I said, thinking out loud. 'Data protection and all of that.' I didn't want to sound too negative, but we had to be realistic. I let out a puff of air. *Realistic.* I was chasing a dead woman.

'Maybe if you go there in person?' Bertie said. 'Tell them a bit about the background, and why you want to know? I've always found if you rely on the kindness of others, it often helps.'

The kindness of others. Since when had I ever relied on that?

'I'd do it myself if I could,' he continued, 'but you're an immediate family member. If your mother did place the advert, then they might release the details to you.'

I grabbed my phone and pulled up the newspaper's website, scrolling down to see where they were located. 'They're in South Kensington, in London,' I said, turning the idea over in my mind.

'Perhaps you could pop in on your way back to Hastings?' Bertie asked. 'You need to connect through London anyway, don't you? You could stay the night here and take the train back in the morning. That should give you plenty of time.'

'Are you two still chatting?' Angus poked his head through the front door. 'I'm running to the shop, Hugh.' I jerked at the name. The man before me seemed so much more a Bertie than a Hugh. I had to agree with my mother on that one, I thought, pushing away the sudden zing of connection. 'Do you want anything?'

'Yes, thank you.' Bertie smiled over at me. 'We're having a guest for supper, Angus. Ella is going to stay tonight and go home tomorrow. Right?' He lifted his eyebrows at me, looking hopeful.

I held his gaze, my mind ticking over. Although I was itching to get back, the sooner I was able to convince Bertie my mother was gone, the better.

'Right,' I said.

'Oh, brilliant,' Angus said. 'Maybe I'll make my famous sausage and mash.'

'Infamous, more like.' Bertie grinned. 'Last time he made it, the sausages burned and stuck to the pan. He said it was the pan, but I don't think so.'

'It was the pan, of course,' Angus mock-protested. 'Okay, then. That settles it. Sausage and mash tonight – if you're okay with that, Ella.'

I nodded, unable to remember the last time I'd had such a homely meal. Usually, I heated up a bowl of soup after work.

'Sounds great, thank you.'

'Right, back soon.' Angus ducked out again.

'That's a good lad, right there,' Bertie said. 'He's taken me under his wing ever since my diagnosis. I don't have any family around – my brother passed away years ago, and we weren't talking by then, anyway.' He sighed, looking off into the distance, as if he could see the past there. 'He got into some financial trouble selling properties off-plan in Spain and asked me to bail him out. I didn't have the money, so he asked me to sell the house. When I refused, well . . . it got a little nasty.'

I shifted in my chair, feeling awkward in the face of such personal information.

Bertie jerked towards me and, for a split second, confusion flashed across his face. Then he cleared his throat and smiled at me. 'Anyway, after years of being on my own, it's rather nice to have someone popping in and out; keeping track of me and making sure I haven't wandered off.' He sounded like he was kidding, but I wondered if he had wandered off before.

'Angus seems lovely,' I said to fill to silence, but for some insane reason I could feel my cheeks getting warmer. Bertie gave me a steady look but, before he could comment, I looked down at my mobile.

'Right, speaking of neighbours . . . I'd better text mine and ask if she can look after my cat a bit longer.' I wrote a quick message, thinking how different my relationship with my neighbour was to Bertie's. I hadn't even known her name until yesterday.

Angus returned from the shops and, despite my discomfort at staying longer, I was surprised how quickly the rest of the afternoon and evening slipped by. Angus and Bertie had such an easy, comfortable relationship that I couldn't help but be drawn into their warmth, finding myself eagerly answering questions about my job and my life in Hastings instead of shying away, like I usually did.

As darkness fell on the mews tucked away in the heart of the city, it felt like it was just the three of us, in our own little world – and, strangely, I didn't long to be alone, back in my sterile flat. This place was crammed to the gills with knick-knacks and it couldn't have been further from the bare confines of my home, but instead of repelling me, it drew me in. Whether it was the men beside me or the house itself, I didn't know, but I felt like I could curl up and sleep for years here.

If only Bertie would stop talking about my mother. As Angus cooked supper, Bertie pointed out where my mother would sit and write music, the place she used to nap, the mug she'd broken . . . it was as if, despite the years, she was still alive in this place for him. I itched to say that I didn't want to know these details – that I didn't want her to come alive for me – but then I thought how tomorrow he may not be able to grasp on to these things. I should let him savour his memories while he could.

We devoured Angus's hearty meal (luckily, not burned) and chatted over yet another cup of tea before Bertie got to his feet.

'That's it for me,' he said. 'I'm absolutely knackered.'

'Ah, you're just trying to escape the washing up,' Angus said, pushing back his chair. 'Are you okay? Do you need help with anything?' I couldn't help being touched by his attentiveness.

'I'm fine, I'm fine.' Bertie waved a hand. 'If you could show Ella where the guest bedroom is once she's ready for bed, I'd appreciate it.' Bertie made a face at me. 'Sorry, I'm not being the world's greatest host here, am I? But you feel like family.' He smiled, and warmth shot through me. Oddly, he felt like that, too. I clamped down on that feeling as quickly as I could. I shouldn't let myself get involved with Bertie and his life. After tomorrow, I wouldn't see him again.

'Good night, all.'

'Night.' Angus and I spoke together as Bertie made his way up the stairs.

I got to my feet and started clearing the dishes, anxious to be doing something to escape the awkward feeling that had slid over me.

'Bertie should be okay tonight,' Angus said, 'but if you need any help, please don't hesitate to call me.'

'Any help?' I froze. 'What do you mean?' I barely knew the man and, as much as I liked him, I wasn't capable of being a carer.

'If he's had a confusing day – a day where he can't get a grip on things – he's more likely to have nightmares, and he may wander a bit,' Angus said. 'But don't worry. He's been great today and it's only happened once or twice.'

'Okay.' I swallowed, fear gripping me. 'It's wonderful that he has you right next door.'

Angus shrugged. 'I'm lucky enough that I work from home, and my hours are really flexible. I can usually fit everything around what he needs me to do. Until quite recently, he's been pretty much fine – just a few minor lapses here and there. Anyway, this is the least I can do for him. He helped me out when I really needed it.'

I nodded, not wanting to pry, but wondering what Angus had gone through. I'd only known him for a very short time, but he seemed so friendly and open – as if nothing bad had touched him.

Angus leaned back, sipping his tea. 'When I first moved in next door, I was in a bad way. My wife, Steph, had got together with my best friend. Such a cliché, I know.' He tried to laugh, and I ducked my head to avoid the pain pulling at his face. I knew only too well the betrayal and bitterness he was feeling.

'I'm sorry,' I said quietly, and although I hardly knew him, I really was.

'Thanks.' He forced a small smile. 'Anyway, she moved out. After she left, I couldn't bear to knock around our house by myself. I sold it and moved in here, and it was . . . well, it was difficult. I just wanted to shut myself in and stay there for ever.'

I nodded, thinking I could certainly understand that. It was what I had done.

'But Bertie wouldn't let me. He took it upon himself to check on me, drag me over to his for meals, take me on walks. I wouldn't say much at first – I couldn't say much at first – but gradually, we started to talk.' He sipped his tea, and I waited for him to continue.

'When it was too much some days and I couldn't even rouse myself to get out of bed or turn on a light, he'd bring me tea and toast. He told me that he knew what it was like to lose someone you loved, but that we were the lucky ones, because we *had* that love in the first place. No matter how we'd been hurt, we would always have that to hang on to.'

I shifted in my seat, turning the words over in my mind. Maybe Bertie could think of my mother's love without the pain she'd caused him, but I couldn't. To me, remembering how much I'd loved her only brought memories of the deep well of long-ing and hurt when she'd gone. The two were inseparable, twisted together in my heart and my mind.

I scraped back my chair, aware of Angus's eyes on me as he awaited my response. Part of me wanted to say he was right – to reinforce his positivity – but I couldn't.

'I'd better get to bed,' I said. 'Good night.'

'Good night.' Angus's voice followed me up the spiral staircase, and I suddenly realised just how tired I really was.

CHAPTER TWENTY-ONE

Ella

I stared up at the ceiling when I awoke the next morning, trying to get a grip on my surroundings. Birdsong floated through the air and light streamed from the window, making me feel like I was in a sunshine-bathed meadow. I shifted on the bed, memories from yesterday flooding in: making my way through the city to Bertie, him telling me he'd seen my mother alive and that he hadn't placed the advert . . . of the hope rekindled in his eyes, and what I'd agreed to do today in order to bury it.

I sat up, rubbing my eyes. There hadn't been a peep out of Bertie's room, but I'd been so worried about him wandering off that I'd barely slept. Tiredness weighed on me, but I couldn't stay in bed a second longer. I pulled off my pyjamas, gasping at the cold air on my bare skin, then yanked on my clothes from yesterday. It might be summer, but someone really needed to turn on the heating.

I sniffed the air as the scent of strong coffee curled into the room. God, what I wouldn't give for a cup or three right now! I padded down the hallway to the bathroom and splashed water on my face then ran my fingers through my hair, peering closely at my tired reflection. As much as I wanted to get back to normality, part of me longed to stay here, in this place so far removed from my life – a place where, strangely enough, I'd felt so safe that I'd let down my guard a bit to connect with others. I couldn't remember the last time I'd enjoyed a supper so much. I couldn't remember the last time I'd enjoyed *people* so much.

I rammed my few belongings into my backpack and made my way down the spiral staircase.

'Morning.' Angus smiled up at me and I jerked in surprise. I'd expected Bertie, not him. 'Thought I'd bring you guys some croissants and make some proper coffee. Bertie lives on tea, and his idea of a good coffee would blow your head off with all the caffeine.' I couldn't help noticing the cute tuft of hair sticking up at the crown of his head. 'I hope I didn't wake you up. I'm an early riser – always have been.'

'I'm the same,' I said. 'There's just something about getting a head start on the day, isn't there? I love the peace and quiet before everything gets going. Even on weekends, I get up early.' I came to a stop at the bottom of the stairs, flushing as I realised I was babbling.

Luckily, Angus didn't seem to notice. 'Do you take milk?'

I nodded, settling on to the sofa. The house was quiet except for the sound of the birds outside and Angus's happy whistle as he prepared the coffee. For a second, a line from one of Bertie's letters to my mother ran through my head . . . how my mum used to sit right here, while Bertie made her coffee just right. Had she preferred her coffee super-strong, just like me? I wondered.

'Actually . . . I'd better get going straight away,' I said. It was better not to linger, no matter how much I could do with some coffee. Suddenly, I just wanted to get out of there. 'Thanks, but I'd better make a move.'

'Don't you want to wait until Bertie gets up?' Angus asked. 'I know he'll be sorry to have missed you.'

I paused. I'd love to say goodbye to him, but I couldn't. I had to go now, head to the newspaper office and find out what I could, then return to my world.

'Better not.' I heaved my backpack on to my shoulders and went out into the cool morning, leaving the fairy-tale house behind me.

◆ ◆ ◆

A couple of hours later, I was on the train to London. Despite my hasty exit, Angus had caught up with me and insisted on driving me to the station. His dirt-streaked four-by-four had rumbled through the streets, with Angus apologising for its 'rustic' appearance. He'd surprised me with a friendly hug after he got my bag from the back and I stood there, stunned, with my hands by my sides. I couldn't remember the last time someone had hugged me; Carolyn knew better than to try. I always felt like I was being smothered, but now, I had to admit I liked the feeling of his arms around me. I felt protected, in a way I hadn't since, well . . . since before my mother had left.

That was ridiculous, I told myself now as the train rumbled through the countryside. I didn't even know the man, and I'd never see him again. I let out a puff of air at the thought, crossing my fingers that visiting the newspaper in person would persuade them to help me. Did they even have the information I needed and, if they did, would they break the rules to let me have it? I prayed they had something to convince Bertie my mother was gone and let him get on with his life as best he could.

For the second time in as many days, I'd called in sick for work. I hated lying to Jane – especially after she'd sounded genuinely concerned, asking if I needed anything – but I could hardly tell her the truth, could I? It sounded fantastical, even to me.

The train pulled into King's Cross and I followed the crowd down the platform and into the Underground, moving in a sea of faces where no one made eye contact or acknowledged my existence.

I felt like I wasn't even there, a stark contrast to the place I'd left behind and the rare connection I'd felt with the people I'd met.

I got off the underground at South Kensington and walked the short distance to the newspaper's headquarters. The sky was blue and the white facades of the buildings around me glowed in the sun. Tourists pushed around me on the street and well-heeled mums and nannies dragged their charges on scooters home from school. Everywhere I looked, life was in full swing. It couldn't be more different from my quiet view out to the sea each morning.

I opened the door of the newspaper office and entered the dingy reception, which looked like it hadn't received any visitors since the mid-sixties. A row of straight-backed chairs lined one scuffed olive wall, a brown coffee table with rickety spindle legs held yellowed newspapers, and a stained beige carpet covered the floor.

'Can I help you?' A woman with shiny black hair and purple-rimmed glasses met my eyes.

'Um, yes. I'd like to speak to someone from Classifieds?' It crossed my mind that maybe I should have arranged a meeting before coming. I hoped this wasn't a wasted trip. I was way too tired to deal with that let-down. I was here now, and I wanted to get this over with.

'If it's about placing an advertisement, you can either email us the text or call this number.' She rattled off the digits so quickly I could barely process them.

'No, no.' I shook my head. 'It's not about placing an advert. Please, can I talk to someone who might have access to the details of previous adverts?'

'You'll be wanting Greg, then. Can I tell him your name, please?' She peered at me over the top of her glasses.

'It's Ella Morgan,' I said, although I was sure he wouldn't have the slightest clue who I was.

'One moment, please.' She picked up the phone. 'Greg, there's an Ella Morgan here to see you.' She paused. 'Okay, I'll bring her through.'

The woman came out from behind the desk. 'If you'd like to come with me?'

I followed the receptionist through a side door and into a large room crammed full of screens perched on beaten-up desks and swivel chairs. So much for cutting-edge newsroom, I thought, lifting an eyebrow. Then again, this paper was hardly known for its hard-hitting investigative pieces, preferring to expose only scantily clad models on its pages.

'Right, here's Greg.' The receptionist gestured towards a man in his twenties, with highlighted hair gelled straight up.

'Hiya.' Greg swivelled around from the desktop. I couldn't help glancing down at his skin-tight jeans, wondering how he could move without splitting them. 'What can I do for you? I'd show you into a meeting room, but they're all taken right now. Anyway, don't worry. Theresa won't eavesdrop, eh, Theresa?' He jerked his head towards his neighbour and smiled what I'm sure he thought was a flirtatious smile but looked more like his lips had got stuck to his teeth. The woman sitting next to him let out a slow breath, rolling her eyes.

'Thanks for seeing me.' I cleared my throat. 'Um, it's about an advert that was in the paper a couple of weeks ago,' I began, feeling awkward hovering over him while he lounged in his chair, manspreading with the best of them. The more I tried not to look at his very prominent crotch area, the more my horrified eyes were drawn to it. 'There was no contact information, and I wondered if you could tell me if whoever placed it left their name or paid by credit card . . . anything that could help me track them down.'

'Oh.' Greg spun back to the keyboard, his crotch now safely tucked away out of sight underneath the desk, thank God. 'Can't help, I'm afraid. Data protection and all that.' He shook his head, clearly enjoying his role as a gatekeeper.

Impatience swelled inside of me. I'd known he might say that, and I hadn't come all this way to be put off by some jegging-clad jobsworth. Bertie's words about the kindness of strangers floated into my head, and I sighed. Maybe I wouldn't rely on the kindness of strangers but on their ego being stroked.

'Look, I really need your help.' I pulled over a chair since he clearly wasn't going to offer me one. I forced myself to smile at him, and I saw something his face twitch in response. This was definitely a man who liked to be flattered.

'My mother disappeared thirty years ago,' I said, launching into my story. 'I thought she was dead – everyone thought she was dead – until I saw the advert in your classified section.' I swallowed. '"I am always with you. I will always be here". Those ten words . . . she used to say them to me every night. That advert appeared on her birthday, and, well, I know it's silly, but I can't help wondering if, somehow, it might be her. If she is alive, after all of these years.' My cheeks coloured as he raised an eyebrow. I felt ridiculous, spouting these words. Of course she wasn't alive.

I paused, my eyes locking on to his. 'Please, if you can help me . . . anything at all you can tell me would be great.' I put a hand on Greg's arm. 'Please.'

Greg held my gaze, then shifted in his chair. 'Okay, okay. They don't call me Mr Softy for nothing.' There was a snort from the woman beside him, and Greg turned towards her. 'Because I have a big heart, okay? Christ.'

I held my breath as Greg clacked away on the computer. 'What date did the advert appear?'

'The twenty-first of July,' I said, watching him peck in information and wishing he'd taken a proper typing course. At this rate, we'd all be dead before he found anything.

Finally, he turned back around to face me. 'I'm afraid I still can't help you,' he said. 'It says here that whoever placed the ad came in person to do it, about a week before the advert appeared. They paid in cash, so I can't even tell you their name.'

Shit. My heart sank at the thought of telling Angus and Bertie I still couldn't find out anything; of leaving Bertie's hopes all stirred up.

'You didn't talk to them?' I asked. 'The person who placed the advert, I mean.'

Greg shook his head. 'No, I was in Ibiza that week and, anyway, taking down adverts is not my job. Whoever did it probably would have talked to Reception.'

'Right.' I stood up. I needed to go and see that receptionist right now. Even if she hadn't been at the desk, maybe she could tell me who'd been working that day. 'Thanks for your time.'

Greg nodded and spun to face the monitor again, and I made my way back to reception.

'Can I help you?' the receptionist asked, clearly not remembering who I was. Dismay rushed through me. If she didn't recognise me from fifteen minutes ago, how could she remember who had placed the advert a few weeks ago?

'This might sound like a strange question,' I started, 'but were you working here the week before the twentieth of July?'

'If it was a weekday, then I was here,' she said. 'I practically live at this place. Unfortunately.' She tilted her head. 'Why?'

'I'm looking for someone . . . someone who placed a classified advert. Whoever it was came in person to do it, and Greg thinks they might have talked to you.'

'Let me think.' She leaned back in her chair and tapped a perfect teal nail against her glossy lips. I stared, afraid to move in case I interrupted her reverie. 'Yes, I do remember . . . if it's the advert you're thinking of. People don't usually come in person to do it – it's so much easier to just place it online these days. It was kind of a strange ad, too. Just a few words, and that was that.'

'That's it!' I wanted to punch the air. 'Was it "I will always be with you. I will always be here"?' The words tumbled from my mouth. The receptionist nodded, and relief swept over me. Thank God.

'Yes, that's the one.'

'Can you tell me what the person looked like?' I leaned against the counter, willing her to remember – willing her to say it was a man, a teen, something to put a definitive full stop in Bertie's mind.

The receptionist closed her eyes, then opened them and stared straight at me. 'She looked a bit like you, actually.'

My mouth dropped open. *What?*

'I mean, not exactly,' the receptionist was saying. 'She was way older, but there is some resemblance around the eyes and the top part of your face. I'm pretty good with faces, my boyfriend always tells me. Anyway, I asked if she wanted to leave her name and contact information – I mean, what's the point of placing an advert if people don't know how to contact you? But she said no, gave me the money, and left. She seemed kind of sad.'

I held her gaze, unable to look away as thoughts ran through my head. My mother was dead. My mother was *dead*. And yet . . .

A woman had come here, to place an ad on the same day as my mother's birthday, with the same words she'd said to me every night.

A woman who looked like me.

A woman Bertie had claimed to see, just two short years ago.

A woman whose body had never been found.

Could she . . . Could she be alive, after all?

The room swung around me and I blinked to try to right it again, but it felt like my whole world had tilted and I was about to slide off the edge.

'Are you okay?' The receptionist's eyes were wide.

I couldn't answer. I couldn't even think about how I might be feeling right now. Scrabbling to grab a foothold, I managed to leave my name and number in case she remembered anything else. My voice sounded far away, as if it was coming from another planet.

Out on the street, I stood for a minute and tried to grasp hold of what had just happened; tried to steady my world. I looked up and down, taking in the busy pavements and the people rushing past. Had my mother seen this exact view just a few weeks ago? Had she stood here after placing the ad, feeling the sun beat down and heat rise from the asphalt?

Was she in this city right now?

I took a step, and then another, moving faster and faster, as if the more distance I put between myself and the newspaper office, the faster I could bury what the receptionist had just told me. All of this . . . well, none of it meant it was her. Anyone could have placed that advert. The receptionist probably thought all women over twenty resembled each other. And Bertie could have spotted anyone that day – he hadn't seen my mother for years, after all. We could spend years trying to track my mum down, and it could all come to nothing. And I couldn't – I *wouldn't* – go through that again. I couldn't let the spectre of hope hover over me once more. I couldn't take the risk of thinking she might be out there, only to never find her.

No. She was dead; she was gone.

End of story.

CHAPTER TWENTY-TWO

ELLA

Rain slanted through the sky when I walked out of Hastings station. Despite the weather, I turned my face upwards. Water splattered my hot cheeks and I breathed in the salty air, willing calm to slip over me. I may have spent the past two days way out of my comfort zone, but I was home now. I'd call Bertie and tell him what I'd found out, and then I was finished.

Guilt pricked me when I thought of how I'd reignited Bertie's hope and, for a second, I considered keeping the receptionist's information to myself. He'd be so delighted that, even though the newspaper hadn't been able to give me a name, a woman who'd looked me had placed the advert. For him, this would be the ultimate proof that my mum was still living. I could already picture his shining eyes; hear the excitement and hope in his voice.

I sighed as I hurried down the promenade in the darkness, the rain seeping through my jacket and jeans. Going to see Bertie had been a huge mistake, but I'd started this and I owed him the information – the truth of what I'd found. Maybe I could temper it with a dose of reality.

By the time I reached my flat, I was wet to the skin and dying for a shower, eager to crawl under the cosy duvet with Dolby and hunker down in the solitude of my home. My space was just that: mine, and mine alone. After the events of the past two days – the past few weeks, even – I needed that peace more than ever. I needed to anchor myself in the familiar and return to the rhythm of my life once again.

I'd only just fitted my key in the lock when my neighbour yanked my door open from the inside. I blinked in surprise and took a step backwards. What on earth was she doing here? My heart dropped when I remembered I'd invited her into my home.

'Oh, hello!' Lou said, grinning at me with my cat in her arms. Lou looked as bright-eyed and bushy-tailed as ever, despite the late hour. 'Just popped in to check on Dolby and make sure she was all right. I wasn't sure when you'd be home.'

'Thank you.' I pushed out the words, forcing myself to smile, even though it was the last thing I felt like doing. I did appreciate her looking after my cat at such short notice but seeing her in my studio with my cat nestled up against her . . . I felt like wrenching my pet away and closing the door; blocking her and everything else out.

'Well, you have the cutest cat ever,' she said, handing over the key. 'I'm happy to look after her any time you like.'

I nodded, even though I knew that wouldn't be necessary. I wouldn't be going anywhere any time soon.

'And maybe we can grab a drink sometime?'

'I don't think so,' I said, the words coming out much harsher than I intended. 'I'm not much of a night-out kind of person,' I added, guilt swooping through me as her face fell. She *was* nice, but . . .

Okay, then,' she said. 'Well, maybe coffee some time. Dolby's great, but I'm dying for some human companionship!'

I could see the hope in her eyes, and I sighed inwardly. I'd never understood being lonely. I was more than fine on my own, and never did I need that more than right now. Lou seemed like Carolyn: you gave her an inch (or a key) and she wanted a mile. I didn't have the energy right now to fend her off, though, so I simply nodded, regret sliding over me as her eyes lit up. She'd never let me forget this, but I'd deal with that later.

'Great. G'night!' She put down Dolby and closed my door behind her. I breathed in the silence, feeling myself unwind. I sloughed off my wet jacket and slicked back my hair, thinking of Bertie and Angus, and how close they were – how Angus kept an eye on Bertie and made sure he was okay. I'd admired their relationship, but I was nowhere close to wanting that myself. I picked up Dolby, breathing in her sweet-smelling fur and steeling myself for what I needed to do next. One final phone call to Bertie and I could put all of this behind me.

I grabbed my mobile. It was late, but I knew he'd be waiting to hear from me. I punched his number into my mobile, absently stroking Dolby as the phone rang and rang.

'Hello?' The voice that answered was a whisper, and my brow furrowed. That wasn't Bertie.

'Angus?' Despite my exhaustion, I suddenly felt more alert. 'It's Ella. Listen, is Bertie around?' Best not to beat around the bush. I'd tell him what I found, wish him the best of luck, then hang up.

'Bertie's sleeping right now,' Angus replied. 'He had a tough day.'

'Is he okay?' I sank down on the futon with Dolby in my arms.

Angus sighed. 'Well, he is and he isn't. He's been a little confused since he woke up this morning, and he kept trying to get out and go down to the river, for some reason. Obviously, that's not such a great idea – he gets a little unsteady on his feet sometimes. I couldn't get him to settle. I just managed to get him into bed about an hour ago.'

Angus sounded exhausted. 'Maybe you should see if a care worker can help out?' I asked.

'There is a community care worker assigned to him, but she can only come once a week or so to see how he's getting on,' Angus said. 'It's not enough now. I've been on the phone to them, and they're going to see what they can do. But for now . . . I'll keep doing as much as I'm able.'

Angus paused. 'So . . . how did it go in London? I hope you don't mind, but Bertie told me a bit about why you came to see him and what you were doing today. If I understood him correctly, you were trying to find out something about your mother? Where she might be living now, or something like that? He was pretty worked up about it, so I'm not sure I got it right. Just tell me if you don't want to talk about it,' he added.

I put down Dolby and crossed to the window. Given how close Angus and Bertie were, I was sure Bertie wouldn't mind me telling Angus about his relationship with my mother and what had happened – if he hadn't managed to already. And maybe . . . maybe Angus could steer Bertie away from wasting what little time he had left on a search that could only bring more heartache. My heart panged at the thought of kind, gentle Bertie using what time he had left chasing someone who'd dumped him years ago – someone who'd *died* years ago. How could he even want to waste his precious time chasing a dream from the past?

'My mother and Bertie lived together, ages ago,' I said. 'She left him suddenly, and he tried for years to find her. But she died – five years after she had me, she killed herself. Her body was never found, but . . .'

'I'm sorry,' Angus said quietly, but I didn't let his words touch me.

'Bertie thinks he saw her, a couple of years ago in London, but it couldn't have been her. And then there was this advert . . .' I stared out at the sea. 'An advert with the same ten words she used to say to me and Bertie, placed on her birthday. That led me to Bertie,

125

but he said it wasn't him who placed it. He's convinced it was my mother reaching out to us, and he wants to find her.'

'Wow.' Angus was silent for a moment. 'And did the newspaper tell you anything? *Was* it your mother?'

'They couldn't tell me much, apart from saying whoever placed the ad was an older woman who looked like me.' I turned away from the window and sat down on the bed. 'Angus . . . I know Bertie will think it's proof my mum is alive and that she's reaching out, but maybe it's not such a great thing for him to go looking for her. She's been gone for thirty years. To pin all his hopes on some random advert, well . . .' My voice drifted off.

The line went silent, and I could almost see Angus's face as he mulled over my words.

'I hear what you're saying, and you might be right,' he responded at last. 'It's not a lot to go on, but it *is* something, isn't it? And Bertie, well, he may look like a pushover, but when he gets an idea in his mind, I can't stop him. If he wants to look for your mother, I won't be able to convince him otherwise. I'll be there for him if he needs me, though, I can promise you that.' Silence fell once again.

'But what about you?' Angus's voice was soft. 'If there is the slightest chance your mother is alive . . . well, don't you want to find her?'

I swallowed as his question hit me. For a split second, I let my mind hover over the possibility I'd shoved away so quickly earlier, that my mother *was* out there . . . that she was alive. Pain swirled inside me as I realised exactly what that meant: that she'd left to live another life, a life where she'd stayed out of touch for thirty years. She hadn't abandoned me because of depression. She'd simply wanted to live a life free of *me*.

My gut twisted, and for a second I thought I might be sick. I gulped in air and glanced around the flat at my familiar things, willing my stomach to settle. What was I afraid of? So my mother might be alive. So what? Whether she'd left to live alone or whether she'd killed herself, she'd still *left*. I'd built a good life without her – a smooth, comfortable life where all I needed was me . . . and Dolby, of course. Whether she was alive or not, it didn't make a difference. She was still dead to me.

'No.' The word tore through my throat, and I swallowed, trying to keep a grip on my emotions. 'No, I don't want to find her.' Not because I feared hope, and not because I couldn't bear it. Because I didn't need her. I didn't *want* her.

'Look, I can't begin to understand what you went through,' Angus said. 'But you must have some questions. You must have things you want to say, stored up all through these years. God knows there's plenty I'd say to – and ask – Steph even now, if she'd talk to me. If your mother is alive, well . . . maybe this is your chance to do that. Maybe this is your chance to finally put everything to rest.'

'I've already put everything to rest, Angus,' I said, and I meant it. Seeing the advert might have stirred something within me and propelled me forward on this unexpected journey, but I was done now. Finished, and that was that. Whatever Bertie chose to do now, it wasn't any of my business.

'Please tell Bertie that I wish him the best of luck in the future, okay?' My voice was hoarse. 'It was lovely meeting you both.' My heart squeezed at the thought of not seeing Angus again, but I couldn't. He was caught up with all of this, and I was desperate to put it behind me.

'Ella, wait. I—'

I hung up. There was nothing more to say, anyway.

CHAPTER TWENTY-THREE

JUDE

November 1981

Jude swiped her cloth over the bar for the millionth time since she'd opened the pub earlier that day. It was almost four in the afternoon, and in one more hour – thank God – she'd escape this dive and walk the short distance home, where Bertie would be starting dinner and humming along to one of the jazz tapes she'd brought by the armload when she'd moved in.

She sighed and surveyed the half-filled room. She'd taken this job at the city-centre pub in the hope of getting on the roster for their weekend music nights, but after three months all she'd managed to develop was an impressive array of skills to deflect men's wandering hands and an ability to jog their memories when it came to paying for their pints. She'd spoken to the manager every week and handed him no fewer than three of her precious demo tapes – even stooping to singing every Scottish classic under the sun – and each time he said that while her voice was 'fantastic, baby', their schedule was full up until next month. Then the next month, he'd say the same thing.

At least it was something to do besides hanging around the house all day, not that anyone here was providing scintillating conversation . . . unless you counted jokes about Dolly Parton's bra size as scintillating. Jude should be using the time to think of her wedding – of setting a date, at the very least. Already it had been over six months since Bertie had proposed, and although they both agreed there was no hurry (they'd need to save every penny, anyway), Bertie was keen to have a confirmed date they could start to plan around. Jude knew that Carolyn would help financially, even if she and Rob were throwing everything they had into doing up their house. But Carolyn still didn't know Jude and Bertie were even engaged. Jude was clutching that piece of information closely to herself, as if by telling her sister she'd let reality intrude on her neat little bubble.

But she had to admit, reality *was* starting to intrude, no matter how much she tried to keep it at bay. After basking in the post-engagement glow for a few weeks, drifting around the house in a happy daze, picturing herself in wedding dresses and buying almost every wedding magazine available to womankind, the urge to get out and sing had filtered in again – to feel alive in a way she never did any time else . . . not even with Bertie, if she was being honest. He was loving, attentive and kind, and she was excited to marry him. But that didn't fill up the longing inside whenever she thought of herself onstage, singing into the darkness.

I'll get there, she told herself, unable to think of any other alternative. She just had to keep putting herself out there, trying to be in the right place at the right time – even if that place was a dingy pub in a city she'd never dreamed of living in before. Everyone had to start somewhere. And once she got her foot in the door of the pub circuit here, she'd be singing every night, she was sure. It *would* happen . . . she just didn't know when. She'd keep plugging away, and maybe . . . maybe she would sit down with Bertie tonight and they could choose a date for the wedding. At least organising it would fill the hours while waiting for a gig.

She bit her lip, her mind spinning. They'd need more time to scrape some money together, and Bertie still had to save up for a ring, so maybe . . . next summer? A summer wedding in Scotland when everything was green and all the flowers were in bloom would be perfect, just magical. Because of course they would get married here, where they lived. The thought of Hastings and the cold wind whipping in from the sea made her shiver. She was sure Bertie would agree.

The last hour of her shift flew by, her mind full of images of what dress she would buy, where they could hold the ceremony, what sort of cake they would have . . .

'Oh!' Jude jumped as someone put a hand on her shoulder.

'Hello, stranger.'

She turned to spot Bertie's brother, Frank, smiling at her from across the bar. What was he doing here? Bertie hadn't mentioned he'd be coming home, but then . . . Jude bit her lip, remembering when Frank had rung last month for yet another 'emergency transfer' because none of the banks in Spain were working. Jude had managed to bite her tongue the first and second times it had happened . . . but not the third. It was the only time she and Bertie had had a real argument.

'He's taking advantage of you,' Jude had said, wanting to protect her kind, generous fiancé. 'We could be using that money for our wedding.' Jude hadn't been in any rush, but she'd known that would resonate with Bertie. Besides, it was true.

But Bertie's eyes had flashed in a way Jude had never seen before. 'You don't know what it's like to have to take care of someone,' he'd said, and Jude's mouth had dropped open. *Take care of someone?*

'Frank's not a child, for God's sake,' Jude snapped back, her body going tense. 'He doesn't need taking care of – and he shouldn't need your money.'

As quickly as Bertie's anger had come, it seemed to fade away, and his long, lean frame sagged on the sofa. 'I'm sorry,' he'd said, squeezing Jude's hand and sighing. 'It's just . . . well, when it comes to Frank, I feel responsible.'

'But why?' Jude asked, holding his steady gaze.

'It goes back to when we were kids.' Bertie sighed again. 'Frank was always getting into trouble, even in primary school. Our father was very strict, and, well . . . let's just say that he had no problem punishing us, with his hands, a belt . . . whatever he could find. Frank got the worst of it, growing up – he was always in and out of the headteacher's office.'

'That's awful,' Jude murmured, tucking herself up against Bertie. She couldn't imagine growing up with a father like that. Her own dad had been full of cuddles and laughter.

'Anyway, when I moved out to go to university, I decided it would be best if Frank came with me. He was about to be excluded from school and I thought a fresh start away from our father would do him good.'

Jude nodded slowly. What a weight for an eighteen-year-old to take on. Her mind had flashed to Carolyn, and for the first time it hit her that her own sister had shouldered a tremendous responsibility at a very young age as well.

'I worked part-time while studying to support us, and I got Frank into the local secondary school,' Bertie continued. 'But things didn't get better. They got worse.' His face twisted. 'I just couldn't hold it together: Frank, my school, my job . . .' He shook his head. 'Frank dropped out. I managed to scrape through my degree. And my father . . . well, he hasn't spoken to either of us since. I know he blames me for ruining the family – for ruining Frank. And he's right.' Bertie cleared his throat. 'If I'd done a better job with him, or maybe if I hadn't taken him away from our father, then perhaps Frank would have finished school. Perhaps he might have a life, rather than going here, there and everywhere, doing whatever work he can find.'

'Or perhaps things could have ended up exactly the same . . . or even worse.' Jude had nestled closer to Bertie. 'Look, Carolyn did everything she could to keep me on the straight and narrow, too,' she'd said. 'But ultimately, I made my own choices. Frank did, too. And if he wants to change his life, I'm sure he will. He's lucky to have an older brother like you.' Did Carolyn beat herself up the same way Bertie did? Jude had wondered. It struck her suddenly how much her older sister was like the man she was about to marry: not only were they the same age, they were both also solid, caring and responsible. Those weren't *bad* things, but the realisation made her a little uncomfortable. She'd balked at those with Carolyn. Would the same be true with Bertie?

Of course not, she'd told herself, pushing away the notion. Bertie was . . . Bertie. He might be like her sister in some ways, but they were miles apart in others – in the ways that really counted. Bertie believed in her dream, and he wouldn't try to change her. And she loved him. She wanted to marry him. She *would* marry him. Now that she understood his allegiance to Frank, that would eliminate the one thing that caused tension between them. Everything else was smooth sailing. What more could she ask for?

'Hi!' Jude tore herself back to the present, focusing on Frank. The scent of his cologne filled the air, taking her back to that night they'd first met. God, it seemed ages ago. Back then, she'd been free as a bird and about to start her life in London, and now. . . For just a split second, regret needled her before she pushed it away. If she'd gone to London, she wouldn't have Bertie.

'When did you get back in town?' she asked. 'Would you like a drink?'

'I should be buying you a drink.' Frank leaned in, his dark eyes twinkling. 'I hear congratulations are in order!'

Jude blushed. 'Yes, thank you.'

'I gotta say, though, I was a little surprised,' Frank said. 'Not at Bertie – he's been ready to settle down and have kids since forever. I didn't peg you as that type, though. Thought singing was your thing.' He shrugged. 'Anyway, congrats.'

Jude forced a smile, despite feeling like she'd been punched in the gut. Settle down and have kids? God, she'd barely got her head around being a wife. Was Bertie expecting her to get pregnant soon? They'd never talked about it, but then they'd never talked about marriage before he proposed, either. She was only twenty, she told herself. They had plenty of time. *She* had plenty of time to get things started before even thinking about children. Bertie would support her, she was sure.

'How is the singing going, anyway?' Frank asked, as if he'd tapped into her thoughts.

'It's not.' Jude sighed. 'I've been trying, but I haven't been able to line up any gigs. It's hard when you don't know a soul in the city.'

'Well, you know me.' Frank flashed a smile. 'Maybe I can help.'

Jude's ears pricked up and hope flashed through her. Perhaps he could finally point her in the right direction. He was from here, he'd worked in the industry, and there must be some help he could give her. Right now, she'd take anything. 'Really? That would be great.'

Frank nodded. 'I'm back here for the next few months and I'm going to be working in a new pub that's opening just around the corner. I know the manager, and I'm sure I can get him to book you in for a night, if you like? No need for a tape or an audition, of course. I've already heard you sing, and you definitely have what it takes.'

'You think so?' Jude couldn't help asking. After months of trying to break into the music scene, she'd started to wonder if maybe it wasn't just down to luck or being in the right place at the right time. Maybe she didn't have the talent, after all.

'Absolutely.' Frank's tone rang with certainty, and a smile grew on her face.

'That would be amazing, if you could talk to the manager. Oh, thank you!' She came from behind the bar and stuck out a hand. 'Thank you so much.'

Frank brushed her hand aside. 'What's this? Come on, you're going to be my sister. Give us a hug.' He opened his arms and she came from behind the bar and stepped into them, her heart racing with excitement. This could be the break she needed. Once she was in, everything would go from there.

'I'll keep you posted,' Frank said. 'I know where to find you. Now, how about that drink?'

CHAPTER TWENTY-FOUR

ELLA

I threw myself into my life with a fervour, religiously observing all the routines I'd created for myself – the neat boundaries I found so reassuring. I rose at the same time each day, ate the same packed lunch, hurried home along the promenade with my chin down, and ignored any outside intrusion . . . including my neighbour's texts to go out and Carolyn's increasingly incessant calls. I hunkered down inside myself, constantly on guard against any rogue thought or emotion that might slip through. I meant what I'd told Angus – I *had* put everything to rest – but I needed to be extra-vigilant now. I couldn't let myself slip backwards, especially not with the possibility – no matter how slight – that my mother might be alive.

Not that it mattered, I reminded myself. Not that I wanted anything to do with her, anyway.

I had my headphones on and my eyes fixed on the screen when a cough right beside me made me look up. Jane was standing there with a friendly smile. I barely managed to repress a sigh, sliding off my headphones.

'Hi, Jane,' I said, trying to keep the irritation from my voice.

'Sorry to disturb,' she said. 'But I have an exciting proposition for you. We're putting together an exhibition to celebrate the new pier, and I'd like you to curate it. I think you're the perfect person. You've been here for years and you know the archive like the back of your hand. "Sounds of the Pier", we're going to call it, and we'll set up sound stations, complete with photos of the old pier and the new one.'

I shifted in my chair, excitement leaping inside. Curating an exhibition was a huge responsibility, and only Jane had spearheaded them before. Her offer was a sign that she trusted and respected my work, and a thrill of pride went through me.

'As well as selecting all the sound files, you'll also need to meet with Marketing and liaise with a photographer and the Hastings librarians. I've also arranged a meeting in London with some people at the British Museum, who've just done something similar. They'll be able to talk you through their process and give you some ideas . . . Would you be up for that?'

The British Museum? I drew in a breath, my pulse quickening. After all these years, could I finally be getting the chance to go there again – not as an overawed student this time, but as a colleague? My mind spun as I imagined talking to the experts about my plans, learning from them, seeing behind the scenes—

But . . . my heart dropped as reality filtered in. *London*. That meant leaving my safety zone. That meant going to the city where there was a chance – no matter how big or how small – my mother now lived. Could I face walking down streets, trying to stop myself from scanning every profile, like I had on that trip to Europe so long ago? Could I stand being in the same city as her, yet not letting thoughts of her consume me every second? My mother *was* dead to me, and I wanted to keep it that way. I wanted to keep her tucked away, out of my life – out of my mind.

'It's a chance to get out from behind this cubicle; to meet some new people and really interact,' Jane was saying. 'You've been stuck down here for ages, and I don't think we've made full use of your skills. I think you're ready.' She smiled encouragingly. 'What do you say?'

I swallowed. Every inch of me was straining to say yes, and yet I couldn't do it. I'd believed I'd been safe before, and all it had taken was one little advert to throw me off. After the upheaval of the past few weeks, I couldn't take the risk; couldn't deliberately put myself in harm's way. I had to stay within my own four walls, both inside and out. I needed all my energy, all my resources, to keep my life on track.

I shook my head. 'I can't. I'm really sorry, but I can't.'

'All right.' Jane's eyes narrowed slightly, but her face was neutral. 'Well, I'll let you get on with your work, then.'

She turned and walked away. I put my headphones back on, disappointment thudding through me. I'd done the right thing, I told myself. I had to protect myself. There would be other projects; other opportunities.

But it didn't ease the sting. It didn't calm the sudden anger flaring inside. If my mum was dead to me, then why was she affecting the decisions I made now? I gritted my teeth, forcing the question away – forcing the emotion away. I didn't want to feel. I didn't want to let anything to do with my mother touch me.

I turned the volume on the monitor as high as it would go, staring at the screen in front of me. Just stick to your world, I told myself. Just keep within yourself and soon, nothing from the past will be able to reach you.

CHAPTER TWENTY-FIVE

JUDE

February 1982

'You coming up to bed?' Bertie leaned over the spiral staircase, and Jude jerked towards him from her spot on the sofa. She'd been miles away, working on a new song to sing next Thursday at the pub where Frank worked. Ever since he'd got her booked in a couple of months ago, Thursday had been *her* night – and her audience had been growing steadily every week. She'd been so nervous the first time she'd sung there, but the crowd had been small and Bertie's encouraging smile had given her confidence, reminding her of the night he'd found her again in the Hastings pub. Finally, months later, she was performing once more. She'd bitten her lip at the thought of all that wasted time . . . time she could have been using to reach for her dream.

But of course it wasn't wasted, she told herself now, smiling up into her fiancé's eyes. She had Bertie. She was engaged to be married . . . if she ever got around to setting the date. She'd been so busy lately, getting ready for her gig, then singing, then writing new songs, that any earlier thought of holding the wedding next summer had been pushed to the back of her mind. They'd stayed there, despite probing questions from Bertie about when they would tie the knot. It was obvious Bertie was more than ready – like Frank had joked, he'd probably been ready since he was born. And she wanted to get married, too. Of course she did. But couldn't Bertie see that she had to pour everything into this opportunity; try to build her audience as much as she could? It'd been hard enough to get her foot in the door in the first place, and who knew how long this gig would last?

Frank understood, probably because he had some experience. He knew how things worked and he'd been incredibly supportive, telling pub punters of her Thursday night sessions and coming back to Bertie's with her from their city-centre pubs, giving her a chance to try out any new music she'd written that day. Bertie was usually already upstairs in bed by the time they got there, and although they tried to be quiet, inevitably the volume would grow as the hours passed. No matter how dire she believed her music was, Frank would always praise it. He'd tell her over and over again how talented she was; how people *would* want to listen to something new by an unknown singer, because her songs were just that good. Bertie was encouraging, too, but he had nothing to compare her to. Frank knew the industry; knew other singers. She could believe him when he said it.

They'd laugh and joke for a while after she finished singing, trading stories about their day at work. Being with Frank was a release after the silence at home and the cacophony of the pub. She was grateful to Frank for his help, but sometimes she wished that she could spend this time with Bertie . . . that *Bertie* could give her this.

She cringed, remembering the time Bertie had interrupted one of her late-night sessions with Frank. They'd been guffawing about some poor bloke whose trousers had caught on a bar stool and been yanked down when he tried to get off. Frank had been re-enacting the scenario, and Jude had been almost hysterical with laughter when Bertie's voice drifted from the staircase above them.

'Would you mind keeping it down?' Bertie had stood there, rubbing his eyes with a cross expression on his face. 'I've got an early start tomorrow.'

'Oh, sorry, honey,' Jude had said, clamping a hand over her mouth. 'Go back to bed. We'll be quiet.'

She and Frank were silent for a minute before Frank shook his head. 'God, no wonder you're in no rush to get married,' he said. 'He acts like he's about ninety, hey? Better get ready for a quiet life. I don't know how you haven't self-combusted with boredom already.'

Jude had just rolled her eyes, pushing aside the reality that she *had* been near self-combustion. There was no need to even think of that now – now that she was singing again; that she had a reason to write. People actually wanted to listen to the music she floated out into the air, and whenever someone approached her after the show, humming the tune and asking if they could get a copy of it, her heart soared.

The bedroom door had slammed shut then, and Jude raised her eyebrows as her heart sank. Had Bertie overheard his brother? Did he think the reason she hadn't set the date was because of any doubts about *him*? It had nothing to do with him. It was just that everything was back in colour again. She felt alive in a way she hadn't since moving here. Guilt swept over her that she was more excited about singing in a pub than marrying the man she loved.

Bertie had been quiet the next day – quieter than usual, anyway, and fear had swept through Jude. Singing was important to her, but so was he. She didn't want to give him any reason to doubt her. So, she'd decided to set the wedding date: 14 August. She'd never seen Bertie so happy. He'd been straight on the phone to book that week off work, and he'd stopped by the travel agents to

140

pick up some brochures to look at honeymoon destinations. He'd given her a huge wedding-planning journal so she could get started. After all, he'd said smiling, August was only a few months away and the summer months booked up fast. They'd need to secure a church quickly. His enthusiasm had been infectious, and she'd found herself looking forward to their big day, too.

But now, once again, something else had eclipsed her excitement. Last night, Frank had told her he'd heard that a big-name music promoter was scouting around pubs in Edinburgh these days, and word had it he might come to theirs next Thursday. Frank was going to do his best to make sure the guy came round. Jude had leaped up and thrown her arms around him in excitement. She'd let him buy her a drink as they talked about her song list and what she might sing. Frank knew her repertoire as well as she did now.

She'd raced home, eager to tell Bertie, but of course he'd already been tucked up in bed sound asleep. And the next morning, he'd been out the door to work before she even stirred, since she'd been way too excited to sleep until late. How could she even think of sleeping when this might be her big break?

'I'll be up in a second,' she told Bertie now. She *did* love him. There was absolutely no doubt in her mind about that, but there was plenty of time for wedding planning . . . It was only February, right? Bertie might think summer was just around the corner, but August was ages away yet. *This* was her chance to begin her music career in earnest, and she'd stay up as late as she needed to in order to knock this song into shape.

Bertie would be asleep again in seconds, anyway.

CHAPTER TWENTY-SIX

ELLA

I dragged myself through the following days, awakening each morning feeling more exhausted than when I'd gone to bed. I'd been tired before, but this was different. This echoed deep inside of me, reaching right down to my very core – a fatigue which sprung from maintaining a defensive position 24/7. I couldn't let myself feel angry again. I couldn't let myself *feel*, full stop. Asleep or awake, I was constantly monitoring my internal landscape, fearful something might slip through. Carolyn kept calling and Lou kept texting, but I didn't respond. How could I deal with the outside world when I was only just managing to keep a grip on myself?

One morning when I opened my eyes, they felt like sandpaper, my head was pounding, and every muscle in my body ached . . . and I was glad. Glad for a reason to curl up in bed all day. Glad to shut myself away, even from my beloved job. Glad that I didn't have to force my muscles to move just to make it through the day, trying to reach the end.

Was this how my mother had felt? I wondered. I shook my head so hard that fireworks exploded behind my eyes. *No.* I didn't need to wonder. I didn't need to know anything about her or how she'd felt. My body might have surrendered, but my soul hadn't.

I was dozing on the bed, off work for the second day in a row, when the mobile phone jolted me awake. My arm reached out and answered, acting on autopilot before I could stop it.

'Ella.' Bertie's voice echoed down the line, and my heart started beating so fast I felt light-headed. Had they found her? Nausea swept through me, and I bit back a groan. I didn't want to deal with this. I wouldn't deal with this. I didn't want to be rude to Bertie, but—

'I wanted to give you some time before I called,' Bertie continued, before I could say anything. 'I hope you don't mind, but Angus told me about your last conversation and that you don't want to try to find your mother.'

'That's right,' I said, my voice emerging scratchy and hoarse. I sat up, mustering the energy to tell Bertie, in a way he couldn't fail to grasp, that I was done. 'I don't want to see her. I don't need to know why she left. All that matters to me is that she *did*.' Anger spurted through me, and I put a hand to my fevered cheeks, taking in deep breaths to calm down. I was fine. I didn't know what I was saying. It didn't matter to me that she left.

'I understand.' Bertie's kind voice made my eyes ache with the pressure of tears, and I rubbed them furiously. I wouldn't cry. I hadn't cried for years, and I wasn't going to start now. God, what was wrong with me? The anger leaped up again, growing in strength.

'But, Ella, the past is behind us,' Bertie continued. 'I don't have a lot of time left in the life that I know. I don't have time to hang on to anger, or pain, or upset. I don't *want* to make time for that. If I have a chance to see Jude again before I fade, then I'm going to do everything I can to make that happen.'

A loud knock at the door interrupted his words, and I jerked in surprise. Who the hell was that? Had my neighbour resorted to

143

non-technological tactics, or had Carolyn finally got fed up with my lack of response?

'Are you okay in there?' Lou's voice filtered through the door, and I put the phone on mute, not wanting Bertie to hear. 'Haven't heard you for a while. Everything all right?'

'I don't know if we'll find her, and I don't know what will happen if we do,' Bertie was saying. 'Maybe she wasn't reaching out. Maybe she won't want to see me. It's a risk, like anything in life. But what's the other option? To shut down and eke out the rest of life in my shell? That's not living, either.'

Another hard knock shook the flimsy door. 'Ella? You okay?' *Bang, bang.*

'Ella?' Bertie's voice buzzed from the handset. 'Ella, are you still there?'

'Ella?' *Bang, bang bang.*

'*Leave me alone!*' The shout burst from me before the words had even formed in my mind. I got to my feet, shocked at my outburst. I never raised my voice, let alone *yelled*. Where had that come from? Lou's footsteps faded as she retreated, and I put a hand to my throat, my heart pounding. Emotion was boiling up inside of me, swirling faster and faster. I took a few steps, uncertain where I was going but unable to resist the urge to move. The room swung around me and I struggled to stay upright, feeling like everything both inside and out was quicksand, shifting and sucking at me.

My hand reached out, yanking open the blinds. I squinted at the light glinting off the sea as the realisation rushed into me. I'd been wrong, and Bertie was wrong, too. The past wasn't behind us, and it could never be laid to rest. The past was *within* us. We could barricade ourselves from the outside world as much as we liked, but it would still be there, lying dormant, just waiting for a chance to break into our lives again.

Until I'd seen that advert, I'd been perfectly fine living in a shell, like Bertie had said. And for the past few days, I'd done everything I could not to disturb the emotions I believed I'd put to rest, even turning down a huge step forward at work. But it didn't matter. It would never be enough, because I could never outrun myself . . . and what my mother had done to me. And all it had taken was one advert, with those ten little words.

Those ten *bloody* words.

Fury exploded inside, a volcano of rage so powerful my muscles shook. I breathed in and out in time with the waves of the sea, anger pouring from me like hot lava. If my mother wanted to be found, I'd find her. I'd find her and tell her exactly what I thought of her reaching out. I'd say that she should have stayed dead, that I *preferred* her that way. She'd chosen to leave me, and now it was my turn to choose to leave her.

I unmuted the phone.

'I'm still here,' I said to Bertie, my voice strong now. 'I'm here, but I have to let you go.' Bertie and I might both want to find my mother, but we were on completely different tracks. I didn't want to hear about love, about last chances. I wanted to vent, to blast this blackness inside of me.

'All right.' His voice was soft. 'Goodbye, Ella. I'll keep in touch.' And before I could ask him not to, he clicked off.

I stared out to sea again, feeling more alive than I had for years. My walls were down. My heart was open – at last. But unlike Bertie, I wasn't full of love. I was full of fury, and I was ready to attack.

God, it felt good.

CHAPTER TWENTY-SEVEN

JUDE

March 1982

'He's here!' Frank poked his head into the small back room where Jude was getting ready for her gig. She turned from the mirror, where she was piling on yet more mascara. Under the pub's drab lighting, she looked half-dead unless she trowelled on the make-up.

'Who's here?' she asked, her mind spinning through her playlist. 'Bertie?' She'd been trying to convince him to come out tonight and relax after a particularly busy day at work, but he'd been exhausted and begged off. Again.

'Mike Fanning! The music promoter!' Frank rolled his eyes as if she was an idiot.

But Jude didn't even have time to respond to his tone with a quick quip, like she usually would, because her mouth was open in shock. The promoter had finally showed up? After Frank had mentioned him a few weeks ago, Jude had spent every minute preparing, and every second of her sets scanning the audience for someone who looked vaguely like they belonged to the music industry, whatever that was. The wedding-planning journal lay empty, buried now under piles of sheet music topped with empty coffee mugs. But as the days went on and no one appeared, Jude started to wonder if the promoter was ever going to turn up.

'Oh my God.' Her heart beat fast at the thought of the promoter waiting out front to see her. This was it. This was her chance to meet someone who could help get her started . . . someone with connections. A steely determination filled her, and she ordered herself to relax. She wouldn't blow it. She'd grasp on to this for all it was worth.

And one hour later, she knew she'd done everything she could. She'd chosen the best songs to show off her voice, which had glided from her like it was pouring from her soul. She'd barely even noticed the time passing as she slid from one number to the other, the audience shimmering before her like a mirage. And when she finished and stepped back from the mic, applause swelling like a wave, she had that glow inside that came from knowing she'd sung exactly as she'd wanted, unsullied by the technicalities of her throat or other physical constraints. No matter what happened now, at least she'd given it her all.

But oh, how she wanted it. Wanted whatever the musical promoter could offer. Wanted something to help her start reaching for her dream.

'Jude?' Frank's voice made her turn. 'There's someone here who'd like to meet you.'

'Hello.' A small, wiry man about her height held out his hand, and Jude tried to conceal her surprise. She didn't know what she was expecting, but it wasn't someone like him. He was probably in his mid-thirties, with hair like a steel brush and dressed all in black. God, no wonder she hadn't been able to spot him in the audience. 'Mike Fanning. Nice to meet you. I enjoyed your singing.'

'Thank you.' Jude tried her best to look calm, but her heart was hammering so much she was sure the man could see her chest heaving.

'Frank here has been trying to get me to come by and see you for weeks now,' Mike said. 'And I have to say, I'm glad I did.' He paused and Jude scrabbled for something to say, but all she could come up with was a nod.

'Look, I'll cut right to the chase,' Mike said, and Jude could hardly breathe. 'I have a band I'm taking on a tour of Scotland and the north of England next month. They're the next break-out band, I'll tell you that for nothing. Really fantastic. We had an opening act lined up, but she's just bailed.'

Jude couldn't make a sound. Her eyes were trained on him as if he was the only thing in the world.

'I like your sound. I like your look, and I think you'd be perfect to come on tour with us.'

'I'd love to!' The words burst out of her almost before he'd finished his sentence, and Mike chuckled.

'Well, that's fantastic. But do you need to take some time to think about it? Any job you need to sort out before you commit? A boyfriend or husband or someone you need to clear it with?' He let out an exasperated sigh. 'I can't be doing with a repeat of the last girl. She dropped out after her husband decided he didn't like her being away for weeks at a time.'

Jude shook her head. 'No, no husband.' She caught Frankie's sidelong look, and felt her defences rise. Well, it was true: she didn't have a husband. Not yet, anyway, and Bertie wouldn't dream of stopping her from doing this, she was sure. Besides, the wedding was still ages away, and they wouldn't be leaving for the tour until next month. She'd get as much done as she could before heading off. How long did a wedding take to organise, anyway?

'Well, it all sounds perfect, then.' Mike smiled and held out a hand again. 'Welcome on board. I'll be in touch to nail down all the details and send you the contract. I look forward to working with you.' He turned to Frank. 'And to working with you again, too. Good night.'

'Good night. And thank you!' Jude called out. She watched him go in silence, barely able to believe what had just happened.

'I'm going on tour!' She needed to say the words aloud to make it real, in case the whole thing disappeared. 'Frank, I'm going on tour!' He lifted her up and swung her around, then set her down on her feet.

'What did Mike mean, working with you again, too?' she asked when the room stopped spinning and she'd caught her breath.

Frank grinned. 'You're not the only one going on tour. I'm going to be hitting the road with you guys, too. I've worked with Mike in the past as a kind of roadie – setting up the gear, doing sound checks, a general dogsbody, really. And while, normally, I couldn't be arsed doing all that shit again, I think Mike is right. This band is going places, and if I get in with them now, it'll pay off.'

'Oh, brilliant.' Jude grinned. As excited as she was about going on tour, she was also a little nervous about pulling off a successful opening act – the only thing she'd ever opened for was a football match on telly. Having Frank around would be a great boost to her confidence. He believed in her. 'But what about the pub?'

Frank shrugged. 'They'll find someone. Anyway, I've stayed here too long. I'm ready for a change.' He shot her a look. 'Aren't you going to call Bertie now and tell him the big news?' He glanced at the clock. 'You're back on in ten minutes.'

'I'll tell him when I'm home,' Jude replied. She wanted to see his reaction to her big news in person. He'd miss her, of course, but she had no doubt he'd be happy for her . . . and pleased that Frank would be along to keep her safe and out of harm's way. Bertie was happy that she was singing at Frank's pub for that very reason.

Jude took a deep breath and got ready to go back out to the mic again, excitement curling inside of her. She wasn't just a regular, run-of-the-mill pub singer any more, dabbling part-time in singing while waiting to get married – not that she ever had been, of course, but she suspected that was how everyone else saw her. She was going on tour now, with a band that was going to be huge. She was on her way.

Life was about to begin.

CHAPTER TWENTY-EIGHT

ELLA

I might be itching to face down my mother but, as the days ticked on, I wasn't any closer to finding her. Anger mixed with frustration as I scoured social media, knowing she wouldn't be listed under her own name, but unable to think of anything else to do. How did you find a person who'd been officially dead for years, anyway? And why the hell would she place an advert without bothering to leave any contact information? Did she expect us to search endlessly for her? I should sit back and wait for her to come to me, but I couldn't. I was through with waiting, with hiding. I needed to act.

I often wondered if Bertie and Angus had found anything, but I needed to do this on my own. Bertie had said they'd keep in contact, but I didn't want to listen to endless stories and reminiscence; to hear how I shouldn't be angry or hurt. Instead, I sat inert in my cubicle at work, the pile of sound files growing as my mind ticked over and I tried desperately to think of some way to track her down.

Was I mad for thinking she might be alive? After all, we still didn't know for sure if she'd placed that advert. Maybe I was crazy, but I didn't really care. I wasn't sure I could stop myself now, even if I wanted to. It was as if some dam inside me had burst, letting out a never-ending torrent of anger. I was burning with so much emotion that I'd taken to running along the promenade each night in a bid to work off extra energy. The only way I'd fall asleep was if my body was bone-tired, even if my mind was still spinning.

I was heading home from work one night when my mobile rang. I squinted at the digits that popped up, thinking it wasn't a number I recognised. In the past, I would have ignored it and let it go straight to voicemail. But now, any call could be a lead that might point to my mother – or my mother herself – and I wasn't going to let anything slip by me.

'Hello?' My voice was breathless as I climbed the stairs to my flat.

'Hello, is this Ella?' It was a young female voice, and my brow furrowed.

'Yes, it is.' Please may this not be an inane sales call, I thought, opening my door. Dolby streaked towards me, and I set down my bag and scooped her up with one hand.

'Oh, thank God. I've been trying to reach you for a couple of weeks, but that idiot receptionist lost the number you'd given her and it's taken until now for her to find it again. No surprise there, given how organised she is. Or isn't, I should say.'

I shook my head as her voice streamed out. Receptionist? Who the hell was this? 'Who's calling, please?' I asked.

'Oh, sorry. God, I was so excited to finally get in touch that I forgot to tell you who I was, didn't I? I'm Theresa Blake from *The Post*.'

'Hello,' I said slowly, trying to figure out why she might be calling. Had the paper found something out about my mum?

'Listen, I hope you don't mind me ringing you out of the blue. I couldn't help overhearing what you were saying to Greg that day you came into the newsroom. About the advert and how you're looking for the person who placed it – how you think it might be your mother.'

Ah. Something clicked in my mind. So that's who she was – the woman who'd been sitting nearby, the one who'd been rolling her eyes at Greg.

'Have you found her yet? Your mother?' Theresa asked.

'No, not yet,' I answered.

'Oh, good,' she said, and my heart sank that she wasn't about to pass on any leads. 'Sorry, sorry, it's just that it'd make such a great story. It's the kind of thing our readers would snap up. And if you are trying to find someone, this might help! We have national circulation, and we post stories on our Facebook page and other social media. I have a feeling this could go viral.'

'That would be amazing.' I raised my eyebrows, pleased at the stroke of luck. This might be just what I needed – all it'd take was just one person who knew my mum now and I'd be able to track her down.

'Great. I was hoping to get the story into tomorrow's afternoon edition – I've just been told we have the space – but I'll need to interview you now. I know it's short notice, but I have to get this written up quickly.'

'Yes, of course.' I plonked down on the sofa. 'Fire away.'

'Right . . . So, let's start from the beginning.'

I swallowed back the nervousness building inside. This was a stranger. Did I really want to open up about my mother leaving and everything that accompanied it?

Why not? I asked myself. Although I hadn't ever talked about it, growing up here, everyone knew my mother had killed herself. I'd been able to deal with it then, and I could deal with it now. And if my mother was reaching out, then she needed to face her past, too.

I *would* need to tell Carolyn, though. Despite my aunt's many calls, I still hadn't spoken to her. She'd no idea that I'd been to Edinburgh and met Bertie. She didn't know that he thought he'd seen my mother, nor what I'd discovered in London: that my mother might have placed an advert . . . that there was a chance she might still be alive.

I closed my eyes, trying to imagine my aunt's reaction. Would she balk at the thought that her sister might be living, like I had at first? The evidence of my mother's existence now was a little flimsy, but then, so was the evidence of her death. Yet Carolyn had always seemed so steadfast and accepting of my mother's passing, as if she'd been expecting it.

I could just imagine Carolyn telling me in her calm tone that the advert could have been placed by anyone, that the birthday date was just a coincidence, and as for Bertie's sighting . . . well, she'd never trusted Bertie, anyway (I still couldn't figure out why she'd tried to hide those letters, but it didn't really matter now). I was sure she'd be sympathetic to his condition, but that would add even more weight to her explanation.

Maybe she was right. Maybe my mother was dead, and I was going mad. Maybe I was on a wild-goose chase. But for the first time since I could remember, I had *energy*. I felt blood running through my veins; heat in my cheeks. Sure, it was anger – an unhealthy emotion. But it was emotion, and it was pushing me out into the world in a way I never could have expected. If that returned my mother to me, then all the better.

Not to embrace and start over, but so I could tell her exactly what I thought of her.

I told Theresa the basics of my mother's disappearance and the journey I'd taken to find her ever since spotting the advert, including visiting Bertie. No matter why she'd left him, my mother had obviously loved him. She wouldn't have kept that necklace around her neck nor repeated their pledge to me if she hadn't, and it was very possible those words in her advert were meant for him as much as they were for me. Perhaps knowing both of us were looking for her would help bring her forward. I wouldn't have a chance to ask Bertie if he was all right with me mentioning him, but I was sure he wouldn't mind.

'Do you have a photo of this Bertie?' Theresa asked, and I shook my head.

'No, sorry.'

'That's okay,' she said. 'But can you send me a photo of you? Just scan one, if you can. I'll email you through the photo specs we need.'

'Er . . . I'd rather not,' I answered slowly. Talking about my mother's disappearance was one thing, but splashing my face across the country? No, thank you.

'It'll really add to the article. People are always more apt to look at things with photos. It might not be used in the print version, depending on space, but we can definitely use it in the online version.'

'All right.' I shuddered, just thinking about it, but the more people who looked at this article, the better. Anyway, I reminded myself, I was through with hiding.

'Great. Okay, I think I have everything I need. I'd love to talk to Bertie, but I'm not going to have the time. I've got to get going on this now, and I think we have enough material. Just one final question: What would you say to your mother if you saw her again?' Theresa's voice lasered into me and, before I could think about it, the words flew from my mouth.

'I'd ask her why she had to go. Why couldn't she always be here, next to me, like she'd promised? What was so terrible that she left a five-year-old daughter behind? And did she ever think about what that might do to me?' I raised my eyebrows in surprise. That wasn't what I'd say! I'd meant it when I'd told Angus I didn't have any questions. Any answer she could give would make no difference. 'I mean, er—'

'No, that's great, that's perfect.' I could almost see Theresa salivating as she scribbled down the words.

'Right, all done,' she said. 'Can you send me through a photo of your mum, too? Something from around the time she disappeared? Someone out there might just recognise her.'

'Um . . . sure.' My mind whirled. The photos in the box that Carolyn had given me were ancient, but perhaps she had a more recent one at her house. I'd have to make a trip to tell her about the article, anyway. I could grab a picture while I was there.

'Can you send those photos in the next hour?' Theresa asked. 'Sorry, but we're on a tight deadline. If it's a hard copy, just scan it or take a picture with your phone and email it.'

'All right,' I said.

'Great.' I could hear Theresa close her notebook. 'I hope you find her.'

I nodded. 'I do, too.'

I hung up and took a photo of the picture on my work pass, then emailed it to Theresa. It was hardly the most flattering image – I looked like I should be wearing an orange jumpsuit – but other than that, the last time I'd had my picture taken had been my graduation from college.

I pulled on my jacket and headed straight to Carolyn's house, steeling myself against what would be her calm rationale. I didn't want to be calm, and I didn't want to be rational. I wanted to find my mother and expel the anger inside.

I rang the buzzer and Rob opened the door, clad in his robe and slippers.

'Now, don't say a word,' he said, gesturing to his outfit. 'I know it looks like I'm about eighty years old, but I wasn't expecting anyone to pop by. Even Carolyn hates it when I wear this old thing.' I squinted at the worn blue robe, which had long since lost its fuzz, as recognition slid over me. I'd given it to Rob one Father's Day, about . . . it must be fifteen years ago now? My heart squeezed that he was still wearing it.

I followed him into the lounge and sat down on the sofa. With the lamps glowing warmly and the crackling fire, the room was the epitome of a calm oasis, and yet there was no way I could relax.

'Is Carolyn here?' I asked.

'No, she won't be back until tomorrow afternoon,' Rob said. 'She's at a conference for teachers in Canterbury, and she's spending the night there.' He shook his head. 'I hope she doesn't overdo it. She really needs to relax.'

'She's okay, right?' I asked.

'Oh, yes. She'll be fine. Now, what can I do for you?'

I ducked my head. I didn't want to tell all of this to Rob and have him repeat it to Carolyn second hand, and I didn't want to tell her over the phone when she was tired after a long day. Carolyn rarely strayed from the confines of the *Guardian* and she didn't have an account on Facebook, so her chances of seeing the article before I spoke with her were practically nil. I'd drop by tomorrow after work and have a chat, I decided.

'Just looking for a photo of my mother,' I said to Rob now. 'Something from the year or so before she died. The ones I have are much older.' I bit my lip, wondering if he was going to ask why, but thankfully, he remained silent. 'I'll scan it tonight and bring it back tomorrow.'

'No rush.' He hauled himself from the chair. 'If memory serves, there's a photo album here with some pictures of her.' He opened up a cabinet in the corner of the room and handed me the album. 'Have a look.'

I lifted the cover and flipped through the pages, hardening myself against the images inside. My mother had been beautiful even in the terrible adolescent phase . . . something about her just shone, in a way I'd never done. In a way I'd never had the chance to, I thought, staring down at a picture of my mum smiling under a blue sky, next to a blue sea in the background, on the promenade. She looked so happy.

The photos jumped a few years – probably when Mum was living with Bertie – resuming again, this time with me. My heart lurched when I turned the pages of the album to reveal photo after photo of the two of us together: playing in the sand, jumping in the waves, Mum positioning my chubby fingers on a keyboard.

I shook my head as I tried to take in the images, trying to frame each one with the knowledge that she'd left me; that she'd broken those ten words she'd said each night. How could you do that to a child? How could you give birth to them, care for them, nurture them . . . and leave them? The same questions I'd had when talking to Theresa hammered in my mind, and I shook my head to dislodge them.

'Everything okay?' Rob asked, raising his eyebrows.

I grabbed the last picture in the album, a photo of my mother standing on the beach. Her hair was blown straight back and her lips were smiling, but the light had faded from her eyes. Perhaps she'd gone from me before I'd even realised, I thought, staring down at the photo.

I forced a grin at Rob. 'Fine.'

As soon as I found her, it would be again.

CHAPTER TWENTY-NINE

JUDE

April 1982

'That was fantastic.' Frank smiled at Jude as she dropped into a chair at the back of the tiny pub in the middle of nowhere, Scotland. She didn't even know where they were half the time and the 'pub' was barely that: a barn with a bar serving only a few drinks. But she didn't care. They were halfway through their six-week tour run, and she never wanted it to end.

She loved the camaraderie of their group as they squeezed themselves into cramped mini-vans after yet another uncomfortable night sleeping in dingy, noisy rooms above pubs. She loved leaning her head against the side of the van as it twisted its way through the back country, closing her eyes to the faint buzz of the other band members reliving comic moments from last night's performance. She loved pulling up into another small town and unloading their gear under the curious eyes of the residents.

And most of all, she loved singing: performing, night after night, honing her songs and feeling her voice not getting tired, but getting stronger. Mike kept commenting how each night's performance from her was better than the last, while the band she was opening for joked that she was stealing their thunder. They didn't have to worry – they would be the next big thing; they were just that good – but hearing praise from such wonderful musicians who she respected and admired made her heart sing. She'd always been alone in her craft – Frank's encouragement and experience in the industry had helped, but he didn't know much about the technicalities of singing. To be alongside others who understood was a real gift. In fact, she couldn't help thinking that this whole tour was just that: a gift. All too soon, she'd be back to reality.

Not that she didn't miss Bertie, of course. She missed him with every part of her – missed his safe, comforting presence by her side, steadying her when she felt like she was about to float away into the darkness. She missed his smile, and the way he looked at her, so full of love and caring. But touring and taking the first step towards her dream, well . . . she didn't want to be steadied. She wanted to float away and keep going, as far as she could, and she'd take Bertie along with her. In just a few months they'd be married, in the cutest little chapel she'd booked not too far from Bertie's. When Jude closed her eyes, she could just imagine the cave-like interior strewn with wildflowers, sun shining down through the stained-glass windows as dust danced happily in the air.

But all of that still seemed ages away. First, she had the rest of the tour to enjoy. So far, Bertie had been super-supportive, as much as she ever could have dreamed. She'd talk for hours on the phone with him after each performance, babbling on about the band when she knew he was stifling yawns and dying to sleep. He'd ask yet more questions and she'd be off again. He was even taking some time off work to see them perform during their last week in York. He was such a good man that sometimes she couldn't help feeling he was a touch *too* good for her. She'd meant what she'd said to him, though: she would always be with him. They might be miles apart, but something between them just worked.

Opposites attract and all that, Jude thought, accepting a beer from Frank. She'd got to know her brother-in-law even better over the past few weeks and realised that, as full-on and brash as he could sometimes be, underneath the surface he was a little . . . insecure, maybe. Despite desperately trying to impress the band at every location, they didn't seem to notice his efforts and rarely even spoke to him except when they had to, which only made him try harder. It was so embarrassing that Jude usually went to her room while the band set up rather than watch Frank run around like an obedient lapdog who'd be lucky if he got within sight of a lap. It was the same reason she disappeared to her room as soon as the show was over – as well as calling Bertie, of course. The days of workshopping her music and laughing together about punters seemed far away now. She cringed, remembering the night she and the band had been huddled together in the corner of a freezing pub, having a post-show drink. They'd been so busy talking about something that they hadn't even noticed Frank standing behind them. It was only when he'd interrupted to tell the same old story about the man whose trousers had caught on the bar stool that they'd realised he was there. But instead of breaking out in laughter at the tale, the band members simply nodded and went back to their drinks, then started talking to each other again. Jude had gone to pull out a chair for Frank to join them, but he'd already backed away to tinker with a light that didn't need tinkering with. She could tell by the set of his shoulders that he wasn't happy, and she'd sighed. She understood his desire to impress, but he really needed to stop trying so hard.

'Right, I'd better go adjust that speaker,' Frank said now, jumping to his feet, 'before it blows. Up for another drink tonight after the show?'

Jude bit her lip. The band had invited her out for a meal at the fish and chip shop down the one village road. She'd hoped they had asked Frank, too, but apparently not. 'Um, I can't tonight.'

'Right.' He smiled, but it didn't reach his eyes. 'Maybe tomorrow. Catch you later.'

'Later.' Jude watched him go, guilt swirling inside. He was the very reason she was here – if he hadn't got Mike to come to the pub that night, she'd never have been invited on tour. She'd make an effort to hang out with him more, she decided. He was going to be her brother-in-law, after all.

'Jude, good work tonight.' Mike sat down beside her and she smiled over at him. She'd been so nervous around him at first, scared to say the wrong thing to someone who had so many connections in the industry. His professionalism and interest in her music had put her at ease, though, and she was eager to take every opportunity to learn as much as she could.

'I'm really impressed with you,' Mike continued, and Jude felt her cheeks flush. 'If you keep improving like this, I think you could go far.'

Jude couldn't help a huge smile growing on her face. 'Thank you. That's so good to hear.'

'So, look. The band has been invited to play at a festival in Budapest this August, and we'd all like it if you could open for them there, too,' Mike said. 'It'll be a huge step up for you, but I think you're ready.'

'A festival? In Budapest?' Jude couldn't stop the words from tumbling out. 'That sounds amazing!' Only one thought held her back: August? The same month as her wedding? 'Um, do you know when in August?' She felt silly asking – Mike was probably wondering why she hadn't screamed out 'yes!'. 'It's just . . .' Her voice trailed off as she remembered the reason she'd been on this tour in first place was because Mike had originally booked a singer with a husband who didn't want her away for weeks at a time. Bertie wouldn't be like that, but she didn't want to give Mike any reason to doubt her commitment.

'They're playing the evening of the thirteenth. Friday, I think.' Mike laughed. 'Unlucky day, if you believe in all of that.'

Jude managed a grin, despite the knot in her stomach. Friday the thirteenth – the day before her wedding. Unlucky, indeed. How could she be in Budapest the night before and make it back to marry Bertie the very next day? Who took off to play in a music festival on the eve of their wedding, when they should be trying on veils and dreaming of bridal bouquets?

Was it possible to delay the wedding, maybe? They may have booked the church, but apart from that not much else had been done. It wasn't like she'd sent out invitations or anything. What harm would it do to change the date? She bit her lip, picturing Bertie's crestfallen expression. He'd been so looking forward to it – they both had.

'So you're in?' Mike met her eyes. 'If this goes well, it'll open up lots of doors for you, I can guarantee it. I might even be able to get you some gigs of your own.'

Jude gaped at him. Mike might take her on; promote her? How could she turn this down?

'I'm in,' Jude said, her stomach churning with a strange concoction of excitement and guilt. It wasn't like the wedding wouldn't happen, she told herself. It was just that it wouldn't happen on the original date. She'd find a way to explain it to Bertie.

Somehow.

CHAPTER THIRTY

ELLA

When the sun filtered through the blinds on my window and Dolby started her usual meowing and morning calisthenics, I opened my eyes. Later this afternoon, the newspaper article would appear up and down the country. Someone who knew my mother might see it. Today, my *mother* might see it. That sounded so surreal, and the now-familiar anger leaped up again. God, I couldn't wait to tell her what I really thought of her. I knew now that the past would stay within me; that I couldn't hide from it. My mother had left me, and I'd ached for ages. Rejecting her wouldn't change that, but it would feel bloody amazing.

After returning from Rob's last night, I'd debated whether or not to call Bertie and tell him about the article. I had mentioned him, after all, and Bertie would be thrilled. But as much as I wanted to talk to him and Angus, I couldn't bear for them to think I was doing this because I'd forgiven my mother. I couldn't be further from it.

I sat up in bed and looked at my watch: six o'clock. Still hours to kill until the article came out. I went through my usual morning routine, patted Dolby on the head, then stepped out into the cool morning. Fog swirled around me and I hurried along the promenade to the museum.

I was just about to eat my lunch when my phone rang. My brow furrowed when I noticed Rob's mobile number. Like Carolyn, he treated mobiles with the suspicion most people reserved for lawyers.

'Ella,' he said, and his tone was grave. 'I don't want you to worry. Everything's going to be okay. Carolyn had a scare, but—'

My breath caught. 'What do you mean, a scare?' I paused, taking in the background noise. He definitely wasn't at home. 'Where are you?'

'We're at the hospital,' he said, and I froze.

'The hospital?' I jerked back from the desk. 'What happened? Is she okay?'

'You know she's been having problems with her blood pressure,' Rob said. 'Well, she was on her way back from the conference this morning when she had a bit of trouble – some chest pain and trouble breathing.'

'A heart attack?' I could barely catch my breath.

'Yes, according to the ECG,' Rob said, and suddenly I felt weak, like the ground I'd been standing on had caved in. 'They're going to do an operation to insert a stent and let the blood flow better to her heart. She's just about to head into surgery.'

'I'm coming right now,' I said, getting to my feet and shrugging on my coat. 'I'll be there in ten minutes.'

I hurried to Jane's desk and told her why I was leaving, too worried to care who overheard me. What did it matter if my work colleagues knew my aunt was in hospital? Soon, they'd know everything about my history – if they didn't already. I took a deep breath at the thought of the article coming out later today. In the face of Carolyn's surgery, I couldn't muster up the same anticipation . . . or the anger I'd felt earlier.

I grabbed a taxi to the hospital then followed the signs through the labyrinth of corridors to the cardiac unit. A nurse showed me to the waiting area, and I hurried inside. Rob was staring at his phone, looking so out of place in the wooden chair that couldn't be further from his comfy perch at home.

'Hi,' I said in a quiet whisper. Rob gave me a tired smile and stood, and before I knew what I was doing, I put my arms around him. I could feel his surprise, but he hugged me back. His embrace was warm and comforting and, despite my shock, I let myself sink into it for just a second.

'I'm glad you're here,' he said.

'Me, too.' I settled into a chair. 'What exactly happened?' I asked, thinking getting him talking would be a good way to distract him. 'Did she just start having pains out of the blue? Did they call an ambulance straight away?'

Rob met my gaze, and I could see there was something he was debating telling me.

'What is it?' I asked.

'Ella . . . why didn't you tell us you were trying to find your mother?' His voice was soft. 'That you still believe she might be alive?'

My mouth dropped open. 'How did you—' My voice stopped as Rob handed me his phone and I took in the Facebook post titled 'Help Me Find My Mother', accompanied by my dour-looking work photo.

Oh, God.

I hadn't even thought of the possibility that the article might appear on social media before the paper came out. Theresa's mention of social media had barely made a dent, since Carolyn and Rob weren't even on Facebook – well, until now, anyway.

So how the hell had they come across it?

I grabbed the phone and clicked the link. The article popped up on screen, complete with a huge photo of my mother, followed by the one of me. I scanned the text, running my eyes over the familiar detail of how my mum had disappeared when I was only five, how my search had started with the classified advert, how Bertie was looking for her, too, and then . . . My heart twisted as I read the questions I'd told Theresa last night: how I'd ask my mother why she couldn't always be here like she'd promised, and if she'd ever wondered what her leaving might do to me. Printed so starkly in black and white, they seemed drained of their anger and so pathetically plaintive.

'One of the teachers at Carolyn's conference saw the post on Facebook, and she recognised you. Carolyn read the article, and she was a little . . . surprised.'

My heart beat fast as guilt flooded through me. Had she had the heart attack because of this? Because she'd seen the article? I'd thought she'd simply dismiss the notion that her sister could be living, but maybe she hadn't. Finding out my mum might be alive would be a shock – a dangerous one, given her heart condition. Tears filled my eyes as I realised that, in my drive to find my mother, I may have risked losing the woman who'd acted more like a mother to me than my real one ever had.

The woman who'd wanted to give me her heart, if only I could have accepted it.

My chest tightened as I remembered the day Carolyn and Rob had sat me down . . . I must have been about twelve? I could tell by their expressions that this was something serious, and fear had rushed into me. Had something happened to my mum? Were they going to say she was never coming back, after all?

Carolyn had slid into the chair next to me – the same chair she'd sat in to tell me my mother was missing that morning, although I was sure she didn't remember – and said that she and Rob would like very much to adopt me, if I would let them. Not to replace my mother, of course. She realised they could never do that. But to a be a family of our own now.

I'd stared into my aunt's slate-grey eyes, the eyes that were exactly the same colour as my mother's but surrounded by wrinkles my mum had never had. Carolyn squeezed my hand and I looked down, noticing her fingers were laced through mine. I hadn't even realised she was holding my hand, and before I knew what I was doing, I yanked it away.

'My mother's coming back,' I said, the words leaving my mouth in a voice I didn't recognise. 'Mum will be here for me again. I know she will.'

Carolyn darted a glance at Rob, who shook his head and shot her a warning look not to push things. Before either one could say any more, I lunged up the stairs. I don't know why, but for some reason I paused at the top and looked down. Rob was cradling Carolyn in his arms, and I could tell by her heaving shoulders that she was sobbing. I flung myself on to the soft, fresh bed and pulled the duvet over me, wanting to stay hidden there for ever. It would have been so easy to say yes. It would have been so easy to fall into a ready-made dream family unlike anything I'd ever had: a mum, a dad, a perfect house.

But I couldn't let go of Mum. And by the time I had, they'd never brought up adoption again. I'd walled myself off, and Carolyn had backed off, too.

That must have been so hard for my aunt, I realised now. She'd wanted nothing more than a child to raise, and she'd got it. But she hadn't got the part she'd really wanted: my love. I wished I could have reached out to her and let her in. I wished I'd be *able* to.

I waited for the anger to flood through me again, but instead all I felt was sadness. Sadness, and a realisation that, even though

I'd believed my makeshift defences had managed to block the past until I'd come across that advert, they hadn't really. The past had shaped everything I'd done; every decision I'd made. From holding myself back from my family, to my job, to my lack of friends and relationships, the life I was living now was a result of my mother's abandonment. Her leaving had become entwined with me as I'd grown. It had affected me from day one.

Was there anything she could say to explain why she'd left; how she could have done this? For the first time, I wanted to find her not just to get rid of my anger, but to talk to her. Her leaving was a part of me, and although I may not ever be able to forgive her, maybe I could give her a chance to speak so I could start to understand . . . start to understand myself, and how to move forward.

First, though, I needed to be there for my aunt.

'I'm sorry,' I said, meeting Rob's gaze. 'I should have—'

Rob held up a hand. 'It doesn't matter, Ella. The important thing is that you're here. The important thing is that we're together.'

I nodded, feeling for the first time that we really were.

CHAPTER THIRTY-ONE

JUDE

May 1982

Jude couldn't believe the tour was finally over – that she'd sung her final show tonight. The past six weeks had been magical, and this week had topped them all: just a couple of days ago, Bertie had come to York to see them perform their best show ever. She'd introduced him to the band (surprisingly, they'd all got on amazingly well), and he'd sat with Frank as she sang, sweeping her up in his arms with a huge hug when she finished her opening act.

God, she'd missed him, and when she'd waved him off the next afternoon after they'd spent all morning in bed making love, she'd felt like someone had cut off a limb. Being with Bertie had reminded her how much she loved him and how much she belonged with him. Spending time together had been so wonderful that she hadn't wanted to sully it by telling him they'd need to change the wedding date. What was the point, when she'd be home next week?

Better to have that conversation in a familiar environment, with no time constraints, she'd told herself, although she really knew she was putting it off. She couldn't stand imagining Bertie's hurt expression when she told him the reason they'd need to move it: that she was putting her musical career over their wedding. Because even though she wouldn't phrase it that way, that was what it really boiled down to, didn't it? It was selfish and it *would* hurt him, and yet she couldn't say no. She needed to do this.

It was just this once, though. Just this once, and then they'd have all the time in the world to get married. She bit her lip. Wouldn't they? What if they set the date again, and something even bigger came up – a gig, like Mike had said; another tour; another thing she couldn't possibly say no to. What would happen then?

One step at a time, she told herself. God, she was really getting ahead of herself.

A knock on her hotel room interrupted her thoughts, and she ran a brush through her hair. The band had asked her out for a final meal at a posh restaurant downtown that was staying open late just for them. Her stomach rumbled, and she slid a hand down to her belly. God, she was starving.

'Sorry, I just— Oh.' Her voice stopped as she spotted Frank lounging in the doorway, holding a beer.

'Brought you a drink,' he said, holding out a beer towards Jude. He didn't even wait for her to take it before barging into the room and collapsing on the bed. Inwardly, she groaned. The band was probably out front waiting and, to be honest, the last thing she wanted was a drink with Frank. Over the course of the past few weeks she'd tried her best to hang out with him when she could, but his stories that used to make her laugh bordered more now on nasty than funny. More than often, he was cracking 'jokes' at the band's expense, and she didn't want to laugh at her friends.

'That's really kind,' she said, still standing at the door. 'But I have to get going.'

'Yeah?' Frank said, slurping her beer. 'Where?'

'Um, just—'

Frank laughed, but he didn't sound happy. 'Don't worry. I know you're all off for a meal. Well, all but me. Doesn't matter, I didn't want to go anyway. Stuck-up bunch of tossers.' His tone was so bitter it was almost unrecognisable. Frank's comments might be caustic at times, but he'd never sounded like this before.

Jude smiled awkwardly.

'You can stay for a quick drink with me, right?'

Jude sighed, reminding herself that he'd got her this tour. 'I suppose so. Just a quick one, though.' She sank down on the bed beside him, the only place in the small room to sit. The space was silent except for the buzz of the bar below them. The more Frank drank, the more bitter he became, spewing venom against the band, Mike, and anyone else who'd ever dared cross him. Jude shrank away from him, thinking if she'd known he would be like this – that he *could* be like this – she'd never have agreed to stay.

'My brother's a lucky guy,' Frank said, and Jude tensed. She could take a lot from Frank, but she couldn't take him slagging off Bertie. 'Always has been. Got the good job, the house, the girl . . . I've got shit.'

'You've got him,' Jude said. 'You know he'll help you if you need it. And when this job is over, I'm sure you'll find something.' She looked at her watch, then out the window, where she could see the band gathered in the car park, waiting. 'I'm really sorry, but I've got to get going.' She debated inviting him along for a second, but in his current state, he'd be more likely to offend than endear himself.

'Well, okay then,' she said awkwardly, when Frank didn't budge from the bed. 'Hope you have a good night.'

Frank put a hand on her thigh, and Jude stared down at it in surprise. What the hell? He was drunk, but not that drunk. Was he?

'Frank!' She decided to laugh it off, like his hand had just ended up there and he hadn't any control over it.

But he didn't move. She tried to get up from the bed, but he took her arm, locking her beside him. A quiver of fear went through her, but she refused to acknowledge it. This was her brother-in-law. Bertie's family – almost her family. He wouldn't do anything to hurt her. If Bertie could be sure of it, then she could be, too.

But when she tried to get to her feet again, he tightened his grip and the fear ballooned, her heart beating fast.

'Frank? Frank, I need to get going now.' She tried again to pull away, but he held her fast. 'Frank, let me go!' Her voice rose in pitch and Frank put a hand over her mouth, stopping her cries. His hand reeked of tobacco and booze and, for a second, she thought she was going to be sick. But she couldn't – she had to use every inch to fight what he was doing now, thrashing and kicking as he pushed her down on the too-soft mattress, using his weight to trap her as he wriggled her jeans over her hips and yanked his own down.

She couldn't believe this was happening – she couldn't let this happen – and yet it was, as the sharp, scraping pain of him forcing himself inside of her, as the squeaking bedsprings protested his movements, as he finally collapsed on top of her, his hand falling away from her mouth.

She had nothing to say now, anyway. Nothing as he pulled out of her and rolled over. She barely saw him. She barely moved.

'If you say anything to Bertie about this,' he said, 'then I'll tell him you wanted it. I'll tell him we were screwing all those nights back at his house, and all through the tour, too. And he'll believe me, you know he will. I'm his brother, and you're nothing but an amateur pub singer. I'll tell him you screwed me so you could get the pub gig, and that's how you got this tour, too. By screwing.'

Frank sniggered, sitting up. 'That's why Mike booked you, you know. Because he thought you might be an easy lay, not because you can sing.' Then the weight of his body lifted off the bed, and she heard him cross the room. The door slammed, and she raised a hand to her necklace, her fist closing around the heart pendant as if it was the only thing that could save her body from rotting, disintegrating slowly into the mattress and fading away.

I am always with you. I will always be here.

CHAPTER THIRTY-TWO

ELLA

I struggled to wake up the next morning. I'd barely slept, but not because I was thinking about my mother . . . because I was thinking about my aunt. She'd come through the operation all right, thank God, but she'd been so groggy that she'd barely been able to open her eyes before sinking back into sleep. I'd stayed at the hospital until Rob had told me in no uncertain terms to go home – he was going to be kicked out soon, anyway – and so I'd hugged him again then climbed into a cab.

Back at my flat, I'd crawled into bed and turned off the light, lying in the dark as my thoughts swirled. All across the country, my newspaper story was being read by thousands of people. Yet I felt so distant from it, as if it was happening to someone else. I hadn't even seen a copy of it. I still wanted to find my mother, of course. I still wanted to hear from her why she'd left. But right now, what was important – what really mattered – was my aunt, the woman who had stepped in to pick me up when the bottom had fallen out of my world.

The woman I'd never let in.

I dragged myself from bed and left another message on Jane's voicemail at work, telling her that I wouldn't be in the office again today. Then, I took a cab to the hospital, retracing my steps from the night before. My aunt had been moved on to the ward, and Rob was already at her side. She looked so pale and small in the bed, and my heart flipped. *Please may she be all right.*

'Hi,' I said in a whisper. Rob glanced up, then stood to hug me.

'The nurse told me that she had a good night,' he whispered, relief evident on his face. 'She woke up for a bit about an hour ago. She'll probably be awake again before long.'

I nodded, my gaze sliding back to her face as guilt poured through me. Rob and I spent the next hour or so looking at our phones, commenting on the weather and staring into space, time crawling by at a pace slower than I'd ever known. Finally, my aunt stirred and opened her eyes.

'Oh! Ella, you're here. I must have nodded off.'

I smiled, wondering how she could go from sound asleep to one hundred per cent alert in one second. My aunt was just like that: completely present, giving every minute her all. My stomach twisted at the thought of how she'd given me everything she could, despite me turning away.

'I'll go grab some coffee,' Rob said, getting to his feet. 'Give you two a chance to talk.'

I nodded, barely registering his words. All I could focus on was my aunt.

'Aunt Carolyn . . .' I sat down in Rob's chair and put a hand on her arm. Even under the sheet, it still felt cold. 'I'm so sorry you saw that article before I had the chance to talk to you. I know it must have been a shock.'

Carolyn met my eyes. 'Yes, it was, and I do wish you'd spoken to me first. I knew you'd been thinking of your mother lately, but I never once thought that, after all these years, you hoped she might still be alive.'

I swallowed. 'I know it might seem far-fetched, but there *is* a chance. There was an advert, and—'

'Ella.' Carolyn's soft voice interrupted me, and I waited for her to launch into her rationale that the advert could have been placed by anyone. She was so certain my mother was dead that I wouldn't have expected anything different.

'I put the advert in the paper, Ella.' She squeezed my hand, and my mouth fell open. *Carolyn* had placed the advert?

'The classified advert?' I asked, unable to believe we were talking about the same thing. 'The one with the ten words? *I am always* . . .' I swallowed, unable to complete the sentence.

She nodded, her eyes holding mine. 'I'm sorry it made you think your mother might still be here. I never in a million years thought you might see it. And even if you did, I'd never have imagined you might believe it was your mother. I didn't realise . . .' She swallowed. 'Didn't realise you still hoped.'

I dropped my gaze, feeling my cheeks colour. *Had* I still hoped? Was that why the advert had slipped through my defences? Was that why Carolyn had placed it, too? Did she think my mother might be out there? It was hard to believe, given how sure she'd always seemed.

I lifted my head. 'But . . . why? Why would you put an advert in the paper?'

Carolyn sighed. 'I've placed one every year since Jude died. It's a way to remember her, I guess. A way to keep her alive in my mind – to say sorry that I couldn't help her. I suppose I could have done it all over the phone, but by going to London I felt like I was fulfilling a dream she'd always had, walking the streets she'd wanted to. The advert was meant only for me and her memory, and that's why I never left a name. I didn't need to.'

I glanced down at our clasped hands as emotions tumbled through me. I'd been so angry at the possibility my mother had

177

left me to live her own life then dared to come back into mine, but she hadn't. My mother was dead. Bertie may have thought he saw her, but given his memory . . .

The same sadness I'd felt last night flowed into me once again, banishing the last lingering flames of fury. The advert that had started me out on this path, well . . . all of this could have been avoided if I'd just talked to Carolyn about it. But I couldn't, because I'd been so afraid to let her in; to be vulnerable. Funny how the journey I'd taken had smashed down those walls now, leaving me more exposed than ever.

'The article mentions someone called Bertie.' Carolyn's voice cut into my thoughts, and I met her eyes. Her face was pinched, and worry shot through me. 'Please tell me you didn't talk to him. I know you had those letters, but . . . Did you speak with him? Did you get in touch?' Her face went even paler, and I shifted in my chair.

'Are you okay? Shall I get the doctor?'

Carolyn shook her head and held up a hand. 'No, no. I'm fine.' Her tone was sharper than I'd ever heard before. 'But please, just tell me. I need to know.'

I drew back, surprised at her urgency. I knew she wasn't happy Bertie had lived with my mum, but surely he didn't warrant this alarm. Maybe if I told her that I'd met him and there was nothing to worry about, she'd relax.

'I did go up to see him,' I said, trying to get it all out quickly so she didn't need to worry any longer than necessary. 'And, Carolyn, he's such a gentleman. He wouldn't hurt anyone. He—' I broke off as Carolyn clenched my hand so strongly it hurt.

'Ella.' Carolyn's gaze was so intense that I couldn't move. 'Promise me. Promise me you'll never see or talk to him again. Please.'

'Okay, sure, but Carolyn, you really don't need to worry. He's absolutely harmless. You know, he's been looking for Mum all these years? He really loved her. He thinks he saw her in London a few years ago, and he's convinced she couldn't have killed herself.'

Carolyn shifted in the bed, still gripping my hand. 'He of all people should know your mother won't be coming back. He of all people should know why she died.'

I sucked in my breath. He of all people should know why she died. Had Bertie been involved in my mother's death? How, if they'd had no contact since she'd left him?

No. It wasn't possible. Bertie was . . . Well, he was *Bertie*.

'Ella . . .' Carolyn's stare lasered into me. 'Bertie's not harmless. He's . . .' She paused. 'You have to understand that I never wanted to tell you this. 'I never would have told you this, if it wasn't for that article. But I failed to keep your mother safe, and I won't fail with you.'

'Okay,' I said slowly, wondering what on earth she was going to tell me.

'Your father didn't die,' Carolyn said, and my heart stopped.

'What do you mean?' I could barely get out the words. 'Why did my mother tell me that, then? Why did *you* tell me that?'

'She wanted to protect you,' Carolyn said. 'The same way I want to protect you.'

'Protect me? From what?' Our eyes stayed locked, and every bit of me was focused on her. 'From *Bertie*?' My heart was beating so quickly now that I felt light-headed. What on earth had he done?

'When your mother first told me she was pregnant, I wanted to throttle her,' Carolyn said, her face tightening at the memory. 'She had so much ahead of her – she was so talented, and she'd barely started living.'

An alarm in the next bay went off, but Carolyn barely noticed. I felt like my senses were hyper-aware, as if everything had gone into overdrive.

'She stayed with me and Rob during her pregnancy,' Carolyn continued, 'and we tried everything to help her; to do what we could. She never talked about your father, so we never asked. Jude was like you: the more you pushed for answers, the further she'd retreat.'

I felt something brewing inside of me, like a storm approaching. The tension pushed against my lungs, making it difficult to breathe. I wanted to move away, but I couldn't. I had to hear, in crystal clarity, what she was about to say. Was I finally going to learn the truth about my mother's death?

'But when she was sleeping . . . It was awful. She'd have nightmares every night, crying and screaming. Calling out for Bertie and asking him to stop. To please stop, to get off of her, to leave her alone.' Carolyn winced saying the words, and my eyes widened in disbelief. Bertie? Gentle, friendly Bertie, who'd loved my mother so much?

No. Carolyn had to be wrong. They'd had a relationship – a *loving* relationship. I'd seen his letters. I knew it was true.

'After a few weeks, I tried to talk to her about it,' Carolyn said. 'But she wouldn't. All she did was ask me to keep Bertie away from her – to make sure he never contacted her. She'd left him, you see. As soon as she found out she was pregnant with you, she knew she had to go to a safe place.'

I stared at my aunt, trying to take in her words. 'Bertie is my father?' My voice was shaky and incredulous.

Carolyn nodded. 'Your mum didn't list him on your birth certificate so he wouldn't have any claim to you, and we agreed we'd say he had died before you were born. We didn't want to risk you getting in touch with him. He *did* try to find your mother at one point. It was the summer after you were born – you must have been four or five months old, I guess. I was leaving the house one day, and there he was. I don't know how he found out where I lived. I suppose he asked around . . . lots of people knew me, of course, since I'd been teaching at the school. He rang the bell and waited for ages, but eventually he left.'

She shook her head. 'He kept writing for years, though. Letter after letter, all addressed to your mother at my house, hoping, I'd guess, that I'd pass them on. I don't think he ever knew your mum was staying with me, thank goodness.'

I sat there, the layers of knowledge piling up on top of me. My mother had been in an abusive relationship. An abusive relationship with *Bertie*. Had Bertie pretended he didn't remember what had happened – that he'd been violent? Had he forgotten, due to his Alzheimer's? He'd remembered lots of other things, though. It seemed a little too convenient to just block that bit out.

'Ella?' Carolyn reached for my hand again. 'You won't talk to that man, not now that you know what happened, right? Your mother would want me to make sure of that. I *have* to make sure of that.'

I wanted to nod, but I couldn't. I couldn't even move as my mind whirled. I had a father – a father who was alive; a father whom I'd met.

A father who'd never even known I existed, and who my mother had fled from the moment she'd discovered her pregnancy.

I drew in a breath. It was just so hard to believe that Bertie abused my mother. I could barely fit 'Bertie' and 'abuse' together in the same sentence. I knew people changed, but I struggled to picture the man I'd met being anything but loving. If he had hurt her, why would she hang on to his necklace? Why would she promise it to me when I grew up? Why would she say those same ten words – the promise they'd exchanged – over and over to me?

But then . . . why would she run from him so suddenly, blanking all contact, if she'd loved him so much? Why would she not even list him on my birth certificate, telling me that he was dead?

Why would she abandon me, ending her life in the sea?

Perhaps Bertie was a different person now. Perhaps he really didn't remember any of what had happened; of what he'd done. Soon, everything – including my mother – would be erased from his mind. I'd never be able to trust his words . . . trust *him*. He might be my father by blood, but I'd never know him. He'd never truly be my family.

Family. I glanced down at my aunt's hand. My mother was gone. I may never understand why she'd left me, but I realised now that she *had* loved me – enough to have me under horrific circumstances, and enough to try to protect me. The pain of the past would always be there, but I didn't want to return to using it as my shield any longer. I wanted to let in the people who'd loved me . . . who loved me now, despite the years of me pushing them away.

I wanted to finally have a family.

I smiled at my aunt and gripped her hand, and only ten words came to mind.

'I am always with you,' I said. 'I will always be here.'

CHAPTER THIRTY-THREE

JUDE

July 1982

'Okay, I'm off!' Bertie dropped a kiss on Jude's lips. She tried to smile up at him from her place on the sofa. She tossed and turned every night now, unable to close her eyes without Frank's face filling her mind's eye. She'd been back from the tour for over two months, and she kept waiting for the day it would get easier – the day the horror, shock and disbelief of what had happened would fade.

But it hadn't. If anything, it was getting worse, like a rotten limb swelling and blackening over time, tainting the room with its smell. Tainting everything, even this wonderful life she had with Bertie.

God knows she'd tried to put it behind her; to block it out and focus on the present. After Frank had left her room that evening, she'd showered, crawled back into her clothes again, and grabbed a cab to the restaurant in York. She'd smiled and laughed, even with the dull ache between her legs, refusing to believe Frank had done what he did. Refusing to let it enter her mind; her consciousness. All she had to do was get back to Edinburgh the next day to where Bertie was waiting, and she would be safe.

Thankfully, by the time breakfast rolled around, Frank was nowhere to be seen. Mike said he'd taken off to Spain, where he'd lined up a job at a hotel as their entertainment manager. He'd never said a word of it to Jude and she couldn't have been more grateful. Frank would be out of her life for the foreseeable future, and she wouldn't think of that terrible night again.

Easier said than done, though, because the more she tried not to think of it, the more it clawed at her brain, demanding to be let in. Those five minutes – if it had been even that – were affecting her every hour, laying siege to her soul and battering every defensive move in her arsenal. She'd been so relieved to see Bertie that she'd thrown herself into his arms when she'd returned, tears streaming down her cheeks. But that was all she could do. Any time he tried to do more than pull her close, her heart started thudding and she had to move away, as if, by making love, he'd know she'd been attacked.

He'd know something was really wrong.

Of course, he already knew there was something wrong. Since she'd come home, she hadn't sung. She hadn't even tried to sing or write music. She hadn't spoken to anyone on the phone, not the pub managers who tried to book her nor the band members who rang to invite her out. She hadn't talked to Mike, either, despite his many messages. He'd probably found someone else to take her place at the festival by now.

A bitter taste filled her mouth. *The festival.* As if she could go onstage and sing in front of hundreds of people. She wasn't talented; she wasn't special . . . not like Frank had led her to believe. He'd only wanted one thing, and the second he'd got it, he'd told her the truth: she was an amateur who might be an easy lay, a dime a dozen. And Mike, well . . . maybe Frank had been lying, but maybe he hadn't. Either way, she'd never be able to trust Mike now. She'd never be able to trust *herself*. Any song inside her had been snuffed out.

She'd told herself to focus on the wedding instead; that at least she still had Bertie. Never in a million years would she attempt to tell him what had happened. She was certain he'd believe her . . . and then she'd recall Frank's threat of telling Bertie they'd been together all those nights at home and during the tour. She'd remember the times she and Frank had been laughing together; of how Bertie might have overheard Frank saying she was delaying the wedding, and a seed of doubt would form. She might be Bertie's fiancée, but he had only known her a short time. Frank was his brother – the brother he still felt responsible for. He'd rescued Frank from scrapes for years. Would he be able to see her as anything other than yet another problem to free his brother from? Who would his loyalty be stronger to?

She couldn't risk the possibility that he might believe Frank over her. She didn't think she could survive that.

So she'd thrown herself into wedding preparations, thankful that Bertie had agreed to have a very small wedding with just the two of them. Jude forced herself to try on wedding gowns, forcing down the bile that pushed at her throat. She tried her best to care about the flowers, the decorations, the shoes she'd wear, the honeymoon . . . but all she felt was numbness, as if a dummy was getting married and not a real, live person – a person who was able to love, to *feel*. Despite Bertie's endless questions about how things were coming along, she'd barely been able to talk to him at all. The silence that had once been so comfortable, curling around them in their little cocoon, now separated them like a cold, icy wall.

'Are you all right?' Bertie was staring at her like she was a toy that needed winding again. He'd asked her a million times since she'd come home if she was okay, if he could do anything, if she was feeling ill . . . She'd latched on to that, saying she was a little under the weather after the tour but she'd be all right. She just needed time to lie low and recover.

At least she hoped – she *prayed* – that was all she needed. And it was true that she wasn't feeling well, apart from what was happening inside her head. Her body seemed to be protesting, too, dragged down with fatigue and fog. Her stomach on fire every time she tried to eat. Even Bertie's special pancakes couldn't tempt her.

When her period hadn't appeared, she'd told herself it was the stress of the tour and the upset of what had happened that had thrown her off. She'd taken her birth control pills, as usual . . . although she'd forgotten that one night when they'd all got a bit (okay, a lot) drunk after a gig that truly was in the middle of nowhere. But one pill didn't matter, right?

Except maybe it did.

She begged any existing higher power that, this month of all months, she would be okay. The universe couldn't be cruel enough to make her fall pregnant now, after what had happened . . . when she wouldn't even know who or what life the baby belonged to: the love of her life, in a romantic idyll with Bertie; or a short, vicious attack by a man she now loathed. Would she love the baby and cherish it with all her might, or dread looking at its sweet face because of the horrific memories it invoked? This pregnancy would be a nightmare – an escalation of the nightmare she was already living; a nightmare where she couldn't even find her voice, let alone carry a melody. That was the reality of it, and she could only hope she'd managed to escape without bringing a baby into it.

She'd brought a urine sample to the doctor Bertie had helped her register with when she'd first moved up here but had never had to see until now. She'd told herself it was only to rule out the possibility, so she wouldn't need to worry about it any more. It was the only way of staying calm – the only way to keep the scream that had been building inside of her from escaping.

That had been a few days ago, and although the doctor had offered to call as soon as he had the results, she'd shaken her head. She couldn't take the chance of Bertie picking up the phone; of the questioning look on his face. She wasn't going to lie to him. She couldn't lie to him. He was the only clean, perfect thing left in her life.

Today, she would go back to the doctor for the results. Today, she would find out if there was a child growing inside of her . . . a baby she wouldn't know whether to love or loathe.

Jude waited a few minutes until she was sure that Bertie was on the bus to work, then pulled herself up off the sofa. She hadn't been outside of the house since her trip to the doctor a couple of days ago, and her muscles felt cramped and achy from the lack of movement. She heaved her body up the stairs and into the bedroom, feeling it was a weight to drag around rather than flesh, bones and muscles that buzzed with energy, like they used to. She wished she could just slough off this body now and float, free, away somewhere.

She had a quick shower, screwed her hair back into a ponytail, then pulled on jeans and a T-shirt. Then she went back downstairs and shoved on her shoes, grabbed a coat and went out into the fresh morning. The sun hurt her eyes after being inside for so long, and she hurried her legs forward, moving faster and faster until her muscles strained and her lungs burned. She kept going, wanting the pain to blot out everything else, to stop her brain from swirling through the different scenarios.

Finally, after a torturous half-hour wait, the doctor called her into his office. She settled into her chair and trained her eyes on him, focusing only on his face and not on the words he might say. It was all she could do to stop from running out.

'Well.' The doctor put on his specs and opened her file, then looked up at her.

Jude breathed in. Then out. Then in.

'You are pregnant,' he said, and her breath stopped.

Her life stopped, and she knew straight away there was no point trying to breathe again.

CHAPTER THIRTY-FOUR

JUDE

July 1982

Jude hurriedly packed her jeans, the thin summer dresses she'd never got a chance to wear, and as many of her T-shirts and jumpers as she could fit inside her bag. She eyed the selection of colourful dresses she usually wore on stage, running her fingers over the crushed purple velvet of her favourite one. Was there any point even packing this? She already knew she wouldn't sing again. The music had dried up inside of her, a cracked, barren landscape that had once been lush with notes and melodies.

She turned from the wardrobe, her mind flitting back to when she'd first packed to leave Hastings and come here. It had only been two years, but it felt like a lifetime ago. Back then, she'd been full of love and hope for the future – with a man she knew better than anyone, despite only having him in her life for a short time. Looking back, the move here seemed rash even to her, but her heart had been right: she and Bertie were wonderful together.

Jude paused, tears coming to her eyes. *Had* been wonderful together. She'd felt safer than ever before. Coming here had made her see what life with a person you love could really be like. But that hadn't been enough for her, had it? she thought angrily, swiping at her cheek as tears spilled down them. She'd wanted more, and look where that had got her. If only she'd just stayed with Bertie, then they could have been happy for ever.

But that wasn't going to happen now, she thought, getting to her feet and staring out of the window, the rush of the river meeting her ears. That couldn't happen . . . not now, not with this baby inside of her. She'd left the doctor yesterday and made her way slowly home, every step like a funeral march. She'd known as soon as the doctor said those words that she couldn't stay with Bertie; couldn't be in his life. How could she, knowing the baby inside of her might possibly be his, but could also be his brother's? She'd made love with Bertie just two days before Frank had—

She pushed away the thought. Bertie must never know about the attack. Even if he did believe her, well . . . Bertie knowing what had happened would shatter them; would break their perfection into a million sharp pieces neither one of them could walk over without bloodying their feet. Bertie would never be able to forgive Frank, and he'd look at her exactly how she didn't want to be seen – exactly how she'd been looked at for years after the death of her parents: as someone to be pitied, as someone who was damaged. They would never be able to move forward from that.

And then the baby . . . this baby, whose father was either the best thing or the worst thing to have happened to her . . . She couldn't stay here, watching Bertie be its father while desperately praying it might actually be so. And she couldn't get rid of it, for even if she wasn't ready – not in a million years – this baby might be the only legacy of her love for Bertie, a light in the dark. She had to believe that. She *would* believe that.

And so she was doing the only thing she could: she was leaving. There would be no wedding. There couldn't be. Bertie would be upset – okay, more than upset – but less than if she told him the truth, that much she knew for sure. She grabbed the pad and pencil that he kept by the phone in the bedroom and bit her lip, her throat tightening when she pictured him returning from work with an eager smile on his face as he climbed the stairs, expecting to find her napping under the cosy quilt. Instead, the bedroom would be empty; the house silent and still.

She zipped her bag closed before the pain engulfed her. She had to keep moving. It was the only way not to let the pain catch her and press down on her. She scrawled a few words that she couldn't do this any more and that she was leaving. Bertie shouldn't try to find her, and she wouldn't be back. She left the note unsigned on the centre of the bed – the bed where she'd first realised what it meant to love; the bed where she'd understood what it was like to be safe. But nothing could keep her safe, not even the man she loved. She knew that now.

She swallowed and tried to lift the necklace from her neck, but she couldn't: every part of her resisted. Her fingers closed around the heavy heart, and she thought of the message inside of it, the words that had only left her lips for two people: her mother and Bertie. Her mother was gone, but she was still in Jude's soul. And even though Jude may be gone from Bertie's life, he would always be a part of her – someone who had shown her how to love, as corny as that sounded.

She wasn't breaking the pledge, she told herself. She couldn't be with him now, but she'd always carry him in her heart. This necklace would come with her, a symbol of her love.

So, it was back to Hastings. She'd move in with Carolyn and try to figure out what to do next. She screwed up her face, just imagining Carolyn's reaction when she turned up at the door, 'I told you so' written all over her smug features.

The thing was, Carolyn was wrong – she couldn't be further from wrong. She and Bertie had been so good together, until . . .

Jude grabbed her bag and swung down the spiral stairs, lifted her coat from its peg, and closed the door behind her. She couldn't stop. She couldn't pause for one second to look backwards, because she'd collapse if she did. Besides the baby inside of her, she was only taking one thing; one token to sustain her through the dark days she knew were ahead.

She touched the chain around her neck and turned away.

CHAPTER THIRTY-FIVE

Ella

I spent the next few days tracing a path from home, to work, to the hospital and home again. Aunt Carolyn was recovering from the operation and would be discharged soon, thank goodness. Sitting by her bed – without her jumping up and buzzing around like usual – made me realise that, until now, we'd hardly ever talked. Much of that had been my fault, of course, and there had always been something for her to do. Rarely had she sat still for longer than a minute. Now, we had hours.

At first, the silence between us had seemed a little awkward, but gradually she'd started talking about my grandmother, what it had been like growing up with my mum, and their childhood together. Before, I would have shut my ears and changed the subject, but now I didn't mind. I wanted to see my mother as a person, not just a woman who'd left her child. Now that I could understand what had driven her from me, I was open to really knowing her.

I supposed I could be angry at my aunt for withholding who my father was all these years; for keeping up the lie my mother first told me. But how could I? She'd been protecting me, the same way I'd been protecting myself all these years, trying to stop anyone or anything from reaching me. My mother's death would always leave a mark on my heart, but it didn't have to be all scar tissue. Underneath, there was a part that was still tender . . . a part of me that was now uncovered, ready to reach out to people once again.

Angus's face flitted into my mind, and I winced as I remembered hanging up on him during our last conversation. Despite the short time we'd spent together, there *had* been a connection between us – a kind of mutual understanding, so rare for me to experience with anyone . . . as well as some chemistry, maybe? I'd been so anxious to protect myself that I'd abruptly cut off anything to do with him. I'd half-expected him to ring after having spotted a social media post about the newspaper article, but the phone had stayed silent. And I couldn't get in touch now, not after what Aunt Carolyn had said about Bertie. Angus believed Bertie was a good, kind man who'd helped him when he'd needed it most. Would he ever believe what my aunt had told me?

Did I?

I shook my head, still unsure what to think; still unable to believe I actually *had* a father. For so long, he'd only been a blank face in my mind, a figure I'd barely even stopped to wonder about. Now the features had been filled in, along with other horrific details that still made me shudder when I thought of them. So much didn't make sense to me about that story, but I couldn't let my uncertainty shut me down again. I had to accept I'd never know the truth in order to move forward – not away from the past, but at peace with it.

Getting to know my family was helping with that. It wasn't just Aunt Carolyn I was forming a new relationship with. Rob and I would often leave the hospital together, stopping at the local Harvester on the way home for a bite to eat. Without my aunt to fill the void like usual, I spoke to Rob more than I ever had before. He'd always been a background fixture in the house but, now, his warm and funny presence shone. He could crack a joke about

194

anything, and the loving way he spoke about my aunt . . . I swallowed. Maybe one day, I'd have someone like that in my life, too.

Now, though, I wanted to make the most out of what I had – out of the life that had always been mine to grasp, if only I'd been able.

A few days after Aunt Carolyn's operation I went into work, early, as usual. But instead of jamming on my headphones, this time I kept them off, listening for Jane's arrival. I hoped it wasn't too late, because I wanted to tell her that I was itching to spearhead the exhibition. And even if it was too late, I had loads of great ideas I wanted to share. Finally, after what felt like forever, I heard her voice.

'Jane!' I popped my head up, and her eyebrows rose.

'Ella, hi. How's your aunt getting on?'

'Good, thanks.' Relief filtered through me that Aunt Carolyn would make a full recovery. 'Listen, I wondered if I might be able to get involved with the exhibition after all?'

Jane grinned. 'Of course! And thank God, I might say. We've been struggling here to come up with anything worthwhile, apart from the usual. It'll be great to have you on board.'

I'd nodded and smiled, then spent the next few days in a whirlwind of meetings with Marketing, Public Relations and my other colleagues in the musical archives. It was amazing how friendly and enthusiastic everyone was, and I had a feeling we were really going to pull together something special. I was enjoying talking with other people who shared my vision and who wanted to make this exhibit as exceptional as I did. We were even planning a trip to the British Museum in the next few weeks.

The past would never be completely behind me. But whatever had happened, I was here, fully present and ready to embrace the future.

To live.

CHAPTER THIRTY-SIX

JUDE

April 1988

Jude faced the sea and drew in a breath. This was it: soon she'd be under the waves, floating weightless in the brine . . . free. She shrugged off her cardigan and kicked off her shoes, wincing as the stones bit into her soles. The effects of the whisky she'd swallowed earlier had vanished and every sense was heightened now, as if her body knew what her mind was planning to do and was living every last second to the fullest.

She waded into the water, wincing again as the cold sea made her toes and ankles ache. An image of Ella sound asleep in her warm bed jerked into Jude's mind, and pain slashed through her. She loved her daughter, of course she did. But she couldn't— She swallowed. As long as she was Ella's mother, she would never be free of him; of what had happened. After six long years, she knew that now, and finally, she accepted it. She took another step forward, stumbling over the rocks underfoot.

'Hey!' A voice behind her made her turn. An older man was staring at her, his dog straining at the lead. 'All right?' The man's eyes were worried, and irritation flitted over her. *Shit.* The last thing she needed right now was a good Samaritan.

'Perfect, actually.' She used every bit of remaining energy to force a bright smile. 'Just wanted to see what the water was like this time of year.'

'Bloody freezing.' The man shivered. 'Right, come on then, Duke.' He gave her a smile and turned to go.

Jude waited until he was gone, then scanned the horizon. Thankfully, for the time being, the dog walkers and joggers were nowhere to be seen. She walked further into the sea, her feet and ankles now numb. This was exactly what she wanted. Numbness. To feel nothing. Not the tug of war between love and loathing; not guilt, and not sadness.

Not fear, and not regret.

Another step. She was up to her knees now. Just a few more and the water would close over her. Just a few more and she would be gone.

Her fingers reached up, automatically closing around the heart pendant hanging from her neck. This pendant with those ten little words had been her saviour when she couldn't carry on, when the darkness and anger swirled around her so strongly, trying to carry her off. She'd clutched on to it, drawing strength from the vow and strength from the love, willing it to anchor her down. She'd even said those same ten words to Ella, feverishly hoping the goodness in them would blot out the bad.

But it didn't, of course. Nothing could erase what had happened to her. Nothing could blot out the life she'd been forced to live . . . not even love.

Jude took another step forward, the water now up to her chest, the pendant shimmering under the surface. She stepped back, jerking the gold heart away from the water's reach and cursing at herself. It was stupid, but she couldn't do this with the chain around her neck. This necklace represented all that was good, and she wouldn't let this darkness claim that, too. She screwed her eyes shut, trying to force away the image of water seeping into the message inside, the ink running and the paper dissolving.

She'd leave the necklace on the beach – leave a piece of what had been the happiest time of her life behind. She'd promised the pendant to Ella, anyway. Maybe her daughter would have something good to remember her by, after all.

Jude clambered from the water and on to the rocks again, shivering as the air whipped around her body. She lifted her hair and pulled the chain over her head, grimacing as it caught on wet strands. She tugged again, but a lock of hair had become trapped in the links of the necklace. She pulled and she yanked, but short of tearing a chunk from her scalp, she couldn't free herself from it.

She let out a cry and sank to the stones. What was she going to do? As ridiculous as it was, she couldn't take this necklace where she really wanted to go. Yet she couldn't go home, either. She couldn't go back to Ella; back to being a mother. Not only would she damage herself, but she'd damage her daughter, too.

She stood, and without knowing where she was heading, she let her feet carry her across the promenade and up the hill. The town was deserted so early on a Sunday morning, and even those who were out barely glanced her way. She knew how she must look, clad only in a T-shirt and jeans and wandering the streets barefoot.

Druggie out for a fix, she could see scuttering through their minds, their lips curled in disdain before their gaze slid away from her. She wasn't a druggie, but she was out for a fix – for something to make her feel less broken. She kept walking until she reached the train station.

Her feet carried her forwards, on to the platform. A train swooped into the station, screeching to a halt. The departures board said it was going to London, and she stepped on board in a daze. She didn't have a ticket. She didn't have cash. But perhaps she could make it that far without running into the ticket inspector.

Maybe London would be an escape, after all, she thought, a mad laugh floating out of her. It wouldn't be a dream, though, that much she was sure of. More like a nightmare.

The dead couldn't dream, anyway, she told herself. Because even if she hadn't walked into the sea, the person she'd been was gone.

And that was exactly what she wanted.

CHAPTER THIRTY-SEVEN

JUDE

September 2018

Jude sat in a patch of sun that fell across the futon in her dingy bedsit. If she closed her eyes, she could almost believe she was lying on a warm, sandy beach, the constant traffic whooshing by her window mimicking the sound of waves. Even after thirty years of living in London, she'd never quite got used to opening the soot-stained blind of her bedroom to reveal row after row of slate-grey rooftops and satellite dishes rather than the sea stretching out before her like an escape.

London *had* been her escape, although not through singing, like she'd dreamed when she was young. After holing up in a women's hostel and starting to make some money giving piano lessons, she'd made a life . . . as much as one could, anyway, staying below the radar. It was amazing how easy it was in a big city like London. Parents paid her in cash, she paid her landlady in cash, and no one asked any questions. She was perfectly anonymous, each day unfolding the same.

The past was another lifetime. She never let herself drift backwards. For her own survival, she couldn't. She'd cut the necklace from her hair as soon as her train had pulled into London that day, using a pair of scissors nicked from the station's stationery shop. The pendant might have kept her alive, but it had no place in this world now. She hadn't been able to throw it away, though, despite several attempts. She'd tucked it inside a drawer in her bedside table, where it had gradually been buried by years and years of receipts and other debris of the life she was living now – the life of an entirely different person to the one Bertie had fallen in love with.

She stared at her reflection in the mirror, thinking she even looked like another person – a bit like her sister. Jude's curly hair was short now and her curves had sagged into 'plump'. Even her wardrobe of matronly skirts and blouses mirrored Carolyn's. Pulling on her 'uniform' made her feel like she was wearing armour, adding another layer to the dowdy middle-aged teacher persona she'd created . . . a woman you'd pass on the street without a second glance.

She fitted the image of a typical, no-nonsense piano teacher, exactly what the parents who employed her wanted. From the moment she knocked on the doors of their West London houses to the minute she packed up her books and left, she was playing the role they expected; a role that came so naturally to her now it felt like it *was* her. Sometimes the mothers or nannies tried to engage with her – to offer her biscuits or an espresso when she finished the lesson, or invite her to stay until it stopped raining, but she always said no. She didn't want to chat. There was nothing beneath the facade she'd created. She was Mrs McAllister, piano teacher, and nothing else.

She wasn't sure why she'd taken Bertie's surname. She certainly hadn't meant to, but it had just slipped out when the hostel workers asked for her name after she had first arrived in London. She supposed it was because she'd linked her name with Bertie's so many times after he'd asked her to marry him. In her mind – in the fairy tale she'd lived for a short time – that had been who she was. But despite the stories she'd spun for Ella, real life wasn't a fairy tale . . . far from it.

Jude placed her bare feet on the gritty floor and threw on her robe, then flicked on the coffee machine. After almost three decades in this room, every step of her morning routine was etched into her mind. She knew every inch of the space as intimately as her own body. Nothing had changed since she'd climbed the stairs that day so long ago and opened the door, breathing a sigh of relief at the empty space before her. There was a small single bed in one corner, a plain white dresser in the other, a tiny counter with sink and hotplate, and freshly painted white walls. After living in a women's hostel, where every inch was clogged with belongings, toiletries and people, the simple space was just what she'd needed.

Jude sighed as she waited for the coffee to trickle down, for the heady smell to fill the air and signal it was time to start her day. She drank it as quickly as she could, then pulled on her light summer jacket and hurried down the stairs, thankfully not bumping into any of the other tenants. There were eight other rooms in this three-storey terraced house, and the faces seemed to come and go seamlessly, one melding into the other. Sometimes a tenant would try to strike up a conversation, but Jude always made it clear she wasn't up for talking, and that was that. What would she talk about? She didn't have a life. Everyone she'd cared about thought she was dead. She wasn't even a person. She was a ghost, and she was fine with that.

Outside, the street was littered with the usual rubbish from the nearby chicken shops and kebab joints, but she was used to it by now. Despite its gritty appearance, Vauxhall was apparently coming up in the world, if the huge posters advertising glossy steel-and-glass high-rises were anything to go by. When she'd first moved here, it was hard to believe anyone with money would want to live 'south of the river'. It had been a little rough, but the room had been affordable and she loved that she could walk to the river.

In the days when she had plenty of time to fill and nothing to do, she used to spend hours there, gazing into the brown water, moving her legs forward as boats glided past. She'd watch the water suck at the wall and, for a second, she could almost envision it pulling her under, too – the same way she'd thought the waves would take her and glide her into oblivion. The river walkway was still one of her favourite places, although her schedule was so busy now she rarely had time to go.

Forty-five minutes after leaving Vauxhall, Jude emerged from the Underground into a world that was vastly different from the one she had left – pristine white houses, where rubbish was whisked away by street cleaners seconds after it dared touch the pavement, and streets lined with wine shops, estate agents and nail bars instead of chicken shops, tatty off-licences and kebab restaurants. Potted plants hung from street lamps, and almost each house had a window box so perfect it looked like it had been curated by an art director.

She'd been lucky to break into this competitive world as a piano teacher. One of the volunteers at the hostel lived in this area and had taken a chance by recommending Jude to teach her neighbour's sons. The boys had been about as interested in piano as they were in painting their toenails pink, but she'd persevered and had managed to teach them the basics. Their mother had been so pleased that she'd recommended Jude to all of her friends, and, eventually, Jude's client base had grown. Parents were happy to pay her in cash, although that was getting more and more difficult as people used cash less and less. Opening a bank account was out of the question, though, for obvious reasons.

She glanced at her watch: half past nine; right on time. Once, she'd been a minute late to a lesson, and the mother had insisted on deducting exactly the cost of that minute.

'Mrs McAllister!' The door swung open and the au pair's face appeared. She was Australian and in her early twenties, and something about her reminded Jude of herself at that age: full of confidence, full of life. 'Come on in.' The au pair turned her head. 'Amelia! Your piano teacher is here!'

Jude stepped inside the house, slipping off her reliable, orthopaedic shoes. They'd cost more than she usually paid, but she did a lot of walking in her job and she'd needed something serviceable. They were hideous, sturdy things that made her feel about a hundred years old, but at least they matched the piano-teacher persona she'd created.

'Would you like a cup of tea?' the au pair asked, ushering her into the lounge, where a gleaming piano that had never been played until Jude had started with Amelia – what, five years ago now – was pushed up against the far wall. Jude would have given anything to have had a piano like that when she was growing up (hell, she would have given anything to have had a piano, full stop), but with her father barely scraping a living working as a fisherman and her mother at home taking care of them, there'd barely been enough money for that week's groceries, let alone extras like a piano. It had been a house full of love and life, though – and music, with her father constantly blasting his favourite songs on the dodgy ghetto blaster he'd picked up from somewhere or other.

Jude pushed the thoughts from her mind. They were gone. Gone, along with everyone else from her past. Gone, along with her.

'Sorry, sorry, Mrs McAllister!' Amelia raced into the room, her long blonde hair flying out behind her. 'Sophie sent me a message, and I had to respond, and then— anyway, I'm sorry. Please don't tell my mum!'

'Sit down,' Jude said, conjuring up her stern voice. 'You've already wasted fifteen minutes.'

The lesson passed in its usual torturous way, with her unwilling student, who hadn't practised all week, murdering the pieces that Jude had heard a million times by now. Knowing there was no point in asking Amelia to play the song again, Jude set another two pieces that wouldn't be practised and would be butchered the same way next week. Sometimes she wondered if parents realised they were throwing away their money just for the privilege of saying their kids were taking piano lessons.

She was packing up her things when the au pair burst into the room.

'Hang on a sec!' the girl said. She shoved her mobile phone under Jude's face. 'Is this you? It is, isn't it?'

Jude blinked, struggling to take in the small type on the screen in front of her. She drew it closer to her face, everything inside her freezing when the letters of the headline swam into focus.

'Help Me Find My Mother,' the bold type said, and underneath it was a photo of her from about thirty years ago. It didn't look much like her now – hell, it didn't look anything like her now – and was that—? She drew in a breath. Was that *Ella*? God, she looked like Bertie . . . like *him*. It was the angle of her chin and that long, straight nose . . .

Her heart beat fast and she felt herself sway. This was her daughter, right here in front of her. It was so unreal it was hard to take in. Jude hadn't thought of herself as a mother since leaving all those years ago. Blocking it out was the only way to survive.

'What is this?' she managed to ask, aware of the au pair watching her with undisguised curiosity.

'It's been going around Facebook, but the link is from *The Post*,' the au pair said. 'That *is* you, right? That's your daughter? Are you going to get in touch? Sounds like she really wants to talk to you!'

'No, no.' Jude forced out a laugh. 'It's not me, of course it's not.'

'Okay.' The au pair looked at her suspiciously but, thankfully, didn't ask more questions.

'I need to go,' Jude said, grabbing her coat and yanking open the door.

The au pair shrugged and nodded, and Jude closed the door behind her. Out on the street, she pulled out her mobile and typed her old name in the search box, her heart pounding as the link to the *Post* article came up. She found the nearest bench and collapsed on to it, certain she was going to pass out.

Her daughter's image filled the small screen once again, and Jude's fingers reached out to touch it. Ella was a grown woman now, a thirty-five-year-old. Jude could see traces of the little girl in that woman's face, and she wondered if Ella had kids of her own . . . if Jude was a grandmother. She pushed away that thought before it could develop. Carolyn would be the grandmother, not her. Carolyn had raised Ella, not her.

She stared into her daughter's eyes, trying to read her expression. Ella looked tentative and uncertain, as if the camera was something she should approach with caution. Did she live her life that way, too? Jude wondered.

Her heart sank as she read the article, published a few days ago. All these years later, and all it had taken was one random classified advert – which, according to this story, had appeared on her birthday – to set her daughter off. Ella still wanted to know why her mother had left . . . Ella still believed she was *alive*. Although Jude was sure Carolyn had done her very best, it sounded as if Ella had always longed for her mother to return

– that despite everything, she hadn't given up hope in the ten little words Jude had said every night. She couldn't have given up hope if she believed there was a chance that Jude had placed that advert; if she thought those generic phrases had come from her mother. For a split second, Jude let herself wonder if maybe the advert wasn't so random – if maybe those phrases *weren't* generic, but from someone she knew. The advert had been placed on her birthday, after all. Was it possible someone was reaching out? She told herself not to be ridiculous, and yet she couldn't stop a face filtering into her head . . .

She froze as Bertie's name leaped out from the text, like it had materialised from her mind. Oh, God. *Bertie.* Had it been him? After all these years, did he still hope she was alive? Her gut twisted as she scanned the words, trying to beat back the emotions rising inside. Finally, she sat back, lowering the phone to her lap and forcing air into her lungs as she tried to absorb what she'd just read.

Bertie hadn't placed the advert, but he was looking for her, too. Had Ella talked to him, or had it just been the reporter? Had they connected the fact that Jude must have been pregnant when she'd left him? Was he wondering right now if Ella was his?

Either way, he'd know that she'd abandoned her daughter, even though he wouldn't know why or how she'd got pregnant. He'd know she'd done something terrible; something no mother should ever do. What did he think of her now? Running out on him, and then her daughter? *God.*

Jude shook her head. She wouldn't think of Bertie or Ella. She wouldn't think of those ten words. They didn't belong to her any more. She'd meant them at the time, but she wasn't that person any longer: wasn't a lover; wasn't a mother. Lovers didn't run away without explanation, and mothers didn't abandon their children.

Time had passed, each year burying her more and more, the same way her pendant had been buried in the drawer.

She scrolled up to the headline again – to her daughter's words imploring for help to find her mother. I'm sorry, she said inside her head, even though she knew Ella would never hear her. I'm sorry, but your mother is gone. That part of her had died the second she'd closed the door of their flat behind her.

Jude closed the browser window on her phone. She slung her bag over her shoulder, then went down the stairs to the underground, feeling the old, familiar numbness slide over her.

CHAPTER THIRTY-EIGHT

ELLA

It was funny how little my life had changed, yet how different it felt. I was still rising at the crack of dawn, performing my morning routine and working flat out at the museum, but now that the cocoon I'd been living in had lifted, it was as if my senses were heightened. The air tasted saltier; the sun felt stronger. The sea was deliciously cold as it lapped my toes, and the colours of the sunset were more vivid, like a painting come to life.

And it wasn't just physical. Inside of me, my heart had expanded, knocking down any remaining barriers and allowing me to feel. I let myself smile at people on the promenade and even exchange greetings. Far from being irritated by interruptions from my colleagues at work, I was actually enjoying collaborating with a team. Aunt Carolyn was recovering well and, more times than not, I was the one who called, not her. I'd yet to go for a drink with Lou, but when my aunt was well again, I'd get in touch.

It wasn't always easy, taking these first steps towards happiness. I was so used to tucking myself away that reaching out and engaging – *feeling* – was foreign and unnatural . . . another language I had to learn. Despite my discomfort, though, I wouldn't go back to building my walls again. Gradually, I was learning. Every day, I was becoming more fluent in the language of life.

I was moseying along the promenade on my way to work one morning, breathing in the salty scent that rolled straight off the waves, when my mobile rang. I squinted at the screen. The number wasn't familiar and I almost shoved the phone back in my pocket, but something made me click 'answer'.

'Hello?' My voice was loud on the empty pavement.

'It's Angus.'

Angus? I nearly dropped the phone in surprise. We hadn't spoken since I'd hung up on him. Why would he be calling? Had he and Bertie finally seen the article? I winced, realising they still believed my mother had placed that advert.

'I hope you don't mind me ringing.' Angus's voice was tense, miles from his usual relaxed warm tone, and my stomach clenched in response. 'I got your number from the list by Bertie's phone.'

'It's fine,' I answered automatically, although already I could feel my emotions swirling as Bertie's face flashed into my head: tenderness towards the gentle man I'd thought I'd met, followed by confusion when I remembered Aunt Carolyn's words.

'Bertie's missing.' Angus said the words bluntly, and I caught my breath.

'Missing?' I stopped walking. 'What do you mean?'

'Ever since you left, he's been very agitated – distressed, even. As you know, he's desperate to find your mother. He's barely slept, and he's become quite confused at times.' Angus sighed, and I could hear his exhaustion. 'Short of going to London to track her down myself, I've done everything I can think of, but nothing seems to calm him.'

'I'm sorry, Angus,' I said, my heart squeezing. That was a lot for him to deal with.

'He's wandered off before,' said Angus. 'Usually in the night, but I was always able to find him and get him back into bed before he got too far. But last night . . .' He paused, and I could hear him run a hand through his hair. 'We were watching a football match at my place – better reception than on his ancient telly – and he wanted to head home to bed. I watched him to make sure he got inside okay, and then I guess I must have fallen asleep. I'd been up late the night before with him, and . . .' His voice broke off, and he cleared his throat.

'It's all right,' I said softly.

'When I woke up, I went to check on him, but he wasn't in his bedroom – or anywhere else in the house. I've looked everywhere for him, up and down the mews, the shops he used to go to . . . he's not there.' He swallowed. 'Ella, he's been talking a lot about watching your mother sing. About the promenade, and something about watching the sunset on the beach. I think he might mean Hastings. That's where they first met, right? What do you think?'

'It sounds like he might, yes,' I answered slowly. 'You don't actually think he's coming here, do you?' *Oh, God.* I sank down on a bench, my heart pounding.

'It's possible,' Angus replied. 'He's very confused about the past and the present. To him, the past *is* the present. There's a chance he thinks your mother is still living there, and he's gone to find her.'

'Could he manage that journey on his own?' I asked. 'Could he make it all the way here?'

'I don't know. Maybe,' Angus said. 'It's amazing how much energy he seems to have sometimes, especially if he's upset about something or driven by a memory from the past.'

I gripped on to the phone so tightly the casing bit into my fingers.

'I went to the station this morning to talk to the ticketing agent, on the off-chance someone might have spotted him last night, or to see if maybe he was still hanging around here. He might have got the sleeper train, which arrived in Euston at around seven this morning.'

I bit my lip, thinking of Bertie in the midst of the chaotic Euston train station at the start of rush hour. There weren't any trains from Euston to Hastings. He'd have to go to Victoria or Charring Cross first, then get on the right train from there. It was confusing at the best of times, but for someone with Bertie's condition . . . I took a breath as worry swept over me, followed in the next breath with uncertainty. Should I even worry about someone who might have hurt my mother?

'I need to stay home in case he does show up again,' Angus said, his voice vibrating with worry. 'Do you think you could keep an eye out? Maybe go to the train station or check out the promenade and see if he's there?'

I drummed my fingers on the desk as my mind flipped back and forth. Even during the short time we'd spent together, I'd connected with Bertie . . . with my father. I couldn't bear to think of the Bertie I knew, alone and confused, miles from home. But that was just it: *did* I know him? Aunt Carolyn had painted a picture of someone completely different – someone horrific. I couldn't bear the thought of helping that person.

'Anything you can do would be great,' Angus said, his tone taking on a note of desperation. 'Really, anything at all. I'll notify the police, but apart from that . . . I don't know who else to call.'

I paused, struggling to answer. I wanted to help *him* – to do something to alleviate his worry and concern – but I couldn't move. I couldn't open my mouth to speak; I couldn't find the words. I was frozen, caught between two poles, and I didn't know which way to move. 'I . . . I don't know, Angus. I—'

'Fine.' Angus's voice cut me off. 'I don't have time to convince you.' And with that, he hung up.

I clicked off the mobile, Angus's voice ringing in my ears as guilt slid over me. He needed me, and yet . . . I promised Aunt Carolyn I wouldn't be in contact with Bertie, I reminded myself, putting my headphones back on. I was conscious it was an easy way out, but I was only too happy to take it.

CHAPTER THIRTY-NINE

JUDE

Jude jerked awake, the sun stinging her eyes. She'd been dreaming she was lying on the beach, the sunshine warming her limbs as Ella played at her feet with a bucket and spade.

She blinked and sat up, an ache so strong it felt like a fist squeezing her heart as she took in her dingy, barren room. For the millionth time since seeing that article, she reached out for her phone and pulled up her daughter's photo, as if staring into this now-stranger's face could loosen its hold; remind Jude that her daughter *was* a stranger. She was grown, and Jude had forsaken any place in her life.

Jude shook her head. She'd been so stupid to even think she could be a mother. She'd been so stupid to even *try*. She sighed, remembering the long days before giving birth when she'd lain cushioned in the house Carolyn and Rob were meticulously resurrecting, vowing to give this child all the love she'd stored up for Bertie – to pledge to this baby never to leave. And she had tried, she really had. She'd even named the baby after Ella Fitzgerald, her favourite singer and the one who'd drawn her and Bertie together the first time they'd spotted each other. Bertie had wanted to play

'Summertime' for their first dance as husband and wife, not that they'd ever got as far as the wedding.

In those first desperate weeks after Ella had been born, Jude had played that song over and over, hoping to soothe her daughter's cries. Ella would cry louder, only stopping when she was safely in her mother's arms. They moved into a council flat and Ella grew. Jude tried to forget, tried to love her, tried to follow through. But she'd failed, and she'd ended up here. Not a mother any more. Barely even a person.

Jude stared into her daughter's eyes again, but the ache still gripped her. Responding to her daughter's call was out of the question, but . . . Jude bit her lip as her mind spun. Perhaps there was something she could do. Perhaps she could give her daughter back the one part of her former life she *had* hung on to, something she'd promised to pass to Ella when her daughter had a love of her own.

The heart pendant.

Jude tilted her head as the thought grew. She could send it by post to Carolyn's address. Her daughter would know it had come from London, but there was no way she'd ever be able to find her. No one knew Jude's real name or anything about her past. But then . . . then, Carolyn and Ella would know she was alive – no one else could have sent the pendant. They'd know she'd left to live another life, and they'd know she was choosing not to return.

Was it better for Ella to know Jude was alive yet not coming back, or to still live in hope she might one day come home? Jude looked into her daughter's eyes again, taking in that uncertain, hesitant expression. Maybe sending this pendant would give her daughter some closure – a final goodbye that Jude had never had the chance to say. Because whether Jude was living or dead, that part of her was gone for ever.

She opened the drawer in her bedside table, slowly peeling back layer after layer of detritus. Empty Nurofen boxes, earplugs, tissue packets and receipt after receipt for God knows what, because she certainly didn't have much purchasing power.

At last the drawer was almost empty. The necklace lay coiled in the corner, like a snake waiting to strike. She gazed at it for a second, breathing in, almost afraid to touch it. It had been years since she'd even seen it.

Jude shook her head, rolling her eyes at her hesitation. For goodness' sake, it was just a necklace; an inanimate object. It didn't have any power. It didn't have a hold over her now.

She reached out and lifted the chain, the heart pendant glinting in the sun. Despite the years that had passed, the weight of it was so familiar, and before she knew what she was doing, she'd raised her arms to place it around her neck once more.

No! She stopped herself just in time, the necklace slipping from her fingers and flying through the air. It clattered on to the hard floor, the pendant snapping open.

Shit. Jude took another breath to steady herself, then reached down to retrieve the pendant. A yellowed slip of paper slid out into her hands, and her heart raced. She knew what this was. She knew what it said.

I am always with you. I will always be here.

She sank on to the bed as the words rolled over her, swirled around her, then vibrated through her body and soul. She could almost feel the hard layers she'd adopted peel away, revealing the soft skin underneath. The memory of the morning Bertie had given her this invaded her brain, so strong and in such vibrant colour there was no way she could even try to stop it.

The singing of the birds; the rush of the river. The love in Bertie's eyes, and how she'd felt so safe.

So *happy.*

She ran her fingers over the letters on the paper, her eyes filling as more and more memories tumbled through her mind. Her mother, smelling of the rose bath cream Jude always tried to steal from her, softly stroking her head as she said goodnight. The way Bertie would say those words so naturally, as if he never could believe anything different. The warmth of her baby's arms and the softness of her limbs as Jude whispered in her ear. How she'd *meant* those words, to both Bertie and Ella.

And how they'd believed in her.

How they still seemed to believe, despite everything.

That ache she'd felt awakening from the dream this morning intensified, so strong that she could barely catch her breath. She'd loved Bertie; loved her daughter . . . she loved them *now*. The bit of her she'd thought had died was still there, stirring painfully within. How that was even possible after so many years had passed – after what she had done – she didn't know. Maybe, just like the words she'd uttered, that love had always been there. Maybe it always would be, no matter how many protective layers she piled on top; no matter who she pretended to be.

She glanced at Jude's photo again, her heart swelling. She could feel the pull in her gut, that visceral response when your child cries out and only you can soothe them. She *was* still a mother: a mother with a daughter who needed her.

But . . . seeing Ella now would mean facing the past. How could she explain to Ella why she'd left without unlocking the fear and anger she'd felt after Frank's attack? How could she even start to tell her daughter that she'd attempted to bury herself first with alcohol, then by running away, and then by becoming someone else entirely? Jude got to her feet again, pacing back and forth across the room as anger slowly poured into her, filling her up until she was shaking with rage.

Frank had taken her relationship. He'd taken her daughter. Hell, he'd almost taken her life. He might as well have, for all she was living now.

How much more was she going to let him take from her?

Jude reached up and put the chain around her neck. The pendant lay against her skin, feeling as if it had always been there. Her daughter was reaching out for her. Her daughter wanted her; believed in her.

And she was going to show her daughter she was right.

CHAPTER FORTY

ELLA

I increased the volume on the clips I was reviewing for the upcoming exhibition, closing my eyes to try to block out the image of Bertie standing alone on a busy platform, disoriented and scared. Clip after clip of sounds from the promenade filled my ears, from the seagulls gliding overhead to the fairground to an accordion, but still that image lingered. I sighed, thinking how ironic it was that just as I'd accepted the past and started to make a new life, here it was disturbing me once more.

And what was I doing, a little voice asked? Hiding away in my cubicle again, attempting to burrow inside myself? If I really had made peace with the past – if I really was open and ready to live – why wasn't I out there now? Why wasn't I able to face my father?

I shook my head. It was one thing to accept living with the uncertainty of what had happened, and it was another to face that person who may or may not have committed such terrible acts. He might not remember, but that didn't erase what he could have done.

I turned the next clip up even louder, and a voice filled my ears, rich and throaty. My lids flew open, and I sat up straight.

I knew that voice.

I clicked on the description of the clip, my heart beating fast as I scanned the words: *Singer, June 1980, Hastings Promenade*. It couldn't be. Could it? And yet, even as my mind dismissed the possibility, I knew it was her. It was my mother, singing 'Summertime' by Ella Fitzgerald, the very singer she'd named me after.

My mind flashed back to the look on Bertie's face when I'd told him my name, and I remembered how he had said this was the first song he'd heard my mother sing; the song that had brought them together. *Their* song, he'd told me – the song they'd chosen for their first dance together as husband and wife.

And now my mother was singing the song, as if to me. I closed my eyes again, listening to the cadence of her voice, the way she released the words out into the air so you could feel them coming towards you, ready to wrap you in their warmth. I could almost sense the sun beating down on me, smell the suncream and the melting asphalt. She cast a spell with her voice, the music spinning from her like magic. I could feel the life streaming from her . . . the love.

Listening to this song felt like my mother whispering in my ear, telling me to leave this desk and go out into the world – to find my father and be strong enough to face him . . . for us both. Whether it would be in love or to stand up against him one final time, I didn't know, but I felt her urging me to close the loop. And even though it might seem silly, I wasn't going to try to block it out. My heart *was* open now, and I was going to follow that voice. I'd hold my mother inside of me and take her to the place where all of this had begun. Back to where she'd met Bertie . . . and where it felt as if, through me, she might meet him again.

I pushed back my chair and got to my feet. I was breaking my promise to my aunt but, somehow, I didn't think she'd mind.

I made my way through the museum and out the door, the sharp sunshine stinging my eyes. For a split second I paused, wondering if I was doing the right thing, glancing back towards the safety of the museum. I pictured the dark silence of my cubicle, then shook my head. No more hiding – not for me, and not for my mother.

I turned to face the blinding light reflecting off the sea. Then I stepped on to the promenade and started to walk.

CHAPTER FORTY-ONE

JUDE

Jude hurried through the station and boarded the train to Hastings. Now that she'd decided to go home, there was no point hanging around. Her daughter had waited long enough already. *Jude* had waited long enough, even if she hadn't known that love and desire inside of her still existed.

She collapsed into a seat, her hand reaching up to close around the pendant as if it could give her strength. Was she really doing this? Was she really going back home . . . back to the place where it had all started? And back to the place where it had ended?

Where she'd thought it had, anyway.

She'd never thought of returning. She'd slammed that door shut, but the article had blown it wide open again. Blown her *heart* wide open again, to reveal what was really underneath. Love, and a longing to show she cared. A longing to see the daughter she hadn't been able to stay with, and the sister who'd always been there.

What would Carolyn say when Jude turned up? Would she ever be able to forgive her? And then explaining to Ella . . . There were so many questions and so many unknowns. But when was life ever a straight line? When was it ever black and white? Only one thing was certain: she needed to do this.

The train pulled into Hastings, and Jude's eyes widened in surprise. The station looked nothing like it had all those years ago, when she'd returned home from Edinburgh, trying to flee from the horror of what was growing inside of her. It was as if she was arriving in a completely different place . . . until she left the carriage and breathed in the air. The salty tang unlocked a tide of memories inside her, and she had to stop and steady herself before she could carry on. She couldn't let them pull her under now. She had to keep moving.

But to where? she wondered as she walked past the taxi rank and the bus stop. She couldn't just turn up at Carolyn's out of the blue, could she? Her sister would be shocked and, anyway, Jude didn't even know if she still lived there . . . although she couldn't imagine her and Rob moving out of the house they'd so lovingly renovated. That place had been the child they'd never had . . . until Ella, anyway.

Jude passed by the house she'd grown up in. She bit her lip, remembering her protests when Carolyn had said they'd need to sell the family home. That house was all Jude had left of her parents – even their memory was fading in her mind – and she'd fought tooth and nail to hang on to it, accusing her sister of wanting to use the money to chuck her out and build her own new house. She'd never even realised that they couldn't afford to keep it any longer. Their parents had re-mortgaged it so many times that everything they'd got for selling it went back to the bank. There'd been nothing left for either Carolyn or Jude, and Carolyn had struggled for the two of them to get by on her teacher's salary until Jude had been old enough to start contributing something of her own . . . not that she'd ever contributed much. God, she'd been a brat.

I really need to see my sister, Jude thought as she went down the hill towards the sea. She needed to say sorry, to say thank you, to do whatever she could to show that she knew how difficult it must have been, and that she realised how strong and brave her sister was to take on her, and then her baby. Carolyn had carried Jude's life on top of her shoulders as well as her own, and now Jude needed to lift that burden from her.

The sea shimmered in the sunshine, and Jude couldn't help but let her feet move towards the promenade. She breathed in deeply and wandered down it, trailing one hand along the railing and squinting against the sun. Her feet stopped, and she jerked herself from her reverie. This was it: her spot. The place where she'd sung, day after day, in the summer months. The spot where she'd dared to hope; dared to dream.

The place where she'd met Bertie and started on a trajectory that would change her life for ever.

She lifted a hand to touch the necklace, her fingers closing around the pendant. She'd come full circle – almost.

Now it was time to find her daughter.

CHAPTER FORTY-TWO

ELLA

I hurried along the promenade, my eyes sweeping the pavement and the beach for Bertie's tall figure. The weather was glorious and the promenade was packed with workers eating their lunch, escaping the office to soak up the sun. Picnic blankets made blotches of bright colour on the beach, with dogs splashing in the waves and children digging in sand.

I stared at every person that passed, feeling slightly idiotic as I met their enquiring gaze. None of them was Bertie. Could he actually have made it all the way here? Despite Angus's belief that he could, it was hard to imagine him travelling this far if his condition had deteriorated so much.

The hulk of the pier came into focus, and I slowed my steps. Sweat beaded on my brow and trickled down my back, and my mouth was dry. I leaned against the rail to catch my breath, automatically scanning the profile of the person beside me.

And everything stopped.

The noise, the heat of the sun beating down, the smell of the sea . . . all of that disappeared as the woman turned to face me. I couldn't breathe. I couldn't move. I could only stare, my mind whirling as I took in her features.

The deep-set eyes that had always seemed so sad. The slightly upturned nose. The dark curls now threaded with grey.

I struggled to assemble them into one picture; struggled to put them all together. I couldn't, because that would mean . . . That would make this person . . .

Before I could say anything, I could see the same realisation dawn on her face. Her eyes widened and she lifted a hand to her throat. I stared at that hand, thinking of the times I'd clutched it, of how she'd stroked my hair, of how she'd held me and kept me safe. Time stretched, then snapped, suspending us in another place.

A place we could make our own.

'Mum?' The word sounded strange in my voice, as if it had been stuck there for a very long time, growing rusty with disuse, but still waiting to be released. Still there, buried underneath it all, despite myself.

I couldn't begin to make out the emotions that flitted across her face: disbelief, then fear, then something like excitement and hope – emotions I was sure were reflected in my own features.

'Ella?' Her voice was a whisper. 'Oh my God. *Ella.*' She reached out to touch my cheek, then dropped her hand as if she wasn't sure she could. As if she was afraid that I might disappear in front of her.

I knew exactly how she felt. I felt the same, like she was a mirage that could vanish at any instant. It didn't seem possible that she was in front of me now. It didn't seem possible that maybe, after everything that had happened, I had been right to hope.

'What . . .' I swallowed, grasping for anything to say as a million questions clamoured at my mind. What had she been doing all this time? Why had she decided to come back?

My mum smiled, lines radiating out from her eyes. She was no longer the woman my mind's eye had pictured all these years, and I tried to match the image with the woman in front of me.

'I came to see you,' she said simply. 'It wasn't me who placed the advert you saw, but once I read that article in the paper, I knew that I had to find you. I had to tell you that I am here – that I always have been, even when I didn't know it myself.' Her voice rang with conviction, and her words burrowed deep into my heart. I couldn't have stopped them from lodging there, even if I'd wanted to.

But I still couldn't move. I still couldn't grasp she was *here*.

'The day that I left you,' she continued, her eyes locked on me as if she could hold me in place, 'I truly believed I was doing the best thing. I might have been your mother, but I wasn't what you needed. I just . . . I couldn't be.' She swallowed, and I wanted to reach out; to tell her I knew why she'd been in such pain. Every bit of me was frozen, though. Every part of me was focused on her words – an explanation I'd waited years to hear.

Words that might fill up that empty space inside of me.

'I told myself Carolyn would be a million times better at being a mother than I could ever be, and I went to the beach. I was going to walk into the sea, and that would be that. I thought it would be better for you, better for me, better for everyone.' She turned towards the sea, a faraway look in her eyes. 'But in the end, I couldn't. I went to London and tried to get through each day – make it from morning to night, that was as much as I could face. Days passed, then months, then years. I told myself the more time went by, the easier it would be. And I almost believed it, too.'

She faced me again. 'But that wasn't true. It never could be. Because love can't be buried under the weight of time. It's not something you forget, or that you can root out. No matter what, it's there, just waiting until the ground has thawed and it can bloom again.'

I breathed her words in, feeling in my heart how right she was. I'd tried everything to stop myself from loving her, and yet . . . I could feel my heart stirring, as if an animal was awakening after a long hibernation. I could feel love seeping into me once more.

'I can't say sorry. Sorry will never make up for what I did to you by leaving, I know.' She drew in air, her eyes glistening. 'Just know that those ten words I always said were true. I may not have been here for you physically, but you never left my heart. I loved you – love you still – and nothing could ever change that. Nothing.'

'I love you, too, Mum,' I said, stepping towards her. I don't know who reached out first, but we were in each other's arms. It was so unlike the embraces she'd given me as a child, yet so familiar at the same time. We had both been through so much. The years had separated us – pain had separated us – yet I knew she was right. Time had not extinguished the love between us. And finally, here we were, together.

'Do you want to sit?' Mum asked hesitantly, as if she was still afraid I'd run off. She pointed to a bench beside us, which had just been vacated by three office workers.

I nodded, and we sank down on the sun-warmed wooden slats. As we crossed our legs, my gaze fell on my mother's serviceable brown shoes, so different from the bare feet that I remembered . . . Yet another reminder that time had passed.

My mobile bleeped and I glanced at the screen. It was a text message from Angus, saying Bertie *had* been on the sleeper train. Angus had contacted Hastings police and he'd grabbed a morning flight to London. He was on the train to Hastings now, but he begged me to please keep an eye out. Guilt surged through me as I recalled my abrupt response. I'd ring him back and tell him—

I lifted my head, a thought entering my mind. I had to tell my mother that Bertie might be heading here.

'Mum . . .' This word still sounded foreign, but this time not as much. 'I have to tell you something.'

My mother tilted her head. 'And I have so much more to tell you.'

'But I need to tell you this now.' I shifted on the bench and scanned the promenade both ways, as if Bertie could be just seconds away. Given Angus's message, he might be. I didn't have time to waste.

'Bertie might be coming here soon.'

'*Bertie?*' My mother's face drained of colour, and my stomach clenched. I hated to think it, but given my mother's reaction, it seemed Aunt Carolyn might be right. My father – Bertie – had hurt my mother. *He* was the reason she'd left without explanation. 'He's coming here? But how . . .' Her voice trailed off and she put hand to her heart, her face so pale it almost matched the white clouds filtering in from the sea.

'Come with me.' I took her arm. 'Aunt Carolyn's isn't far. We can be there in five minutes. You won't have to see him.'

But my mother was shaking her head. 'No. I'm through with running – through with hiding. I can't do it any more. I won't do it any more.' She drew in a breath, almost vibrating with emotion. 'I want to see him. I need to see him.'

I met her eyes, realising I'd just thought the same thing: we were done with hiding. We didn't need to; we weren't alone any longer.

This was our story. The two of us were entwined, and together we'd face my father.

CHAPTER FORTY-THREE

JUDE

Jude's fingers clutched the heart pendant as she tried desperately to take everything in. Just a few hours earlier, she'd been holed up in a barren bedsit in London. Now, she was here. She'd found her daughter again . . . or maybe her daughter had found her. And Bertie might be on his way, too? Why?

She shook her head, trying to calm the volcano of emotion inside. Was it crazy to hope that maybe she could mend the rifts of the past? Could she finally say what had happened to drive her away – from both Bertie and Ella? She'd already hurt them so much. Would the truth hurt them even more – *could* it hurt them even more, any more than she had?

Jude turned to look at her daughter. Her head was down as she clicked away on her mobile. Ella was so beautiful, although she could see that her daughter hadn't a clue how lovely she was. Everything about her, from her short hair to her clothes to her sturdy shoes, was designed to hide herself away, to fade from sight. Jude understood that only too well. But even with those measures, Ella couldn't cover up her gorgeous long-lashed eyes, her milky skin and the strong jaw that reminded Jude so much of Bertie. She pushed out the other face that filled her mind, refusing to let it in.

He was gone. All she wanted to see – all she *did* see – in her daughter now was love.

Ella glanced up to meet Jude's gaze, and once again Jude felt a jolt that this woman in front of her was her daughter.

'I need to call Bertie's neighbour and let him know I haven't seen him,' Ella said. 'He asked me to keep an eye out.'

'Sure.' Jude closed her eyes and leaned back, the questions still hammering in her head. How did Ella know Bertie's next-door neighbour? Had she gone to see Bertie? How would she even know where he lived? The sun warmed her face as Ella made her phone call, stinging her cheeks as if she'd suddenly emerged from years of darkness.

'Right.' Ella's voice rang in the air, and Jude opened her eyes. 'I've talked to Angus, Bertie's neighbour. He's here in Hastings with Bertie.' Jude felt her heart beat faster. 'Bertie had a fall on the platform, and they took him to hospital. Angus was his emergency contact, so the hospital called him. They're going to meet us here as soon as they can.' Ella swivelled to face her. 'I suggested maybe Aunt Carolyn's place, but apparently Bertie was adamant they come here.'

Jude smiled. Of course Bertie would want to meet here, for the very reason that she had come to this place. It was where everything had started – where their life together had begun.

'So how. . .' Jude swallowed. 'Did you meet up with Bertie – talk to him?' Had Bertie asked her age? Had he noticed how much Ella looked like him? Oh God, did he think Ella might be his child? She could be, but . . .

Ella nodded. 'I went up to Edinburgh after I found a box of letters from him.'

'What box of letters?' Jude asked, her brow furrowing. Bertie had never got in touch. He couldn't, anyway – he'd had no idea where she was. Even if he'd guessed she was in Hastings, he wouldn't have known where to write.

231

'At Aunt Carolyn's,' Ella said. 'They were all addressed to you at her house. I have them back at the flat, if you want to have a look.'

'I would. Thank you.' So Bertie *had* written, somehow finding out Carolyn's address. Carolyn had followed Jude's request and not passed them on. 'And did he ask . . .' Jude paused, choosing her words carefully. 'Did he ask about your father?'

'I told him my father was dead,' Ella said, 'and he seemed to accept it. He didn't ask any more questions about it. I reckon he just wanted to think about his life with you. He made it sound idyllic, actually. But I'm not sure how clearly he remembers everything.' She bit her lip. 'Bertie has Alzheimer's.'

Jude's chest squeezed. Alzheimer's? Bertie, who'd remembered the exact date and time they'd first met, was starting to lose his memories?

'How bad is he?' she managed to ask through the questions circling her brain. He must remember something, or he wouldn't be on his way here.

'Some days are better than others,' Ella said. 'Angus has been helping out a lot when things are bad. It sounds like he's got worse in the past few weeks.' She swallowed. 'I'm not sure why he thinks you're here, but he does believe you're still alive. Angus says he's been very confused and distressed lately.' Ella touched her arm. 'I found all of this out before I talked to Carolyn. If I'd known what had happened between you and Bertie, I never would have gone to see him.'

Jude tilted her head. What on earth had Carolyn said? She didn't know the truth. What *had* she known?

Jude's mind flashed back to her words from so long ago, when she'd told Carolyn to keep Bertie away from her – that she never wanted to speak to him again. It was the only way she could protect herself and him. And then all the nightmares she'd had, and the time Carolyn had asked if she'd been hurt . . . Oh, God.

But surely Carolyn wouldn't tell Ella that *Bertie* had hurt her? They'd both agreed the best course of action was saying Ella's father had died.

'What exactly did she tell you?' Jude held her breath.

'That Bertie was abusive, and that you left him when you got pregnant.' Ella's voice was shaking. 'He never knew he had a child, and you told me he was dead only to keep me from learning what had really happened.'

Jude stiffened, her heart plummeting. Poor Ella. Her poor, poor girl. She'd thought she'd protected Ella from the truth. What on earth had her lies done?

'Carolyn only told me after the article appeared in the paper,' Ella continued. 'She was worried about me meeting up with Bertie again.' She looked into Jude's eyes. 'I know you said you want to see him, but . . . are you sure?'

Jude stared at Ella, admiring her strength. Her daughter had been through terrible traumas, believing that her mother was dead and that her father had been capable of horrible actions. And yet here she was, not only accepting Jude back into her life, but caring about her. If Ella could do that, then Jude could be strong enough to tell both Bertie and Ella what had really happened.

There was nothing else she *could* do, anyway. She'd thought that by running she could escape those memories, but she'd never been more wrong. The past didn't die, and it didn't fade away. It lived on, affecting every action and emotion. You couldn't escape – not physically and not emotionally . . . no matter how much alcohol or whatever else you tried. You could only be honest, open and keep loving the best you could, with all the cards on the table.

'I'm sure.' Jude had never been more certain. 'He needs to know the truth, and so do you.'

CHAPTER FORTY-FOUR

ELLA

I caught my breath at my mother's words. *The truth.* Was I finally going to hear it? Was I ready to hear it? I faced my mother as certainty filtered in. I was. No matter what she said, I was ready.

'Ella, Bertie didn't hurt me. He loved me, and I loved him.'

I swallowed, trying to take in her words as hope leaped inside of me. 'So . . . what Aunt Carolyn said . . .'

My mother shook her head. 'I couldn't tell her the truth. I couldn't tell Bertie the truth. And I sure as hell didn't want you to know the truth.' She sighed. 'Looking back now, maybe I should have said what really happened. But after the attack, things were so jumbled in my mind.'

'Attack?' I gulped at the word. So my aunt had been right about one thing: my mother had been hurt by someone.

'I was on tour as an opening act, and it happened on the last night. He came into my room, and then . . . then, he forced himself on me.' My mother's face twisted, and she looked away. 'He threatened that if I said anything to Bertie, he'd tell him we'd been together all through the tour.' She sighed. 'I didn't think Bertie would believe him, but I couldn't be sure.' She met my eyes once again. 'It was Bertie's brother, Frank.'

'Bertie's brother?' Oh my God. My hand flew to my mouth. How awful, that someone she had trusted – someone who'd practically been family – could do something so terrible to her.

'Bertie loved me, but his brother, well . . . they'd grown up together in a difficult situation. Bertie would have done anything for him; anything to keep him out of trouble. How could I tell him what his beloved brother had done to me? Even if he did believe me, it would have put him in an impossible situation. So I tried to pretend.' She gazed out to the sea.

'I tried to pretend nothing happened. I tried to pretend I was all right. I tried to pretend that Bertie and I could carry on as normal; that the life I was living was intact.' She shook her head. 'And who knows, maybe it could have been.'

'But then you found out you were pregnant,' I said in a flat voice, realising what had happened next. My mother turned from staring out to sea and looked at me.

'Yes. And Ella . . . I . . .' She took a breath. 'I wasn't sure who your father might be. I was on the Pill but I'd missed one earlier that month, and, well, that was the only protection I'd had.' She winced and I shifted on the bench. 'I couldn't bear telling Bertie the baby was his when I wasn't sure, and I couldn't bear telling him what had happened with his brother. The only thing I could do was leave.'

She paused. 'I told myself that you were half mine, too. Half of me, and I'd love you no matter what.' She put a hand on my arm. 'And I did love you. I do. You are a part of me, and vice versa. I have always been with you. I have always been here – inside of you; a small piece of what makes you *you*.'

She stared back out at the water, her eyes filling with tears. 'He stopped me from being the mother you deserved. The memories of the attack and what I'd lost closed me off. I had to stop caring about anything in order to survive, but then I stopped caring about surviving, too.'

'So why didn't you walk into the water that day?' I asked softly. I didn't want to upset her, but I had to know.

My mother met my gaze. 'Do you remember the necklace I always wore?'

I nodded slowly. 'Of course. You said that you'd give it to me one day. For a while after you left, I thought the fact that it wasn't found on the beach meant you were coming back.'

My mother's face tightened. 'I was in such a state that morning . . . I wasn't thinking clearly. All I knew was that I couldn't let the sea swallow me with the pendant around my neck. Bertie gave it to me when he proposed and, to me, it was pure joy. It felt so wrong, taking it with me. I got out of the water to remove it, and then, well . . . I couldn't go back in.'

My eyes widened as she drew it out from under her jumper. This necklace had saved her life, and she was still wearing it. It had been given to her by a man who loved her – whose pledge had lifted her up when she'd needed it.

'I'm sorry, Ella.' Her voice was soft. 'I wish I'd done things differently. I wish I could have been a mother to you. I wish I could have been here, like I'd promised.'

I swallowed. Nothing could erase the pain I'd felt after she'd left me and the numbness of the following years as I tried to protect myself. Like her, I wished she could have been here for me – that she'd stayed. But neither of us could change what had happened. The past had affected us, twisting us in certain directions. But now we had come together, and we could make the future what we wanted. *She* could make the future she wanted, too. God knew she'd been through enough.

'You're here now,' I said, touching her arm. 'And, Mum, you don't need to be afraid to tell Bertie the truth any more. Frank died

236

a while back, and by the sound of things, he and Bertie weren't talking. I'm sure it won't be easy for him to hear what happened, but I think their relationship was long since over, anyway.'

My mother's eyes were wide and she nodded slowly. Her face eased, as if some invisible strings had relaxed. She almost looked like a different person.

We sat in silence as the minutes ticked by. The stream of people on the promenade became a trickle, and the sun sank lower in the sky. I leaned back on the bench and closed my eyes, tipping my face up as I tried to get a grip on my feelings . . . on the truth of what had happened. I'd thought for years that my father was dead. Then, I'd been told I was the product of an abusive relationship, but had struggled to believe it, hoping my aunt had been wrong. And now, even though the details had shifted, the end result was much the same: my father was either the love of my mother's life, or the man who had ruined it.

My head was spinning, but one thing was clear: Bertie's sincerity and kindness were genuine. He'd loved my mother with such strength that it had lasted all these years – that even as his memory was fading, his love for my mother wasn't. He'd stood fast by those ten words. This reunion wouldn't be one of anger or hatred, but of love.

Suppertime came and went, the sky pinkened and the air cooled, and there was still no sign of Bertie.

Sighing, I picked up the mobile to call Angus, but the phone rang out. It wasn't far from the hospital to here, but perhaps they'd got delayed? I shook my head, thinking how fortunate it was, in a way, that Bertie had needed medical assistance and they'd called Angus as his emergency contact. Otherwise, we might not know where Bertie was . . . although I couldn't help feeling that, somehow, Bertie would have made it here.

The sky darkened and the promenade lights came on, bathing the pathway in a golden glow. Beyond us, lights twinkled from the houses on the hill, and the whoosh of the sea seemed louder as silence blanketed the town. Apart from the odd dog walker or jogger, Mum and I had the promenade to ourselves now. I pulled my light coat around me, every inch of me sagging with exhaustion, but there was no way I'd leave my mother here alone.

If she was going to wait, so was I.

I jerked forward as something in the dark caught my eye. Two figures were making their way down the pavement. One was moving very slowly and unsteadily with the other one keeping him upright. I held my breath as they got closer, not wanting to blink unless they disappeared into the night. My mother still hadn't noticed, staring in the opposite direction as the lights on the pier flashed on and off. I watched as the two shapes got closer and closer, their features gradually coming into focus.

And my heart grew, bigger and bigger, until I could hardly breathe.

There, almost in front of us now, were Angus and Bertie. Bertie looked awful, with a huge white bandage around his arm, his hair tousled and his face grimy. Angus didn't look much better. But they were here. They'd made it . . . at last.

'Mum,' I said, and she turned my way.

CHAPTER FORTY-FIVE

JUDE

Jude sat on the bench, barely noticing anything except her daughter by her side. She'd told Ella several times that she didn't have to stay, but her daughter refused to go; refused to leave her on her own. And even though Jude knew she'd done nothing to deserve it – even though she was more than used to being alone – she was relieved to have Ella here as she waited for Bertie. Ella was a part of this, too.

Jude could see now that everything was connected; that everyone was connected. Good and bad, for better or for worse . . . you couldn't simply chop out one piece of the fabric without damaging the rest. You had to take life as a whole and cherish the good without letting the bad blacken you. She hadn't been able to do that in the past, but maybe she could now.

It was hard to wrap her mind around the fact that Ella knew now what Jude had tried to hide from everyone – even herself – for so long; strange that the first one to know the truth was the person who'd been the outcome of that horrific event. What would Bertie say when he found out what had happened? Would he even be able to remember that time – remember the tour, her singing, the listless days and nights when she came back again? How much was clear and how much lost in the fog of time and disease? The events of the past were as vivid in her memory now as if they'd just happened, like they'd been waiting, perfectly preserved, beneath multiple layers.

But even if Bertie's memory was hazy, he remembered *her*. He'd never have come all this way if their relationship hadn't affected him. He'd never have written all those letters. Even without knowing why she'd gone, she'd left a space in his life that had reverberated through the years.

Would he be angry that she'd never told him – never told him that he might have a daughter? Would he be able to take in her words about what had happened with Frank, or would they be too much to bear? Even if he had fallen out with his brother, he was still just that: his brother. Perhaps he'd come expecting a happy ending, only to be told of her damaged past. Would he walk away after finally finding her?

Whatever happened and whatever he remembered, he deserved to know why she had left. He deserved to know that he may have a daughter . . . or a niece.

He deserved the truth.

'Mum.' Ella's voice cut into her thoughts, and Jude turned to smile at her daughter, her heart swelling with love.

'Yes?'

Ella's face shone as she gestured towards two people approaching them on the pathway. Jude squinted, unsure at first what why her daughter looked so excited. That wasn't Bertie, hobbling along like an old man. It couldn't be, could it? But as they got even closer and his face came into focus, she knew in an instant it was the man she'd loved; the only man who had made her feel safe. A huge bandage was wrapped around his arm and his face sagged with fatigue, but the familiar blue eyes and jutting chin were just the same. And it wasn't only that: it was his expression when he looked at her, as if he really saw her. So much had changed, but that hadn't.

She leaped to her feet. Her muscles screamed in pain after sitting for so long, but she barely noticed as she closed the gap between them, stopping in front of the man she'd tried everything to forget. Her heart beat so loudly that it drowned out everything else, and her mouth went dry. Her eyes locked on his and, despite the years etched on to their faces, the time that had separated them melted away.

Bertie let go of the man who was supporting him, reaching out a trembling hand to touch the heart around her neck. His fingers were warm on her cool skin, and Jude's mind flipped back to the first time he'd placed the necklace over her head. His hands had been warm then, too.

'You're here,' he said, in an echo of the phrase that had drawn them together. He gripped her hand. 'I can't believe you're here.' Jude nodded, unable to grasp on to the many words that were pouring through her. It was enough right now to stand here, facing each other, with the sound of the waves colouring the night air . . . the same way it had when they'd camped out on the beach their first night together. Bertie squeezed her fingers. 'Come on, let's sit down.'

Jude took his arm and helped him over to the bench, noticing Ella and Angus chatting on the next bench over. Apart from the low murmur of their voices and the occasional cry of a gull, the promenade was silent.

'Do you remember that night we first met, when we took our fish and chips down to the beach?' she asked, then she bit her lip, realising he might not remember.

The corner of Bertie's mouth lifted. 'I'm hanging on to it as much as I can,' he said. 'Some days it's clearer than others. Right now, it feels like yesterday.' He met her eyes. 'Ella probably told you that I have Alzheimer's,' he said simply, and Jude nodded. 'It's an unpredictable thing and I don't know how much longer I'll be able to keep everything straight in my head. Often, especially lately, I can't. But it's teaching me one thing, and that's to live in the present . . . to cherish the here and now, because I may not have the past to rely on, and I've no idea what my future may hold.' He took her hand again, and she gazed down at his fingers closing over hers. Their skin was much more wrinkled than the smooth surface of their youth. It was a reminder that time passed, and that you had to grasp on to the people you loved while you still could.

Jude swallowed. 'Bertie, I need to tell you why I left.'

Bertie met her eyes. 'You don't,' he said softly. 'You don't need to tell me anything, not now. Like I said, I'm happy to see you again; to be in this moment. I don't need anything else. I always wondered, of course. I'm not going to lie about that. But that's behind us now. It's over and done with.'

'But it's not,' Jude said, turning to look at Ella's profile on the next bench over. 'It's not over and done with, and I need to tell you this, as much for Ella as for me.' She didn't know what Ella might do with the information that Bertie could be her father, but if she needed Bertie's help to investigate further, then Bertie needed to know. Jude paused, hoping what she was about to say wouldn't distress him too much. It had been years ago, but . . .

'Frank raped me when I was on the tour.' Jude let out her breath. She hadn't meant to be so blunt, but there was no delicate way to say it. Even after all this time, it was still difficult to say those words aloud, but she wouldn't let that terrible event control her any longer. 'He threatened that if I told you, he'd say we were having an affair.'

Bertie was so still and unmoving that Jude wasn't sure if he'd taken in her words. What happened had been brutal, and she couldn't soften the blow even if she wanted to. Frank hadn't just taken her body that night. He'd taken her life, too.

'Frank,' Bertie said, spitting out the word in a tone she'd never heard him use before. 'Frank . . . attacked you?'

She couldn't blame him for not wanting to utter the word. It was so ugly that she could barely bring herself to say it, but she'd had to. Jude nodded, and Bertie's other hand covered hers.

'Oh my God. Oh, Jude.' He squeezed her hands, as if he could give her the strength now that he couldn't before. 'I'm so sorry.'

'I tried to carry on after the tour and pretend everything was fine,' she continued, desperate to get it all out. 'But then I discovered I was pregnant, and I couldn't be sure if you or Frank was the father. And so I left. I left you, and I raised Ella on my own.'

'*Ella.*' Bertie's voice was soft in the darkness. 'You got pregnant with Ella on the tour?'

Jude nodded. She couldn't trust herself to speak now.

'Ella's my daughter?' Bertie was shaking his head, and Jude's heart dropped. Perhaps he hadn't understood. It was a lot to take in at once.

'Well, I'm not sure,' she said slowly. 'You'd been down to visit two days before Frank attacked me. I was on the Pill, but he . . .' She dropped her eyes, then forced herself to look up again. There was nothing to be ashamed of. None of this had been her fault. 'He didn't use anything,' she said, 'so we can't be certain.'

But Bertie was still shaking his head.

'You're wrong,' he said, a look of wonder in his eyes. 'I *can* be certain.' He was squeezing Jude's hands so tightly now that it almost hurt. 'Jude, Frank couldn't have children.'

'*What?*' Jude drew in a breath, her heart pounding. Frank couldn't have children? So was Ella really—? She interrupted her thought. She couldn't go down that road until Bertie explained. 'What do you mean?'

'Frank had some sort of infection when he was young,' Bertie said. 'Something to do with the tube that stores sperm. I don't know all the details, but I do remember it resulted in him not being able to have children. He never minded, actually. Always said he wasn't interested in kids, anyway.'

Jude sat in silence as the words washed over her, trying to understand. Ella was Bertie's daughter. There'd never been a chance she was Frank's. Jude had run – first from Bertie and then from her own daughter – for nothing.

She wanted to pound the bench, to scream, to laugh. If only she had known. If only she'd talked to Bertie and told him what had happened. It would have been horrific, of course, telling him about Frank. But with their baby on the way, the two of them could have got through it together, she was sure. Life would have – could have – been completely different for her and for Bertie . . . and for Ella, too. By keeping quiet, she'd destroyed that chance. She'd cheated them of the life they should have had.

'I'm sorry,' she said, her voice shaking. 'I'm sorry I didn't tell you. I thought I was protecting you, keeping you safe from what had happened. I thought leaving you was best for everyone.'

Bertie was silent, staring out at the sea, and a fist of regret twisted Jude's insides with such force she thought she might be sick. Then, Bertie turned and smiled that same old smile, the one where his eyes gleamed with warmth and love. She could see back to the man he'd been when she'd first met him . . . the man she'd fallen in love with.

'I wish you'd told me,' he said. 'I wish you'd let me be there for you . . . for Ella.' Jude gazed down at the bench again, and he tipped her chin up to meet his eyes. 'But I meant what I said. The past will be lost to me soon. I don't want to waste time thinking about what we could have done differently.' He got to his feet, staring down at her. 'So . . . can you take me to meet my daughter? *Our* daughter?'

Jude smiled and stood up beside him. 'With pleasure.'

CHAPTER FORTY-SIX

ELLA

While my mother and Bertie chatted on the next bench over, Angus and I watched the lights of the town blink on and off in the darkened night. I breathed in his warmth, thanking God we'd finally found him and Bertie . . . or they had found us.

'What took you guys so long to get here?' I asked in a low voice, not wanting to interrupt my mother and Bertie. 'I tried to call you.'

Angus made a face. 'We were about to leave the hospital, but Bertie started to feel a bit dizzy so they wanted to check all his vitals again. Thank God he had me as his emergency contact number, or he would have been there by himself.' He shook his head. 'I tried to get him into a hotel to rest up until morning, but he insisted on coming here. I knew he wouldn't relax until he did, so . . .'

'My mum was the same,' I said. 'She wouldn't leave until he came.' I bit my lip, wondering what state Bertie was in right now. 'Is he . . .'

'He's okay,' Angus said. 'He's had a hard couple of days, but he seems to be clear right now. Did you tell your mum about his condition?'

I nodded. 'I did. And, Angus . . . I'm sorry for not jumping to help you. I . . .' I sighed. 'Well, I was worried Bertie wasn't who I'd first thought him to be, and that threw me.'

Angus tilted his head. 'What do you mean?'

I twisted towards him, meeting his steady gaze. And for the first time, I realised I *did* want to open up to someone. 'Ever since my mum left, I've had a really hard time connecting with people.' I shifted on the bench, thinking of Aunt Carolyn, Rob, everyone at work, my neighbour . . . of all the people who'd tried so hard to interact with me and who I'd turned away. I'd told myself I didn't need anyone, but maybe that was true: in my self-contained, closed-off state, I didn't. But once those ten little words had reached out to me, they sent me on a journey where I did need to connect with others – if nothing more than to learn the truth about my mother. And now that I knew that truth, I didn't want to hide away any more.

'Bertie was the first person in a long time I felt comfortable with. Well, Bertie and you.' My words hung in the air, and my cheeks coloured.

'I trusted Bertie and his love for my mother,' I continued. 'But then, well . . . things got a little complicated, and it scared me. I thought that I'd been wrong about him, and it made me close up again.' I took a breath. 'I'll fill you in on all the finer details later. But the one thing I need to say is that I do want to be open now. I want to connect. With you.'

My last words came out as a whisper, and I could barely hear them over the pounding of my heart. For a split second, I wanted to take them back. What if Angus was just being nice, and that spark I'd felt between us was all in my mind? But I knew that however he responded, I didn't want to spend years of my life alone, like my mum and Bertie had.

Angus took my hand and squeezed it, and happiness gushed into me. 'I want to connect with you, too,' he said, his lips curving in a gentle smile.

I stared down at our entwined hands, my heart full of hope. No matter what lay ahead, I hadn't closed myself off. I'd given us a chance – for love, for life.

We sat listening to the waves lap the sea wall as the stars peered down from above us. Finally, the scuffle of feet made us turn.

'Ella.' My mother's voice cut through the darkness, and I shook my head. I still couldn't believe she was here. That she was alive, and she was standing right in front of me. 'Ella, I have something to tell you.'

I gazed up at the her, wondering what else this day could reveal.

'Bertie is your father. We can be sure of that now.' Her voice was clear and certain.

I stood, feeling my legs shake beneath me. I'd gone from believing my father was dead, to finding out Bertie was my father, to thinking he might not be, to hearing this. I wasn't sure what I could grasp on to now. 'How do you know? I thought you said . . .' My voice trailed off.

My mother smiled. 'Frank couldn't have children. It had to have been Bertie who got me pregnant.'

Something lifted inside of me, a heaviness I was strong enough to carry if I had to, but now didn't need to. I hadn't been the result of an attack. I'd been the result of love. It didn't change what had happened in the past, but the knowledge made me feel light and almost giddy, as if I might float away.

'I met you first as your mother's daughter, Ella,' Bertie said, his voice sombre yet his eyes full of joy. 'And I'm beyond thrilled to meet you now as your father.' He reached out a hand and I took it in mine. Then, I gripped my mother's hand.

The loop had closed. The three of us were connected, through love and blood.

Through those ten little words.

CHAPTER FORTY-SEVEN

ELLA

'There's one last person I need to see.' My mother's voice broke the still air. 'I need to see my sister. To explain everything . . . and to say thank you. I've caused her – and you and Bertie – so much pain over the years. It's too late to change that. But maybe if I explain . . . maybe she'll understand. I can only hope that she won't turn me away, although I wouldn't blame her.' Her face tightened, and I could see how much my aunt's forgiveness meant to her. I couldn't offer her that, but I did know that Aunt Carolyn would never send my mother away; that she was keen to keep my mother's memory alive. The advert she'd placed every year was proof of that.

'That advert,' I began. 'The one with the ten words. The one that started me on this journey.' I paused, placing a hand on my mother's arm. 'It was Aunt Carolyn. She was the one who put it in the paper.'

Both Bertie and my mother turned towards me in surprise.

'Carolyn.' The name left my mother's lips as a shuddering exhale. 'Those words . . . our mother used to say them to us. It was something that held us together, wrapping us into a neat, protected bundle . . . until she died. I never said them again until Bertie . . .

and then you.' Her brow creased. 'But why? Why would she do that? Did she think I was still alive?'

'She told me that placing the advert was a way of remembering you,' I said, watching tears form in my mother's eyes. 'That every year she'd travel all the way to the newspaper office in London because you'd never got the chance to go there.'

My mother was silent, but I could feel her body trembling under my hand.

'Come on,' I said softly. 'Let's go. I know she'll be thrilled to see you.' I took my mother's arm to move forward, but she held back.

'Should we ring first?' she asked. 'Even if she will be glad to see me, showing up after all these years might be, well . . . I don't want to give her too much of a fright.'

I nodded, thinking it might be a good idea to call, especially given Aunt Carolyn's health condition. 'I'll ring now,' I said, sliding my mobile from my pocket. I paused for a minute before pulling up her number, shaking my head in wonder. I was about to tell her what I'd longed to say for years: that she'd been wrong to believe my mother was dead. My mother was alive. My mother was here.

But I couldn't even start to conjure up any sense of triumph over Aunt Carolyn's steadfast belief in my mother's death. In her own way, my aunt had felt the loss as keenly as I had – felt it still, even after all these years, resulting in her annual pilgrimage to London.

I hit 'call' and held my breath, my pulse quickening as my aunt's cheery 'hello' echoed down the line.

'Aunt Carolyn? It's Ella.' I paused, holding the words in my head, savouring them until I was ready to let them go. I'd buried them, pummelled them, tried my best to eradicate any thought, then covered them with anger, but now . . . 'It's my mum. She's alive – she's with me, here on the promenade. We're on our way to you.'

There was silence on the other end, and fear flashed through me. Was my aunt okay? Had my news been too much of a surprise? 'Aunt Carolyn? Are you all right?' Angus shot me a worried look, then reached out to take my arm. I'd almost forgotten he was there, but I was so pleased he was.

'I'm all right,' Aunt Carolyn said. 'Just a bit . . . shocked. I never . . . I need to sit down for a moment.' I could hear her pulling out a chair, then the low tones of Rob's voice behind her asking what was happening. 'But . . . Where is she? How did you find her? Was it the article?'

'We're on our way to you now. We can explain everything then,' I said. 'But if you need more time, we can head to a restaurant for a bite to eat first.'

'No, no.' Aunt Carolyn's voice was vehement, and I could just picture her shaking her head with that no-nonsense expression. 'I can't believe it. I can't believe she's here, but I don't need more time. How could I wait any longer? It's already been years.'

I nodded, even though I knew she couldn't see me – my throat was too tight to say any words. Silence fell between us.

'Are you okay?' Aunt Carolyn's voice was soft. 'How are you doing with all of this?'

I paused, trying to get a hold on what I was feeling. So many emotions were swirling through me, from joy to disbelief. The one thing I did know was that, for the first time in years, I was all right.

'I'm fine,' I said, and even though I'd said that to my aunt a million times before, this time it was different. This time, I was more than fine. 'We'll see you soon.'

I hung up and met my mother's anxious gaze. 'Aunt Carolyn can't wait to see you.'

My mum drew in a shaky breath, a smile slowly spreading over her face. 'Shall we call a taxi?'

Bertie shook his head. 'No,' he said. 'I've been waiting all these years to walk along the prom with you again. I'm not going to get in a taxi now. Come on, let's go.' He took my mother's arm, and the two of them made their way down the pavement, their bodies merging into one shape in the darkness.

Angus and I followed behind, a younger version of the couple up ahead. He took my arm and I leaned into him, loving how the warmth of his body filtered into mine. Moving slowly, it felt like it took forever to reach Aunt Carolyn's house, and yet when we stood in front of my aunt's door, it felt like no time at all . . . like we were outside the boundaries of the world around us.

Angus paused. 'Would you rather I let you all talk in peace?' he asked, his voice tinged with uncertainty. 'I'm sure you have a lot to catch up on.'

I tightened my grip on his arm. He was part of this story – a part of our lives, no matter what the future held for us.

'Stay,' I said, and he grasped my hand as footsteps approached. I swallowed as the door opened, preparing for the past and present to come together. No matter what complications the future may hold – how lives might collide; how illness might take away precious memories; how tragic events could spin us off in different directions – we were all connected by an invisible wire of love.

And when we wanted to – when we *chose* to – all we had to do was follow that line home again.

CHAPTER FORTY-EIGHT

JUDE

Jude clutched Bertie's hand as she waited for Carolyn to open the door, feeling like she was in a dream. She couldn't believe she was in Hastings now, with her daughter and Bertie, back in the house she'd run to after leaving Edinburgh . . . where she'd lain on the sofa and tried to make sense of everything; where she'd tried to deal with becoming a mother; where her sister had done everything she could to help her.

But it still hadn't been enough. It never could have been, although Carolyn hadn't known that then, of course. Jude had abandoned her daughter for Carolyn to raise, leaving her to believe Jude was dead. After the loss of their own parents, it was almost unforgiveable.

Would Carolyn ever be able to forgive her? The advert gave her hope she wouldn't be turned away, but Jude couldn't be sure of anything more. She just knew she had to try to explain. The truth was the only thing she could say.

Carolyn's face appeared around the side of the door, and Jude's eyes widened as her brain tried to merge the image of her youthful sister with the older woman standing before her now – an older woman who, funnily enough, looked a lot like her: short dark hair threaded with grey, sensible shoes and nondescript clothes. The years had brought them closer together in appearance than they ever could have guessed.

Before Jude could say anything, her muscles propelled her forward and into Carolyn's arms. She gripped her sister, breathing in the same talc her mother used to wear, praying Carolyn wouldn't push her away. She couldn't remember the last time they'd hugged – maybe not since that awful night their parents had died. Jude had pushed her away ever since, despite her sister's best attempts.

But now . . . Jude lifted her head and stepped back, feeling her cheeks wet with tears. Tears brimmed in Carolyn's eyes, too, and Jude noticed the rest of the group move past them into the lounge to give the two sisters a moment alone.

'Carolyn, I . . .' Her voice faltered. What could she say to the woman who had always been there for her – the sister who had raised her child when she couldn't? How could any words express the overwhelming gratitude she felt and the sorrow at the pain she had caused?

Carolyn cleared her throat, then took a tissue box and held it out to Jude after blowing her own nose. Jude couldn't help smiling. After all these years, Carolyn was still taking care of her.

'Thank you,' Jude said, wiping her eyes. She met her sister's gaze. 'Thank you, for everything.' It didn't even come close to what she was feeling, but she was desperate to show Carolyn how grateful she was. It was a start – a small one – and she knew she'd never stop trying in the years ahead.

Carolyn's eyes welled up again, and she swallowed. 'I thought you were dead. I thought you were gone and I'd failed you. That I couldn't help you when you needed it most.'

Guilt shot through Jude. She'd caused so much hurt to those around her, but she'd been in so much pain back then that she hadn't been able to help even herself. 'No one could have helped me, Carolyn,' she said, touching her sister's arm. 'Not even the best doctor in the world. I . . . I needed to go. I needed to leave. That was the only way I could carry on.'

Carolyn leaned against a chair, her face so pale that for a minute Jude was afraid she might faint. 'What did make you come back? *Was* it Ella's article?'

'I did see Ella's article, yes,' Jude said. 'But if it hadn't been for that classified advert – the advert *you* placed – then Ella wouldn't have started her search in the first place.' She paused. 'I'm here because of you . . . because you never forgot me. You may have thought I was dead, but you never let me go. Not in your heart.' Tears streamed down her cheeks now and she let them fall unchecked, noticing that Carolyn was weeping too. And this time, it was Jude who handed her sister a tissue.

'Come,' she said, taking Carolyn's arm. 'There's someone I want you to meet.' She led her sister into the lounge and over to where Bertie was sitting.

'This is Bertie,' Jude said simply, and Carolyn recoiled at the name. 'He never hurt me. He'd never hurt me.' Her heart squeezed at the lies of the past; the protective walls she'd thrown up around her. It was time to knock those all down. 'He *is* Ella's father, though – that much is true. He's part of our family.' She met Carolyn's eyes. 'I'll explain everything later, I promise.'

Carolyn smiled, despite her evident confusion. 'We have plenty of time.'

Jude and Carolyn sat down on the sofa, and Jude thought how odd it was that, all these years later, she had brought Bertie home to meet Carolyn – along with her daughter and Angus, a man she didn't know but could see meant something to Ella. They were all here under one roof after so many years and secrets had separated them.

I am always with you. I will always be here.

Those ten little words had made her feel safe, had saved her, and had found her again, but it wasn't the words that held the power. It was the people – the ones who'd hoped, longed and loved.

The ones she'd never let go of again.

CHAPTER FORTY-NINE

ELLA

Six months later

I stood in the middle of the gallery, breathing in the silence and trying to quell the nerves inside of me. In just a few minutes, the doors to the exhibition would open and people from all over Hastings and beyond would pour in to 'Sounds of the Pier'. The past few months had been crazy, trying to get everything just right, from arranging the banks of headphones, to selecting the clips, to choosing accompanying photos and material that showcased not just the pier, but also the surrounding areas. But as I gazed around the airy room filled with the history of my hometown, I couldn't be prouder at what I'd achieved – what my whole *team* had achieved, because there was no way I could have done this on my own. Through endless meetings and discussions – many that had spilled over into drinks at the pub, which we'd jokingly dubbed 'the conference room' – we'd managed to pull off something really special.

And now it was time to show everyone else.

'Okay,' I said to the security guard, my voice trembling with anticipation. 'I'm ready.'

She nodded and swung open the doors. Almost immediately, the room was engulfed in a flood of people tugging on headphones, peering at photos, and sharing their own memories. I stood still for a second, unable to move, savouring the moment when the exhibit finally came to life. Without people, it was nothing – an empty shell, waiting to be filled up. I smiled, thinking how my life had been like that, too. Now that I'd let people in, I felt more alive than ever.

'This is amazing!' Angus appeared at my side, and I turned towards him.

'Hey.' I slid an arm around his waist and pulled him close, happy he was here. I hadn't seen him for a bit – he'd met me in London a few weeks ago, and we'd had a wonderful weekend together – but we spoke on the phone every day. He'd listened to me natter on endlessly about the exhibition, and I was so excited to show it to him. And now that I'd finished work on it, I'd have time to investigate other opportunities . . . opportunities that might be closer to Edinburgh, if not in the city itself. In a way, I was grateful for the distance of the past few months. It had enabled us to move slowly; to get to know each other at a pace we were both comfortable with. But now, after absorbing all I'd learned about my family and adjusting to the huge changes in my life, I was ready to make a move – both professionally and personally. The past was a part of me I could embrace, and I was excited about what the future might hold.

'I'm so proud of you, Ella.' Carolyn and Rob came up behind Angus, and I drew them both in for a hug. 'I'm going to have to organise a school trip for the kids to come here! I know they'd love it.'

I grinned, knowing that, for Carolyn, organising a school trip was the highest endorsement she could give. She was back at work after making a complete recovery from her heart surgery, still driving Rob crazy with her inability to sit still for longer than a second. She'd even recruited me for a nightly power walk on the promenade, and as a result I was in better shape than ever before. She'd become a regular part of my life and I loved our jaunts along the waterfront, whatever the weather. Sometimes we didn't even talk – it was enough to be doing something together, striding in tandem as the sea stretched out before us.

'Have you seen Mum?' I asked, craning my head to try to catch a glimpse of her. 'Or Bertie?' Even though I knew he was my father, it still felt odd to call him that. We'd agreed to stick with Bertie for now, but whatever label I used, he did feel like a father figure. We'd had a connection since the day we'd first met.

Mum and Bertie had made the journey down from Edinburgh, where they were now living together in Bertie's house. Mum had said she didn't want to waste any more time, and watching them together on one of my recent visits, it seemed like she'd never left. Bertie had his bad days – and we all knew they'd come more frequently as his condition progressed – but right now, they were savouring every moment. They were even talking about getting married in the coming weeks.

Carolyn shook her head. 'They came in with us, but we lost them somewhere in the crowd. Shall we have a look around for them?'

'That's okay,' I said. 'I have an idea where they might be. Let me go find them.' I cut through the crowd, nodding and smiling as people told me how much they were enjoying the exhibition; what a wonderful job we'd done. By the time I spotted Mum and Bertie, just where I suspected they might be, I was bursting with happiness and pride.

I paused for a second, watching them huddle together as they shared a pair of headphones. Their arms were around each other's waists and their eyes were fixed on a large photo in front of them.

I knew without even looking that it was a picture of my mother busking on the promenade, with the pier stretching out in the background. Her cheeks were red, her hair was tousled and her mouth was wide open in song – perhaps the very song they were listening to now, years later, together again at last.

Perhaps the same song that had brought me back to her.

My mother glanced over, as if she sensed me standing there. 'Ella!' she said, reaching out towards me. 'Sorry, we were trying to find you, but then we spotted this.' She nodded towards the photo, then touched the headphone on her ear. 'This music . . .' She shook her head and put a hand to her mouth, unable to continue as tears streaked down her cheeks.

Bertie drew her closer and I laid a hand on her arm. She didn't need to speak. She didn't need to say any more. I held her gaze, and I could see into her heart. No barriers and no secrecy existed between us – not any more.

And I knew that, no matter what, she would always be with me.

I knew she would always be here.